Shards of Love

A SAFE Security Trilogy

Mercenary Hearts 3

Michele Zurlo

www.michelezurloauthor.com

Shards of Love (A SAFE Security Trilogy: Mercenary Hearts 3)
Copyright © July 2018 by Michele Zurlo
Print ISBN: 978-1-942414-51-3

Editor: Nicoline Tiernan
Cover Artist: Nicoline Tiernan

Published by Lost Goddess Publishing LLC
www.michelezurloauthor.com

This book is a work of fiction. While reference might be made to actual historical events or existing locations, the names, characters, places and incidents are either the product of the author's imagination or are used fictitiously, and any resemblance to actual persons, living or dead, business establishments, events, or locales is entirely coincidental.

Warning: This book contains sexually explicit scenes and adult language and may be considered offensive to some readers. It is not meant for underage readers.

DISCLAIMER: Education and training are necessary in order to learn safe BDSM practices. Lost Goddess Publishing LLC is not responsible for any loss, harm, injury or death resulting from use of the information contained in any of its titles. This is a work of fiction, and license has been taken with regard to BDSM practices.

Shards of Love (Mercenary Hearts 3)

"I'd wanted the fairy tale, and somewhere along the line I'd forgotten that everyone in a fairy tale paid a price."

All Jessica ever wanted was a family.

When the unthinkable happens, Jessica finds herself adrift in a sea of grief. It's going to take everything she has to pull her life together and fight for the life she wants.

Warning: Bondage, D/s, rape (not romanticized)

A Note to Readers:

The Mercenary Hearts trilogy begins in the prequel, Forging Love, and it's meant to be read in order:

Forging Love (alternating viewpoints)
Drawing on Love (Jessica's viewpoint)
Broken Love (Mostly Jesse's viewpoint)
Shards of Love (alternating viewpoints)

Chapter 1

Dean

Looking through my scope, I double-checked that the reticle was centered on my target, and then I radioed to David. "I'm all set. Locked and loaded."

"Tell me again why you had to be here instead of with Jesse?" David liked to wait until I couldn't escape his jabber to ask stupid questions.

"I'm a sharpshooter. You need me to cover your ass."

Rather than acknowledge my skills were necessary on this job, David chose to poke the bear. "Seems like Jesse could have used a sharpshooter more than me."

"More than I." The correction was automatic because I didn't want to have this conversation. While a sharpshooter would have been useful to Jesse—or Frankie—on their mission, the pair of them were quite capable of extracting their target without my particular skills. David, on the other hand, needed someone who could cover him from a distance as he transported ten million dollars worth of rubies for our client.

Given the mountainous terrain of the Denver area, air support was necessary. Once he was in the vehicle with Brea, I would follow them by chopper, ready to pick off anyone who tried to mess with our transport system.

"Are you going to tell me why you're still avoiding him? Jessica isn't mad at you for all the shitty things you did to her." Brea chimed in for this one. The pair of them needed to fucking leave me alone.

Jesse hadn't told anyone the things I'd said to him, not even Jessica. Otherwise these two would know because Jessica told Brea everything, and Brea didn't keep secrets from David. It was a tad annoying the way adding this pair to our lives had eradicated any sense of privacy we used to enjoy.

The things I'd done to Jessica had been designed to capitalize on her breakup with Jesse to bring her to me. I'd fully expected a spectacular argument, but with my charm and suave sophistication, she'd end up in my arms and in my bed. Once she was there, she'd realize she'd made a terrible mistake—I was the man for her.

Shooing away the unnecessary distraction of my failure, I used my binoculars to check the surrounding area. My position was perfect to cover David and Brea as they exited the museum where the rubies had been on display. We'd been tasked with making sure they arrived at Colorado Springs where our client had a massive vault. As long as we were vigilant, this job was easy money.

"Dean?" Brea's question came through crystal-clear on the private communication devices Jesse had designed and built. He'd even made different sizes to fit different ear canals.

"Yes?" I kept it short because I didn't want to talk about Jessica. Staying away from her was good for both of us. Okay, it was mostly for my benefit because she didn't think of me as anything but a friend.

I'd been friend-zoned.

"If we don't know what happened, we can't help."

I didn't fucking want help. "We had a disagreement, the details of which are none of your business."

She sighed, which was probably accompanied by a dramatic rolling of the eyes. Brea was queen of the eye-roll, which wasn't one of her more endearing habits. "Dean, sometimes talking helps. We could give you a different perspective on the problem."

"Thanks, but I've covered all the perspectives. We're okay, Brea. It's just going to take time. Now, quiet on the comms for this next part."

I listened as they greeted their contact person and confirmed the contents of what we were transporting. This part of our dealings were non-negotiable. We didn't care if we were transporting rubies or horse sperm—we obtained a visual of the goods. This was to protect our asses because sometimes people were unscrupulous. Whether it was a substitution or hiding of drugs—we didn't break laws like that—or falsifying cargo to come after us for lost or missing items, we covered our asses at the beginning and end of each job of this nature.

Brea snapped photos of the cargo and sent them to me. I loved having her on the team for assignments like this because she was good at doing things without anyone noticing.

Of course, Jessica was just as good with all these covert skills, but she had no interest in pursuing this kind of occupation. Now that she had a kid, she divided her time between mom duties and her business repurposing furniture. I'd been keeping track of her from afar, through friends and by checking her website. She'd recently begun using social media, and she had amassed quite a following simply by posting tips about adding artistic touches to furniture—and by posting lots of pictures of Bailey. That little girl was beyond adorable, and the public seemed to have responded to her harrowing tale of preeclampsia, having a daughter in the NICU for six weeks, and recovering from an unexpectedly difficult pregnancy.

Just this morning, she'd posted a picture of Bailey wearing a pink headband and a pink camo-patterned shirt that said, "Daddy's Girl."

I didn't think Jesse had any social media accounts or that he'd check it from Guatemala if he did. Of course, nobody would believe I now had a secret account or that I followed Jessica. I could admit it wasn't helping me get over her.

Ten miles into the trip, Brea went live on comms again.

"Dean, what happened between you and Jesse?"

From the chopper, I checked out the surrounding traffic, looking for tails and other dangers. I kept an eye on a pair of Hummers that seemed to be driving in a two-man tail formation. I glanced over at Joss Blaese, my pilot, and thanked goodness he wasn't on this comm line.

"Brea, I appreciate your concern, but this is between him and me. We'll work it out eventually."

David chuckled. "She can't get anything out of Jessica, though that's because Jessica isn't sure what's going on either. It'll be easier for all involved if you just told us instead of letting us speculate."

Since I wasn't paranoid by nature and I kept my emotions under wraps, I wasn't worried that they'd picked up on my crush on Jessica. Until I'd said something, neither Jesse nor Jessica had known how I felt.

"We're not letting it affect the team, and neither should you." My phone rang with Frankie's number. Since I wasn't expecting to hear from her until the scheduled check-in four hours from now, this was cause for concern. "This is Dean. Go."

"Dean." She was breathing hard. "We were captured. Jesse pushed me out of the plane, but he didn't get out. I watched the plane, and an engine caught fire, and then it lost altitude. It went down southeast of my location, but it's all mountains and jungle. I'm trying to track him, but I'm hurt. I've been shot, and I'm losing blood."

"Where are you?"

"I don't fucking know. I was knocked out for a while, and when I came to, we were tied up in a small cargo plane with two pallets of cocaine. My GPS isn't working, and Jesse isn't here to fix it."

"Keep your phone on. We'll come to you." I hung up and called Jessica. We might not be best friends anymore, but I knew Jesse kept tracking equipment around, and he'd put more bugs in more of our stuff than we knew about. It wasn't invasive as much as it was a dedication to making sure we could always be found. He'd done it for situations like this.

"Hello, Jessica's phone. This is Sylvia."

Sylvia was Jessica and Brea's mother. She and Warren, their father, lived with Jessica and Jesse because Jessica needed the help.

"Sylvia, this is Dean. I need to speak with Jessica now. It's an emergency."

"She's in the studio. Hang on." In the background, I heard her shout for Warren to go get Jessica. She also lamented the fact that Jessica had left her phone inside while she'd gone out to work on her art.

I didn't blame Jessica. Creating art took time and concentration. A phone was a distraction.

"Dean? What's wrong?"

Of course she would jump to worst-case scenarios because why else would I call? Keeping my tone calm, I said, "Jessica, I need you to go to SAFE Security headquarters and turn on Jesse's tracking equipment. We're looking for anything he's tagged to Frankie."

"Oh, he has that all set up here. I'm going to his office right now. Shit, it's locked."

I smiled. "Since when is a lock an obstacle for you?"

"You're thinking of Brea. She picks locks. I forge things."

"I didn't confuse the two of you, but I assumed it was a keyhole lock, and I know you have a bump key."

"Also a Brea thing. Deadbolt. Tumblers." She went silent for a moment. "I think I know where the key is. Yes. I found it. I can't believe he'd lock me out of a room in my own home." She kept up the nervous chatter as she logged onto his computer.

"He locked the door, but he didn't password protect his equipment?"

"He did, but I know how his brain works."

"It's Bailey's birthday, isn't it?"

She laughed. "I'll never tell. Okay, I'm in. Here's his tracking stuff. Oh—fucker has a tracker in my cane? That's a conversation we'll be having when he gets back."

I didn't want to tell her we'd lost Jesse, so I didn't. She was already nervous enough about the idea Frankie was lost.

"Okay, I have coordinates for her. I'm texting them to you right now."

"Thanks, Brat. Think you might throw Jesse's on there as well, just so I have all the information?"

"Yeah, sure. Dean, I don't want to ask what's gone wrong, but I need to know. Are they okay?"

I wasn't going to lie to her, but I also didn't want to tell her the extent of the problem before we had a solution. There was no sense in freaking her out when we could still salvage it all. "They encountered some problems and got separated. I'm working on locating them right now, and they'll work on reuniting. In the meantime, we'll stay in touch, and I'm going to need you to stay on the trackers, okay? Send updates every fifteen minutes."

"Dean, this sounds serious. If there's more I can do, you'll let me know, right? I know I'm not part of the team, but I know how to do all of this covert stuff."

"I know, Brat. That's why I called you." We really needed to expand our team. With this much going on, we needed someone to manage all the missions. They could also take care of the billing and paperwork, like Brea had done when David had prohibited her from active participation in missions. It had been nice to have someone around to do the things I hated doing.

Next I called Frankie back while I kept my eyes on my target. The chopper pilot was an old SOCOM buddy who'd been in the Navy until he'd lost his right arm below the elbow. He could still fly, but men with missing limbs weren't considered combat ready. He mostly worked for local news stations, taught flying lessons, and sometimes freelanced because he had his own chopper.

The line crackled, letting me know she was far away from a cell tower, and her signal was piggybacking from the satellite as backup—another modification Jesse had made to our equipment. "Dean? What did you find out?"

"I sent coordinates for where you are and where he is. You're in the southern part of Guatemala right by the Honduran border, and he's in Honduras. I have Jessica updating your locations every fifteen minutes."

"For fuck's sake, Dean. Don't tell her what's going on."

It looked like a reminder was in order. "I'm not a moron, Frankie. She just knows you got separated. It happens, and it's often not a big deal."

She exhaled hard, the kind of sound someone made when they were in pain. "I'm in guerilla territory."

That meant she needed a guide, someone trustworthy who knew the terrain. It also meant she was hurt worse than she was letting on.

"Frankie, list your injuries."

"Gunshot to the leg. It missed the femur and femoral artery. Broken ribs, maybe three or four. Mild concussion from the rifle butt I took to the head. I'm fine."

Extrapolating brought me to dangerous conclusions. Broken ribs could easily puncture a lung, and that wasn't good under any circumstances. This was why I was the de-facto leader of our small gang—I was gifted at thinking about the big picture.

Brea and David were out of Denver and headed toward our drop-off point. Everything in this mission was going according to plan, while Frankie and Jesse were half a continent away and in dire need of backup.

I made a quick decision.

"Frankie, stay put. Find somewhere to hole up. We're on our way."

Next I informed David and Brea of our change in plans.

"Jesse is missing and Frankie is hurt. Rescue mission leaves in one hour."

"Um, Dean?" Brea's frown and concern managed to come through in her tone. "Are we finishing this one?"

"You are. Joss will cover your six. Pull over and let David out of the car."

Joss heard my end of all conversations, and he was intelligent, so he put it together without asking questions. I handed him my comm so that he could stay in touch with Brea. He dropped a ladder to pick David up off the side of the freeway, and then he set us down on the roof of a nearby building. All of this, he accomplished without losing sight of Brea.

"Are you good to fly and shoot?"

He shrugged. "I guess we'll find out."

When he was gone, David scowled. Along with Frankie and Jesse, David was not only my friend, but he was family. We'd met at the tender age of 18 when we'd both joined the Marine Corps, and we'd bonded instantly. Even being separated—I'd chosen to become a sharpshooter while he concentrated on explosive ordinance disposal—hadn't dampened our friendship. We'd been paired again in the field where we'd met Frankie and Jesse. The four of us had been an effective Special Forces team even though we'd come from different branches, and we'd decided to stick together for our post-military careers.

I motioned to the retreating chopper. "I know you don't like leaving her to do this without you, but give her some credit for knowing more about this kind of thing than you do. She planned it all, and she prepared for this scenario."

Even I'd been impressed by that nugget of wisdom, but Brea had merely informed me that it was stupid to not plan for people suddenly not being in play. She'd been thinking of what might happen if we were ambushed, one of them became incapacitated, and they lost air support.

David nodded. "How bad is it?"

On the way down the building, I briefed him on the details.

A cab waited on the street. We slipped into the back, and the cabbie turned around. "I'm not on duty."

"There's an extra hundred in it if you can get us to the airport in ten minutes." I'd already booked a flight.

"You're not listening." The cabbie turned around and pointed a gun at us. He was an older man, thin and stooped. "I'm waiting for my daughter."

Neither David nor I blinked in the face of this threat.

"A thousand," David said. Everyone had a price.

His lips pressed together with a refusal.

"Two thousand."

"Five," he countered.

"Done," David said. "Going to need an ATM, though."

The man gestured to the building from which we'd just emerged. As David got out to get the cash, a woman in her fifties put something into the trunk and climbed into the front seat.

She brushed her frizzy blonde hair back from her face and noticed her father's gun. Her eyes widened as she peered into the back where I sat. "Dad, what's going on?"

"Detour to the airport."

She frowned. "We were going there anyway."

He scowled, and I rolled my eyes. "You'll still get your money, and you can keep the ride off the books."

David returned. "Let's go."

As the cabbie navigated traffic, David got on his phone. "Sugar, what's your position?"

Brea gave him her coordinates. "Everything is proceeding according to plan. You just get Frankie and Jesse and bring them back in one piece, okay? I called Jessica. As soon as you text your flight information, she's sending travel bags to your destination."

I closed my eyes. Jessica didn't need to know the details. David and I could purchase the supplies we needed once we landed.

"Sugar," I said, using David's term of endearment for Brea because it used to piss him off but now it was just her nickname. "I wish you hadn't done that. I was trying to keep the details from Jessica."

"She doesn't know that Jesse is missing, only that they got separated and Frankie is injured." Her frosty tone cooled my ire. "She's worried, but we both have every confidence that you'll bring them back. Of course, if you need us to follow you down and save your tender asses, we're game."

With a three-month old baby who'd only been home from the hospital for about seven weeks, I doubted that Jessica was as eager to undertake a rescue mission as Brea believed. "We'll keep you on standby."

Jessica

I knew they weren't telling me everything. Now that I had a baby, I was suddenly too delicate to understand the dangers Jesse faced whenever he took on a mission that involved a Central American drug cartel.

Fuck that. Jesse had never lied to me. He'd told me the parameters of this mission before he'd left, and I knew from the coordinates they were miles away from where they were supposed to be.

The real reason Jesse had locked the door to his office was to keep my parents from accidentally wandering into information they shouldn't have. Despite their trusted position in our lives, Brea and I had not disclosed the actual nature of what David, Jesse, Dean, and Frankie did. Now that Brea was part of their coalition, keeping the dangerous nature of their jobs from our parents was even more important.

My parents thought SAFE Security installed security systems for businesses. They thought Jesse developed technology for protecting buildings, personnel, and intellectual property, and they thought the rest of them monitored those businesses and worked with law enforcement whenever there was a problem.

That was not at all what they did, but right now, I wished it was.

Brea had just called to tell me that David and Dean were on their way to the airport, and she was finishing a four-person mission with two people.

I transferred the active tracker feed to a tablet. Shoving it into my bag, I hightailed it to the other end of the large house Jesse had purchased while I'd been in the hospital on bed rest. We'd been trying to delay Bailey's birth for as long as possible.

She'd been born eleven weeks early, and she had some vision problems that would require corrective surgery in a couple months when she was bigger and stronger, but things could have been so much worse.

I found Bailey in my father's arms. He danced around the living room, singing a Bee Gees song as he gazed into her crossed eyes.

Sylvia, my mother, sat on the sofa, watching them with a smile on her face. She glanced up as I came in, but her smile was already maxed out, so it didn't grow upon seeing me. "She's so much like you when you were a baby. You used to love listening to your dad sing."

My dad had a pleasant voice. I still liked listening to him sing. He danced her over to me, and I kissed her forehead.

"I have to go," I said. "Brea needs me to run to her place and send David something at the airport."

Warren's brows lifted. "Is everything okay?"

"Yeah. They just need some equipment. Can you watch Bailey? I'll be back in a couple of hours." I knew they were already watching her, but I'd been planning to take her back after lunch so we could spend time together. I loved being a mother, and I loved that Jesse, Sylvia, and Warren supported me in my artistic endeavors. Right now, my life was pretty perfect.

"Of course," Sylvia said. "Did you put more milk in the fridge?"

I had so much milk in the freezer that I could dry up, and she'd still have a month-long supply. I'd even donated some locally for babies in need. "There's some in my fridge."

Already my boobs ached.

Warren's gaze flickered from my face to Sylvia and back. "Sylvia, why don't you drive Jessica to Brea's house?"

Because I didn't want to answer questions about why I was hiding money in different currencies in the lining of their bags. I couldn't ship guns through their luggage, but they were going to need firepower once they landed.

"I'm okay."

"You're not cleared to drive." He eyed me regretfully. "Sweetheart, I know you've been seizure free for three months, but it's better not to take chances."

I was convinced my seizures had not indicated a problem with my brain injury. They'd been triggered by preeclampsia, and they'd gone away after Bailey had been born. However I knew I would get out of there faster if I didn't argue, and I could pump while Sylvia drove to the airport.

"Fine. Let's go."

In the car, Sylvia didn't say a word.

"Let's go to Dean's house first. It's closer."

Dean lived less than a mile from us in a house even larger and more impressive than mine. If ours was large, then his was practically a mansion. It had been built in the Forties by mobsters, and Dean had updated it without destroying the historic charm. I loved Dean's house, and Jesse knew it. I think it played into his selection of the house we now lived in.

The curved drive let us stop in front of the door, and I used the key I'd taken from Jesse's office to get inside.

Not one to wait in the car, Sylvia followed me inside. The large foyer featured a curved staircase along one side. In the center was a table with a huge bouquet of fresh flowers. Sylvia's gaze took in the carved banister and the elegant wainscoting. "Dean has impeccable taste."

I agreed with her sentiment, but not with her awed tone. Dean hid behind trappings like this to prevent people from looking beneath the surface. Except for his numerous comments he and I were alike, I honestly had no idea what made that man tick.

Having been here dozens of times, I guessed his backup travel bag would be in his bedroom, so I headed up the stairs.

"Can I help you?" A man in a three-piece suit met me at the top of the stairs. He was older, maybe seventy, and his clothes were simply elegant.

I'd never set eyes on him before. I figured that Dean had a housekeeper—I had a housekeeper now—but I didn't expect to meet a... valet? Butler? What was the difference between the two?

"I'm Jessica," I said. "Who are you?"

"Corban Whitley." He bowed his head. "I am Mr. Alloway's man."

Completely unsurprised that Dean had a "man," I continued. "Dean sent me to get his travel bag."

He nodded and turned. "Very good, Ms. Zinn. Let me show you where it is kept. Mrs. Zinn will please wait in the foyer."

Okay, this was going to be easier than I'd thought. I shot my mom a raised-brow look and followed Mr. Whitley. She shrugged and sat on a bench near a door to the library.

Though my house wasn't as large, the architecture was equally as impressive. However, I'd never live this kind of stiff, formal existence. I gained a new appreciation for the fact Jesse had never bothered to make a bed in his life.

Of course, Dean probably had his man do it for him.

"How long have you worked for Dean?"

"I've been with Mr. Alloway since he was seven years old."

I stumbled. Dean had a valet as a child? Dean was a year younger than me, so I did the math. "You've been with Dean for almost thirty years? Even when he was in the Marines?"

"Yes, Miss. Of course I didn't follow him on deployments. I waited stateside at his residence in Maine."

Of course. "Why haven't I met you before now?"

"I don't work evenings or weekends, Miss, and Mr. Alloway tends to entertain during those times." He opened a door to an adjoining room. Along one wall hung six black travel bags. "Mr. Alloway has several bags. Where will this one be sent?"

"I'm not sure yet, but either Guatemala, Nicaragua, or Honduras." I lifted one bag from the hook and looked inside. It had the basics—boots, socks, a change of clothes, and survival gear. Really it looked like items one might take camping. "This'll do."

I felt around the inside lining for hidden compartments. Either I could hide the money here with Mr. Whitley, or I could do it in front of my mother and have to answer some hard questions.

"It's stocked with a thousand in small bills."

With the instability of the currency in most Central American countries, US dollars were still the safest bet.

I was not surprised that Dean had all his bases covered. "Cool. Now I need to get one for David."

"I have just the thing. Mr. Alloway keeps supplies for all members of SAFE Security on hand." He ushered me out of the closet and to a room down the hall.

In seconds, I was holding a bag that had all the same supplies, but the clothes and shoes were in David's size. I was tempted to hug Mr. Whitley. I smiled brightly. "Thank you for your help, Mr. Whitley. Now I understand why Dean is so efficient. It's really you."

A small blush traveled up his neck. "Thank you, Ms. Zinn. I see now why Mr. Alloway speaks so highly of you."

Before I could process the idea Dean had talked to his "man" about me, my phone chimed with a text containing flight information for David and Dean. They were flying to Guatemala, and the flight left in an hour. I'd ship the bags on a flight that would arrive at the same airport at around the same time.

"Do they have passports?" Sylvia asked as she drove to the nearest airport.

"Always." Because they never knew when they'd have to fly to another country to mount a rescue.

I got out my pumping equipment and set it up. It was going to take more than fifteen minutes to get to the airport.

Fifteen minutes. Fuck. I'd almost forgotten.

I fished the tablet from my bag and found no movement in the coordinates for Jesse and Frankie's trackers. I knew Frankie was hurt, but now I questioned whether Jesse was lost, hurt, or captured.

Dread pooled in my stomach as I texted an update to Dean and David.

Chapter 2

Dean

Finding Frankie took two days. Even with the help of a local guide who'd spent years wandering the thick mountain forests, it was rough going. At one village twenty miles from the last set of coordinates Jessica had sent, we found a man with a chopper and no fuel.

David and I were more than happy to front the cost of obtaining gas.

The battery on Frankie's phone had long since gone dead, but the beacon Jesse had installed had an independent power source for situations just like this.

We flew over the last known location, looking for places she could hole up.

David pointed to a jaguar picking its way down a rocky area on the slope of the mountain. "Let's set down here."

"Where there's a jaguar?" I wasn't sure I wanted to tangle with that thing. I'd win, but it would be a hollow victory.

It was a majestic creature with yellow-orange fur and those rosette-shaped black spots. I estimated this one to be around 150 pounds and about four feet long.

"Where there's a large mammal, there's food and a water source nearby, probably a spring." David tapped our pilot and indicated that we wanted to be let down. "Also, we're within fifty feet of Frankie's coordinates."

"Do a fly around to check out the area," I said to Alberto, our guide. "Radio back in twenty minutes."

This chopper didn't come equipped with a ladder for us to climb down, but the pilot did oblige by giving us a large, knotted rope to tie to the landing skids. I went down first, and David followed.

Once we were down, I waved off the helicopter. As the echoing sound retreated, I checked my GPS to see where we were in relation to Frankie.

David did his search the old-fashioned way. "Frankie," he called. "Frankie, we're here to rescue you."

I joined in with the call as I dragged David in the direction of the coordinates. When I got to the exact place, I paused and looked around. We were under a grove of trees, so I looked for where she might have set up a camouflaged shelter. The underbrush wasn't thick enough here to build much of anything.

Then I looked up. A dingy white hammock stretched from one branch of the tree to another. "Frankie?"

A small noise came from up there. David bent down and wove his fingers together, forming a platform to catapult me to the lowest branch. How the hell had she climbed so high with her injuries?

With David's boost, I caught the lowest branch and pulled myself up. A little more scrambling, and I approached the hammock.

Frankie was inside. She was pale, the dusky skin she'd inherited as part of her Indian and Persian ancestry alarmingly gray. She didn't open her eyes, but she murmured, "Jesse."

"It's Dean. David is on the ground. We haven't found Jesse yet." I touched a hand to her forehead and shouted down to David. "She's burning up."

Remembering the damage report she'd given me, I noted that she'd wrapped her torso to protect her ribs, and a bloody piece of cloth was tied around her leg.

"She's in bad shape," I peered down at David. "We need to get her down, and then we can see what kinds of field care we can give her."

Fever meant infection, which probably came from her leg. At least she wasn't showing signs of bleeding internally.

"Can we rig a system of pulleys to lower her hammock to the ground?" David bit his lip. While we both loved rope bondage, David's skills were more utilitarian. Jesse and I were the ones who were into the fancy stuff.

I dug out the rope from my backpack and wound it around a smooth section of branch. Once I had a configuration David thought would work, I connected it to the ends of her hammock. Then I cut the places where she'd connected the parachute material to the tree.

Truly, I was amazed by her resourcefulness. Having known her all these years, I shouldn't have been, but I was. Hopefully Jesse had been as ingenious where he'd landed. It concerned us all that we hadn't been able to establish contact, but that was easily explained by him having lost his phone.

Which meant that when we got to his coordinates, we might find just his cell phone and not him. I pushed away those negative thoughts. This was my team, and I was going to bring them all home.

The rope only let us lower Frankie halfway before running out of line, which was enough for David to reach her. He lifted her from the makeshift hammock and set her down. I clambered down the tree and jumped from the lowest branches.

"Frankie," David said her name as he checked her leg. "Francesca Sikara, I'm going to cut open your pants."

She stirred at his use of her full name, a frown wrinkling her brow. She hated when we called her by her given name. She said we were condescending bastards who pronounced it with the wrong inflection.

I thought it was because she didn't want us to see her as a woman, but I kept that idea to myself because Frankie would maim me in my sleep.

Since that had elicited a reaction, I used a soothing tone as well. "Francesca, can you open your eyes?"

They fluttered open, her thick lashes shading her dark brown irises. I knew she was trying to glare, but she didn't have enough strength. This was worrisome.

"There are those daggers. We love you too, buddy. How long has your leg been infected?"

"This morning," she gasped. "It was okay until around four this morning."

As it was late afternoon, she'd been fighting this all day. Hope was not lost. "How about some water?"

"Have to pee," she said. "Really bad."

David poured a travel bottle of whiskey over the wound, and Frankie screamed. It was a pathetic scream, like a pissed-off kitten.

"Sorry, Frankie, but it'll help sanitize the wound. We need to keep the infection from getting into your blood." He capped the bottle and stowed it back in his pack.

I ripped up a pair of skivvies in my pack that I hadn't yet worn, and we used it to bandage the leg wound. Then we helped her with her relief issue. David cut off her pants the rest of the way, and we held her up as best we could without aggravating her broken ribs.

She hadn't been kidding about having to go. We briefed her while she did her business.

"It's been thirty-seven hours since we got your SOS call. We're in southern Guatemala, and there's a friendly village about twenty miles from here. Our bird should be back any minute to pick us up." I looked over at David. "I'm thinking you shimmy up the rope, and drop a second one. Then I'll attach her hammock, and you pull her up?"

He nodded.

Frankie said, "Jesse?"

"We think he's in Honduras." David helped her into a pair of his pants, which fit her vertically but gaped horizontally. At least they were loose enough not to aggravate her bandage. "Once we get you to a hospital, we're going after him."

He laid her in the hammock while I reinforced the lines with stuff I'd salvaged from higher up in the tree.

"Plane went down over the mountain," she gasped. "Didn't see a jumper. No time to waste. Take me with you."

"No." It wasn't up for discussion. She needed immediate medical attention. There was no way in hell I was going to delay that.

With a gasp, Frankie closed her eyes against the pain, and she stopped arguing because she knew I was right.

Two hours later, the sun disappeared behind the mountain, and our pilot refused to fly at night because he didn't have lights on his chopper.

We left Frankie in a poor excuse for a medical clinic where they were giving her IV antibiotics, for which we'd paid top dollar. Thank goodness Whitley kept extra cash in all of my travel bags.

At first light, we set out. The chopper pilot flew us to a village near the Honduran border, and we had to bribe our guide double his fee to take us into the Honduras half of the mountain. I would've abandoned him, except the locals spoke many different dialects, and I spoke none of them. I knew enough Spanish to ask for a bathroom, but some of the indigenous people in these parts did not speak any Spanish.

We walked for most of the day before the vista cleared enough to show a scar in the trees below. A plane had gone down here recently, leaving a swath of downed trees and blackened greenery in its wake.

Adrenaline rushed through my veins. Jesse had to be here somewhere.

Alberto pointed to the west. "Village down there, by river."

In the distance, I noted land cleared for farming, and on this side of the river, I spied the glint of sun from several corrugated roofs. I checked our position, and I estimated the crash site as the location of the tracker signal from Jesse's phone.

I had a bad feeling about this.

David and I picked our way down the mountain, our eyes peeled for signs of danger. If Jesse survived this, then it was likely some of the Magas mercenaries had as well.

"I know what you're thinking," David said. "Quit it."

Keeping my eyes peeled for anything that could be hostile, I said, "I don't know what you mean."

"You're thinking that you should have come down here with Frankie and Jesse because maybe with three, they wouldn't have been overpowered and captured."

I hadn't been thinking any such thing. Mission assignments were made after careful consideration of data. All signs pointed to this being a two-man job. It seemed David was feeling responsible because he always insisted on partnering with Brea. "Perhaps your training would have worked here better than mine. You could have blown up whatever needed blowing up."

He considered that. "You're right. We were both stupid. This was clearly a four-man job, but I hate having Brea work without me, and you've been busy arranging to not work alongside Jesse ever since he came back to work. We're both at fault."

Though he made a valid point, I didn't react. I couldn't because he was right. Once we found Jesse, I would do whatever it took to make amends, and then we'd be a full team once again.

"We should bring in more associates." I'd been thinking we needed to expand for a while, but I hadn't acted on it. Having Jesse on leave for almost six months had limited the jobs we'd been able to take on, though having him at home to coordinate missions and keep our technology on the cutting edge had been really nice.

"Work is steady enough." David agreed. "I wonder what it would take to get Malcolm Legato to come on board full time?"

Malcolm was a former FBI agent with tech and field talent that we sometimes tapped when we needed a sixth man. I was completely in favor of bringing him on board, but he had a wife and two kids in Michigan, and his whole family lived there. I couldn't see him relocating to KC.

"We'd have to let him work remotely," I said. "Let's throw him some more jobs first to see if this is something he wants to do more than a few times a year."

We'd have to run all this by Jesse and Frankie, but I didn't think they'd take issue with any of it. Brea didn't get a vote. She was an employee, not a founding partner. However I didn't make the mistake of thinking she wouldn't voice her opinion. She had a strong personality and a passionate nature, and if we didn't listen to her, she would make sure we regretted it. I had mad respect for her tactics.

We'd reached the site of the wreckage. Plane parts littered the area and black streaks of ground surrounded us. David and I fanned out to search for survivors, while still making our way toward the fuselage.

Inside, we found no bodies. The cargo bay had been stripped of all usable parts. Even the radio was missing from the cockpit. It was savage on one hand, but on the other hand, this plane was never leaving the site. Salvaging parts and letting time take its toll were the only likely outcomes for this husk.

"Traces of blood." I pointed out brownish stains in a splatter pattern on pieces of the wall and ceiling that had not been burned or torn away.

David shined his flashlight on it for closer study. "Times like this, I wish I carried Luminol and a blacklight."

I was fairly sure he'd find a lot more than just blood. I couldn't imagine drug smugglers taking the time to clean and disinfect the interior of the cabin before a run.

We searched the rest of the wreckage, hoping Jesse had somehow survived and could hold on until we got to him.

Emerging from the fuselage, I found Alberto holding a cell phone. "I found over there." He pointed to the forest behind us.

It was Jesse's cell phone. I took it from him and tried to turn it on. The battery was dead, so I took the one from my phone and put it in his while David searched the area. Jesse's phone booted up, and I looked through it for anything that might help.

Nothing.

I joined David in widening the search. We used a standard grid pattern to look for evidence anyone had been there, and we found tracks that led in the direction of the village Alberto had pointed out to us. More than tracks, we found drag marks.

"Careful." My warning was mostly for Alberto. He was trespassing in Honduras same as we were. He didn't know the village or what we'd find there. Some of these villages were connected to the smugglers and cartels. Due to their remote nature, the cartels were their only defense against other cartels that might murder or enslave them. "Stay between us."

Dusk was falling by the time we reached the village, and so we showed up in time for dinner. Most people were inside their homes.

Alberto knocked on the nearest door, and as he conversed with the inhabitant, David and I measured the lay of the land.

It was a small village with perhaps forty homes dotting the fields and edging the forest. I estimated the population at around two hundred, but I could have been way off, especially if there were more homes spread out up or down the river.

"Dean, Fernando says the men in the village went to the crash and brought back the men from the plane."

Fernando took a step back as David and I gave him our full attention. He was a short man, probably of Mayan descent. He had a round, wide face with almond-shaped eyes, and his dark hair had been crudely cut, probably by a knife.

Alberto gestured, introducing me and David. I knew this because when he said our names, Fernando nodded in our directions.

"Please thank Fernando for his help," David said. "Assure him that we aren't a threat. We're just looking for our friend."

Alberto spoke, and Fernando launched into a long speech as he led us down a path to the very end of the village.

"He says they came two days ago," Alberto translated. "They had many injuries, and they did not survive the crash. The villagers tried to help them, but they have no medicine."

That sinking feeling in my core felt like rocks in my stomach.

We came to a larger wooden building with a cross on top. Around it was a fenced cemetery. Fernando pointed to several patches of freshly turned earth and said more things.

"He says the men did not survive. They buried the bodies yesterday and the priest said a Catholic mass for them. He says they will mark the graves with crosses."

I stared at the small mounds of dirt, my mind refusing to believe what I was seeing. "We'll need to dig them up. I want proof."

Alberto stepped in front of me. "Mr. Dean, it is bad luck to disturb a grave. The villagers believe it will bring death to them all if you disrespect the bodies."

Unless I saw proof that Jesse was dead, I wasn't going to believe it, and if he had died in this godforsaken place, I wasn't going to leave his body in an anonymous and unmarked grave. Dread gave the world a surreal feeling. I floated closer and dropped to my knees. I sank my hands into the dirt and flung it aside.

David put a hand on my shoulder. "Alberto, take Fernando back to his home. Ask for shovels for us. The villagers don't have to be present for this, but we need to verify our friend's identity."

"Mr. David, do not disturb the dead."

"Alberto, if our friend is in there, we're taking his body home with us. He has a wife and daughter waiting for him, one way or another." David's voice caught toward the end, so I knew he was as close to losing his shit as I was.

Alberto and Fernando left, and David joined me in my quest to dig up these graves.

"It's not him," I insisted. "He jumped clear. He's out there in the jungle, surviving on his wits as he makes his way to where he can contact us. Just wait. Any minute, we'll get a call from Jessica saying that he's sitting at an airport waiting for us to send a new passport."

David didn't say anything, which I appreciated. I didn't need a different perspective right then, and neither did he.

Alberto came through with the shovels and more expressions of disapproval. I threw myself into digging with renewed vigor, and David was beside me. We worked feverishly into the night until we couldn't see our hands in front of our faces, even with the help of our flashlights.

We stopped for the night, setting up camp outside the perimeter of the yard. We might be desecrating graves, but that didn't mean we would further upset the villagers by setting up camp on hallowed ground.

The next morning, we were invited to a hut for breakfast. As we were running low on food, we took advantage of the hospitality. The eggs, thick tortilla filled with refried beans and cheese, and plantains made for a filling meal. Afterward, a stream of men, women, and children headed off to the fields to work and tend livestock.

Several men stayed behind talking with Alberto.

David and I headed back to the cemetery to find that some villagers had been here in our absence, and they'd filled in the progress we'd made the night before.

Alberto appeared behind us. "Mr. Dean, this is Father Juan. He says you cannot dig up the graves. He says you will have to visit the Honduras police and ask for permission."

I opened my mouth to argue, but Alberto motioned to Father Juan.

The priest came forward and spoke. Alberto translated. "Four men came, all burned from the fire, but they were alive. Two spoke Spanish, one spoke English, and one did not speak."

The priest set down wrapped bundles at the foot of each grave.

"He says these are clothes and possessions of each man. He says you will look through these to find your friend. He says he also has pictures, but they are gruesome and he doesn't think you should see your friend like that. Your friend is with God, and you will let his spirit rest."

I wasn't on board with not exhuming the bodies, but I recognized this wasn't going to be a simple operation. This village might be remote and third-world looking, but they operated within the law, and I had to respect that.

David started at one end of the line, and I went to the other. The first bundle had singed and torn pants with a camouflage pattern, a knife, an assault rifle magazine, and a leather billfold full of cash that had somehow avoided being burned.

"Dean." The note of panic in David's voice had me skipping over the second bundle.

I knelt next to David and looked at the itemd he'd laid out. Jesse's backpack was there, though all of the contents were missing. David unfolded a shirt with the SAFE Security logo on the sleeve. It was dirty with blood, sweat, and grime, and it was full of burn holes.

Snatching the shirt, I examined it for proof that it hadn't been on a person when it had been damaged.

David pointed out the center of a bloody patch. "That's where Frankie said Jesse was shot."

My knees felt weak. I'd lost men in the field before, and it always hit me hard, but not like this. Jesse wasn't just part of my unit—he was part of my heart.

I dropped back to the ground, frantically looking through the rest of the items, but everything there only confirmed Jesse's identity—his boots, shreds of his pants full of more blood, and his wedding ring.

"I told him not to take his wedding ring." David's voice came out in a whisper.

I held the simple gold band that he'd bought when Jessica got out of the hospital. They'd had another wedding, a small ceremony inside their home, because Jesse hadn't technically been present for the first one.

The priest spoke to us, probably offering comfort, but I didn't listen. I thought about the awkward and stilted conversations we'd begun having the night Bailey was born. I'd gone to the hospital to talk to him, to apologize for the things I'd said. They were true, but they were my burden to bear. Telling him I was in love with his wife had damaged our friendship.

What the hell had I been thinking? I'd been selfish on so many levels.

And it had cost me the last few months I would ever have with one of my closest friends.

"You want to see the picture?"

No, I didn't want to see it, but I forced myself to look. I owed it to Jesse.

Father Juan called up the image and handed his cell phone to me. The man in the photo barely looked human. Soot painted his face black, and dried blood stained his skin, but there was no doubt I was looking at a photo of Jesse. The shirt and boots were the ones from the bundle at the foot of his grave. Gunshot wounds to the abdomen and leg were in the same spots Frankie had reported.

David stumbled away and fell to his knees, and he lost his breakfast.

For all I knew, he could have been sleeping. I scrolled through the next few photos, and I found a close-up of Jesse with his eyes open, his vacant stare and cyanotic coloring leaving no doubt that he wasn't alive.

I lost it. I fucking lost it.

The composure I'd prided myself on always having fled, and I roared. My pain echoed through the valley, and I sobbed like a baby.

Chapter 3

Jessica

Arranging for Frankie to come home from Guatemala was a bitch. The government there insisted her injuries warranted an investigation, and they knew if she flew home to the US, they'd never see her again.

Palms were greased, and Brea and I got her home.

We waited in the designated area in the surgery wing. Frankie's infection was severe, and they needed to go after it more aggressively, and they also wanted to repair the damage to her leg. The bullet had missed the bone, but it had torn a huge chunk of muscle and skin away.

"She's going to have one hell of a scar to show off." Brea laughed nervously.

I considered the extent of her injury, and I suspected her days of field work were over. She was going to need her cane back. While I worried for Frankie, I had faith the doctors here would save her life.

My main concern was Jesse. He should have called me by now. Frankie was the one who had been lost and injured, not Jesse. The three of them better not have tried to salvage the mission.

"My boobs are ready to bust. I'm going to pump." Long past caring about other people's delicate sensibilities, I slipped the pump up my shirt and into place.

Brea glanced over. "Your boobs are enormous."

"I'm aware."

Jesse had gone out and bought me a whole set of nursing bras. I was amazed at his ability to pick out the right size and a comfortable style. He'd also bought me an entirely new wardrobe full of clothes that were more forgiving of the baby weight. It did not escape my notice that most of the shirts had scooped and V-necks that showed off my swollen breasts. Jesse loved my boobs almost as much as he loved my ass, and he preferred me in shirts that showed off my natural assets.

"I read that if you pump less, then you'll produce less milk."

Five minutes provided a lot of relief. I stowed the milk in the portable cooler I carried in my extra large purse. "When they're full and I don't pump, they hurt. I'm not much of a masochist."

With a sly smile, she shot me a side-eyed look. "David?"

That wasn't anything close to what I had anticipated her saying, so I looked to where her gaze had gone. David had arrived, and Dean was close on his heels. I was surprised to see them because they hadn't called or had us arrange flights back. Also, where the hell was Jesse?

David bypassed Brea and stopped in front of me. From his somber manner and Dean's ashen face, a horrible realization dawned on me.

"No."

He sat down next to me and put his arm around my shoulders. "Jessica, I'm sorry."

"No." I shook my head, denying anything he might try to say. None of it could be true. I shrugged out of his hold. "This isn't funny, David. Where is Jesse?"

"He didn't make it." Dean's quiet voice broke through my rising hysteria, arresting the flow of my emotions. "He saved Frankie by pushing her out of the plane, but he went down with it."

"NO." Shoving David away, I jumped to my feet.

Dean grabbed my shoulders, forcing me to face him. "We found his body, Jessica."

When I tried to struggle away, he took my hand and put something in it. I opened my palm to see Jesse's wedding ring. Tarnished with smoke and stained with dirt, it bore the inscription I'd had engraved inside: Love endures.

My brain stopped working. Unable to think or feel, I froze, my gaze pinned to the thick band of gold that didn't hold nearly enough memories.

"Jessica?" Dean brushed hair away from my face. "It's going to take time to get his body home. The Honduras government isn't cooperating with our requests, but we're not giving up until his body is home."

His body? That was such a cold way to talk about Jesse. He was more than just a body. He was love and warmth, compassion and understanding, strength and power. My mind couldn't accept the idea he wasn't coming home.

He'd promised.

Without warning, my hand flashed, lashing out, and I slapped Dean full across the face. The sound reverberated through my consciousness, and I clapped the offending hand over my mouth to contain my shock.

"It's okay," David said. "We've all wanted to do that at one time or another."

Brea broke through the pair, and she wrapped her arms around me. That's when the world fractured. I collapsed against her, sobbing uncontrollably.

"He promised," I cried into my sister's shirt. "He promised to come back." He'd made reservations at the restaurant where he'd taken me on our first date, and we had tickets to a musical. This was supposed to be a short trip, a momentary interruption in our new life together.

He'd planned to tie me up.

We were going to take Bailey to the park.

His sister, Olivia, and her family were due to visit next week.

We'd planned for a life together, not this.

I didn't remember getting home, but I found myself in my bed with Brea curled against my side.

My whole life, no matter what else was going on, Brea was always by my side. She was the single constancy, the person I could always count on, but she couldn't salve the ache inside. She couldn't close the gaping hole in my chest that made even breathing painful. I wanted to die. I wanted to crawl into the grave with Jesse and stay there forever.

As if she knew the drift of my thoughts, she shifted and threw her arm over me. "I'm here," she said. "I'm right here."

That's what Jesse had said all those nights I laid awake worrying whether Bailey was going to make it another day. *She's just like you and me—stubborn and strong. She's a survivor.*

I slept in fits and starts, adrenaline bursts making my heart race as I looked expectantly toward the door and waited for him to walk through it.

I spent the next few days lying to myself.

He's just checking on Bailey.

He's working out with Frankie, and he's going to come home sore.

His head is in some program he's writing, and he's forgotten the time.

He's making breakfast.

He's having a drink with my dad.

He's helping my mom plant flowers.

The only thing that helped was Bailey. I held her constantly, crying when she cried and when she didn't. I cried harder when Sylvia took her away from me for changing or naps.

Brea was always there, the voice telling me to eat or take a shower or change my clothes. Warren held me when I couldn't move. Leon made sandwiches and talked about the things he'd liked about Jesse. Time passed, leaving me behind and shrouded in a miserable fog.

One day I sat by the side of the pool with my bare feet on the first step and stared into the clear depths. The tile edging the pool was dark blue, so much darker than Jesse's eyes. Bailey had Jesse's eyes. Crystal blue and bright with joy, they brought to mind every single time Jesse had smiled at me.

"I hope you're not thinking of jumping in."

I looked up to find Dean standing over me. His broad shoulders and tall stature cast a shadow over me, blocking the sun so I could look up. As always, he was impeccably groomed, and he wore tailored pants with a polo shirt. I hadn't seen him since he'd delivered the news at the hospital. I didn't even know how many days had passed since then.

"I'm sorry about slapping you."

He waved a dismissive hand. "I'm sure I deserved it for something else." Without waiting for an invitation, he removed his shoes and socks. Then he rolled up the cuffs on his pants and put his feet in the water next to mine.

"I can't swim," I said. I didn't know why I'd shared that obscure fact. Maybe it was because I no longer knew how to talk to Dean. At one time, we'd enjoyed an easy camaraderie, but after that first failed attempt at a relationship with Jesse, he'd come out firmly against me. Until he'd kissed me. Then he'd put distance between him and Jesse.

I'd hated that I'd come between them.

"If you want to learn, I can teach you."

His offer didn't require a response, and I didn't give one. We sat in silence for a long time.

"I miss him." Dean's soft admission didn't carry far, but I heard him. "He always made sure I didn't take myself too seriously."

Silence, and a sigh.

"I fucked up our friendship."

I didn't know what had happened between Jesse and Dean except that Dean was against Jesse and me getting back together. Jesse had felt betrayed, but I'd tried to help him see that Dean's opinion and actions, though hurtful, came from a place of love. I knew it was just a matter of time before all the fences between them were mended.

"I never told him you kissed me. He asked me to be honest with him all the time, but I wasn't. I know you regretted it, and I didn't want one mistake to stand between you."

"I told him." Dean traced circles on the tile between us. "I was... stupid. He punched me. We argued."

I peered at him curiously. "He never said anything to me. I thought he was just mad at you for all the shitty things you did to me."

"He wasn't happy about that." Dean folded his hands in his lap and swirled the water with his feet. "I was a dick to both of you, and I'm sorry. There are so many things I want to say to him. I want to apologize for not being the friend he deserved. I want to tell him I'm happy he found love and has the family he's always wanted."

He broke off, squeezing his eyes shut too late to prevent the tears from coming.

I scooted closer and slid my arm around Dean's waist as I rested my cheek on his arm. "You were dicks to each other. I'm sure it evened out. And with me—I understood why you did what you did. In your place, I would have done the same thing. When Brea wanted to break up with David, I was on board with helping her disappear from his life. If he'd hurt her, I would have done anything to make him feel pain."

He moved the arm I leaned against and slung it around my shoulders. We remained that way for a long time, drawing strength from each other.

If only Jesse was here to take part in this reconciliation. He would have been ecstatic to have Dean back as his friend. Of course, he would have couched it in macho terms, and they would have ended up slugging each other and probably grappling in the pool—maybe even ending up soaking wet—but things would have gone back to normal.

"Jessica?" Sylvia's voice jerked me from the peaceful cocoon of Dean's embrace.

I lifted my head from his shoulder and turned to my mother. "Hi, Mom. Is Bailey awake?"

"She is, and your dad is giving her a bottle right now." She held my cell phone out to me. "It's Sheila."

Sheila called every day. She wanted me to make funeral arrangements even though we didn't have a clue when the Honduras government planned to release his remains to me. Every day, she pressed me until I broke down in tears.

For the first time in days, I felt a shaky sense of peace. As tenuous as spider's silk, it would fall apart the second I moved.

I didn't want to talk to her.

Dean took the phone and pressed the button to unmute it. "Hi, Sheila. This is Dean. Yes, I know. I'm sorry too. I can't imagine what you're going through right now."

He went silent, and from where I sat, I heard Sheila's voice but I couldn't make out her words. I didn't need to. I knew what she wanted.

"Mmm-hmm. I think it's a little premature now. There's so much red tape. I'm trying to cut through it, but it's going to take time. Yes. As soon as I know, we'll make arrangements for a memorial service. Um, no."

Dean disengaged his comforting arm from me and got to his feet. He paced to the other side of the yard, and his lowered tone still carried to me.

"No, Sheila, I am not going to ask her that, and neither are you. Jesse wouldn't want to be buried next to Josie. First off, he wants to be cremated, and second, he'd want to be kept here, near his wife and child." He paused. "Yes, he has a will. He left everything to Jessica and there's a provision for a trust fund for Bailey."

How did Dean know about Jesse's will while I knew nothing?

"When we have a death certificate. I'm working on it. Like I said, lots of red tape." He listened some more. "I'll contact you as soon as I know something, but please understand that we're talking months, not days."

He came back around to my side of the pool and handed me the phone.

I took it. "Hi, Sheila. How are you holding up?"

"Not well. I bore two sons. They were supposed to outlive me."

How was I supposed to respond to that? She was angry, and I felt like a hollow version of a human being, empty and alone.

It turned out not to matter. She talked for the next hour, reminiscing about Jesse as a child and how he'd sent her a picture of Bailey every single day. Sheila had come to visit soon after Bailey was born, but she hadn't stayed long. As Jesse liked to say, Sheila couldn't survive without her cigarettes and bingo—and he wouldn't let her smoke at all when she was here.

When I begged off, citing Bailey as an excuse, I found Dean in the living room with my parents. He held Bailey up in front of a mirror, showing her the features of a baby.

"That's a cute nose, which you got from your mom because your dad had kind of a large schnoz. Those are your eyes, which you got from your dad because green eyes are a recessive trait, and it's exceedingly rare for even two green-eyed people to have green-eyed offspring. Your grandparents are bucking the odds with three green-eyed children."

I cast a glance at my parents, who were watching Dean and trying not to laugh.

"These are your cheeks, which are cute and babyish and utterly your own at this point. This is your chin, which is also adorable and a little pointy. That's from your dad's dad. He had a long, oval face and a pointy chin. Your dad had more of a square-thing going on, and your mom's is rounded."

Dean's gaze shifted from the reflection of Bailey's face to catch me watching him. He turned around, tearing Bailey from her reflection.

29

"And there's your mom. From the wet marks on her shirt, I'm thinking it's time for a snack."

I glanced down to see the wet circles over my nipples. "I ran out of the pad things." Jesse usually picked those up when I ran low. I hadn't needed to ask; they'd just appeared.

"I'll pick some up this afternoon," Warren said.

Dean handed over my baby, and I settled on the sofa to nurse. "I heard what you said to Sheila. Thank you."

He smiled, and he sat on the chair across from Warren. "You're welcome. I know she can be a bit much sometimes. Everyone handles grief differently, and her coping mechanism is to power through it as quickly as possible."

"She lost her son," Sylvia said. "I know what that feels like."

I reached over and squeezed her hand. Though she had Brea and me back now, she'd mourned us for more than two decades without knowing what had happened to us. Then I faced Dean. "I meant for telling her he wasn't going to be buried next to Josie. He wouldn't want that."

Warren frowned. "Who is Josie?"

"Jesse's first wife," I explained. "He met her in high school and married her right after. She'd asked him for a divorce the day before she was killed in a car accident. Jesse had been deployed overseas at the time." I left out the part where he was pretty sure Josie had cheated on him. It didn't matter now.

Dean frowned. "I didn't know she'd asked for a divorce."

I shrugged. "He didn't see a reason to make a big deal out of it. I think he preferred to remember the good times." I hoped Dean took that to heart and didn't let guilt eat away at him. Time healed all wounds, and I knew they would have repaired their friendship.

Our gazes met across the space. A sheen of tears wet his eyes, and I knew he understood my message.

And I realized I'd been so wrapped up in my grief that I hadn't made it to the hospital to see Frankie.

"Dean? Bailey is most likely going to nap after this. Maybe you can take me to go see Frankie?"

"Yes, of course."

I left twenty minutes later, the first time I'd been out of the house in six days. My parents assured me they didn't mind watching Bailey for a couple hours. I was lucky to have them in my life.

"Frankie is in rough shape," Dean warned. "She's had three surgeries on her leg, but they finally got the infection under control. Her parents and brother flew in from California. Her mom's name is Samira. Her dad is Mr. Sikara. His first name is Ramesh, but he's a little old-fashioned. Her brother's name is Elijah. He's a hotshot software developer in Silicon Valley, and her parents are extremely proud of him."

"Do they know what Frankie does?"

"No. She told them she does the books for a security firm."

I stared at Dean. "Seriously? Did they know she was in Special Forces?"

"They don't talk about her time in the military. Her parents didn't approve of her joining up. They wanted her to have a more traditional life—marry rich and spend her time doing charity work. If they knew a fraction of what she's done, they would have a collective heart attack."

This explained why Frankie had a chip on her shoulder large enough to drive her to become one of the best operatives in the world. "So what do they think she was doing in Central America?"

"Digging wells for villages that don't have access to fresh water."

It was a plausible reason for being there. "And she was attacked by guerillas?"

"Something like that. We're not discussing details. Her parents don't want to know, and she doesn't want to tell them anything. She's focusing on recovery so they'll go home and leave her alone."

"That's so sad." I thought about the place my family—my extended family—had come to occupy in my life, and right now I was even grateful for Sheila's daily calls.

"She has us." Dean found a parking spot in the garage. "She's going to cry when she sees you."

I frowned as I got out of the car and leaned on my cane. "Why?"

"Because she blames herself for what happened to Jesse."

I wanted to say it was ridiculous for her to blame herself, but truthfully it was everybody's fault in equal measures. They'd all planned the mission, and they all bore responsibility.

Just as Dean had predicted, her room was full of people when we got there. The first person I saw was around my age. Like Frankie, he was tall and lanky, and he had her dark hair and eyes. His skin was a few shades lighter. He wasn't quite as tall as Frankie, but his eyelashes were just as dark and long. He gazed at me curiously as I entered.

Once I was past the bathroom, the room opened up. On the near side of the bed were a man and woman who appeared to be in their sixties. My artist's eye picked out the way their faces had blended to form Frankie's stunning features. Her father had the same quiet intensity she had, and her mother was built like a dancer.

My attention focused on the woman in the bed. Her skin was ashen, and she had dark circles under her eyes. She was swollen from the IV fluids, but none of that dimmed her spectacular beauty.

The moment she saw me, her eyes welled with tears.

Wordlessly, I limped to her side and bent over to hug her.

"Careful of her ribs," Dean cautioned. "Four are broken."

I kept the hug mostly around her shoulders and head, which put her face squarely in the middle of my girls. "I'm sorry I wasn't here sooner."

She clung to me, sobs tearing from her chest and wetting through the shirt I'd changed into after feeding Bailey. "No, I'm sorry. I can understand why you wouldn't want to see me."

"It's not that. I'm not mad. I just... couldn't get out of bed."

She pushed me a little, angling her face so she could breathe. I let go of her and stepped back. She closed her eyes against a wave of pain, but I wasn't sure if it was physical or emotional.

I sought to reassure her. "This is the first time I've left the house."

Dean guided me to a chair on the other side of the bed. "Samira, Mr. Sikara, this is Jessica Zinn. She's a friend of Frankie's, and she's Jesse's widow."

I did my best to smile at her parents, but I only managed something tremulous. "It's nice to meet you. I wish the circumstances were better."

Her father nodded, and her mother gave me a sympathetic smile. "We're so sorry to hear about Jesse. He was a good man."

Rationally I knew Jesse was gone, but I wasn't ready to hear him talked about in the past tense. I wasn't ready for Dean to refer to me as a widow.

Dean kept a hand on my shoulder, and that's where I found the strength not to fall apart again. "This is Elijah, Frankie's brother."

"Elijah is Francesca's older brother. He's a successful software developer." Samira's smile morphed to proud and maternal. "He owns a large house and he also has a vacation property in Vale."

If Dean hadn't warned me, I would have thought she was trying to set me up with her son. Her daughter was lying in bed, too weak to sit on her own, and she was bragging about her son's accomplishments? Not only that, but Frankie risked her life to make the world a safer place. Maybe she didn't have a large apartment, but she could if she wanted.

Frankie coughed. When I looked at her, she chuckled. "Mom, Dad, Elijah, how about you go get some lunch? My friends will stay until you get back." Once they were gone, she wrapped her arms around her midsection and broke out in giggles. "Oh, the look on your face, Jessica. Priceless."

"What look?"

"Incredulity."

I didn't want to criticize her mother. "Sorry. I wasn't going to say anything. Dean briefed me on the way in."

The laughter fell away, and her gaze turned somber. "I've thought about this a lot, but I don't know what to say to you except I'm so, so sorry."

"I am too." My voice came out hoarse and whispery. "We all love him. We all lost him. I'm not going to sit here and pretend my loss is greater than yours. He was my husband, but the four of you were best friends." I wiped a tear away. "He would want us to pull together, to be here for each other. He was really big on being supportive."

She leaned her head back against the pillow, and tears streamed down her cheeks. "He kept that picture of you and Bailey next to his heart. Every little while, he'd touch his hand to it."

Dean handed tissue to both of us, and he dabbed at his eyes as well.

We sat in silence for a few moments, each of us lost in thoughts of Jesse.

Finally I looked at Frankie, who was wiping her cheeks, and I asked the million-dollar question. "Are you going to want this cane back?"

She laughed. "I'll get a new one, I'm sure. That one was too short for me anyway. I could never bring myself to tell Jesse."

Chapter 4

Dean

"Blueberry muffins." Brea set a platter in the center of the table in the conference room.

She didn't have to say she'd made them because they were Jesse's favorites. They were the ones he asked for every time she said she was going to bake. That, and chocolate cake. I preferred cranberry almond or banana walnut. I liked complementary flavors blended together to produce something new and tantalizing.

"Thanks, Sugar." David kissed her cheek and took a seat to my right. Brea sat next to him, and Frankie rounded out our crew.

Three months had passed, and we were on our third debrief about the mission that had gone so terribly wrong.

Frankie looked much better. Having been in peak physical condition beforehand, she'd bounced back faster and more efficiently than the physical therapist had expected. She didn't even use a cane to walk anymore, and thanks to reconstructive surgery, it didn't look like she'd lost a chunk of muscle from her leg.

She folded her hands on the table. "Let me begin by saying that it's good to be back."

"It's great to have you back," David said. "Shall we get started?"

"Yes," I said. "First order of business is backup teams. I'd like to discuss recruitment and pay structure for keeping a backup team on retainer for every team we have in the field."

Frankie met my gaze. "When we formed this company, we meant for it to stay small so we could better control the moral compass. When you bring on more people, then they're going to have opinions and want to take jobs that go against our mission statement."

"Things change in seven years." David quietly backed me up. "We get older. We start underestimating the manpower a job requires."

"It was a two-man job." Frankie's ruddy color betrayed her emotions. "We fucked up. We got cocky about how many mercs we could take on at one time. We should have used a more covert strategy."

"It took us two days to get to you," I countered. "We left Brea on a job with someone she'd never met, and it still took us two days to find you. If we had backup teams in better positions, then they could have extracted you faster."

David nodded. "They could have gone in earlier, when you and Jesse were captured, and they could have freed you. Or maybe the backup team could have been there to help Brea finish the delivery job."

Brea snorted. "Delivery job. You make it sound like I was driving a cupcake van."

For the first time, I considered the position into which we'd thrust Brea. I'd been so preoccupied with the tragedy of losing Jesse that I hadn't thought about how we'd left her with half of the original team.

I said, "Sugar, you're downplaying the significance of the situation in which we left you."

"Dean, I'm amazed at the lengths you'll go to just to avoid ending a sentence with a preposition." She flashed a cheeky grin. "Seriously, I was fine. Joss was a great partner. He kept an eye on me from the sky, and when we had to re-route because he spotted an ambush, he kept his wits about him."

I leaned forward, folding my hands on the table. "You were almost ambushed?"

She shrugged. "We expected it, right? We were prepared. The rubies made it to their destination an hour late, but they made it."

Rather than respond—because what more could I say?—I turned back to Frankie. "We all fucked up. We are all responsible for what happened down there. We were supposed to be a team, and we weren't. Either we all work on one job at a time from now on, or we expand our employee base to include backup teams."

Frankie gestured to Brea. "She's not exactly an employee."

I dismissed her concern. "She's not a partner."

Brea scowled. "I'm seeing fewer muffins in your future."

As David was her husband, there was no way he was going to field this one, not if he ever wanted to get laid again, so I responded gently. "Simmer down, Sugar. While we value your opinion and your input, you're not a partner. The question becomes, if we hire more employees, will they also have input into what missions we accept and how we plan them?"

David snagged a muffin, and he peeled it as he voiced his opinion. "I think it depends on who we hire. Brea has practical experience that comes in handy in some of our missions, but in others, she has to trust us to know what we're doing. Someone like Malcolm Legato would have valuable input as well. I see where we don't want to give up control, but if we bring in good people, they're going to have something valuable to add."

Frankie pressed her lips together. "So, we're doing this? We're not even going to discuss taking fewer jobs?"

"We could do that," I said. "What are your arguments for pursuing that resolution?"

"We keep it small, just us."

Brea leaned over and set her hand on Frankie's. "It would be nice to have more women at the table. It's been a testosterone fest around here for too long."

I had no objection to hiring women, but that didn't change facts. "Finding qualified women for this line of work is more difficult than you might imagine."

"But not impossible." Brea spread her hands, indicating herself and Frankie. "Check us out."

Frankie regarded Brea thoughtfully. "Jessica could—"

"No." David and I spoke at the same time.

"She doesn't want to," Brea explained. "She's never liked the life we used to have, and now that she can leave it all behind her, that's what she's doing."

"Why do you all want to expand SAFE Security?" Frankie pounded her fist on the table. "This is our family. We don't need more people in our family. We don't need to put more people at risk."

"We'll always be family," I said. "Nothing is going to change that. The main reason for backup teams is for safety. Even if the four of us go on every mission together, we still don't have backup."

Frankie's face fell. "I feel like this is all my fault. If I'd grabbed Jesse when he pushed me out of the plane, he'd be here. He might be hurt, but he'd be here, and then we wouldn't be having this conversation." She sniffled, and I handed her my handkerchief, but not my sympathy.

David chimed in. "Frankie, I hate to burst your bubble and ruin this lovely pity party you're throwing for yourself, but this isn't the first time we've needed backup. We've had more and more close calls in the past few years. Even last fall in San Tesoro, if Brea and Jessica hadn't come after us, we'd either still be rotting in those prison cells, or we'd be dead. We should have addressed the problem a long time ago, but we didn't, and Jesse paid the ultimate price."

"We all failed Jesse," I added, "and I'm determined not to fail anyone ever again."

She wiped her eyes and kept the balled-up linen square. "Let's talk about how we're going to structure payment and go about finding talent."

Brea said, "I propose that we keep the male-to-female ratio here at no lower than forty percent female."

I hadn't expected that, and frankly she had no standing to make such a demand. Still I wasn't going to shut her down, because Frankie would kill me. "How about we see who is most qualified, and we can vote on each candidate as they come up?"

Brea looked at Frankie. "Girlfriend, I think we have our work cut out for us."

Later, when everyone was gone for the night, I opened the program where we kept our financial data, and I set to work trying to figure out what we could afford to spend on new hires.

I hated paperwork and recordkeeping. These were not my skill set. Jesse was great with this stuff, and Brea was equally as wonderful. Together, the pair had forced me to actually do my paperwork and participate in the bookkeeping. Now when I looked at the numbers, I heard Jesse in my head telling me about expenses and profit margins.

About the time the numbers blurred in front of my face, I heard a noise in the hall. I looked up to find Jessica standing in my doorway.

In the past three months, she'd lost a considerable amount of weight—too much, if she were to ask me. Her skin was ghostly pale, which made her brown hair seem even darker and duller, and her green eyes were eerily luminous. Her stylish shirt hung on her frame, and the leggings were splattered with paint and spit-up stains. The only time I saw her smile was at her daughter, and the only time she seemed to find some measure of peace was when she was working in her studio.

Though she was bereft of joy, her furniture creations were increasingly bright and whimsical, as if she was trying to create happiness to fill the void.

I forced myself to visit her every few days, and each time it tore at my heart to see the shadow she'd become. I wanted to help her, but I didn't know how.

I got to my feet. "Jessica, I wasn't expecting you."

"I came to clean out Jesse's office." She peered down the hall, and I knew what she wasn't saying.

"David and I took care of that. I didn't think you wanted his computer equipment." Besides, it belonged to SAFE Security, and it contained sensitive information we needed.

She shook her head, a small movement that betrayed how many miles away her thoughts were. "I've been going through Jesse's things at home. He has a lot of stuff."

I went to her and guided her to the sofa in my office. "If you want help, just call me, Jessica. I'm willing to help you sort through anything."

"I found his will." Now that she was sitting, she seemed to see me for the first time. "He wants me to give his mom a thousand dollars a month for bingo."

I chuckled. "Sheila does love her bingo."

"She expects me to call her every few days, just like Jesse did."

"You and Bailey are her connection to him."

Jessica grabbed my hand. "Dean, I've met her twice. I suck at relationships."

It was wrong, but I reveled in the fact that she was touching me and that she'd come to me in her time of need. "The more you practice your relationship skills, the better they'll get."

Her gaze lost focus as she thought. When it came back, she studied my face. "Did you know Jesse is wealthy?"

All of us had enjoyed lucrative paydays since we'd launched SAFE Security seven years ago. "I know he's not hurting for cash. None of us are."

"No, Dean. *Wealthy*, as in he's a multi-millionaire. Did you know he sold patents and technology to major companies and the government? He gets royalty checks that make what he sends to his mom a drop in the bucket. No wonder he bought her a condo and he pays her bills and he sends her spending money on top of her pension and retirement."

I hadn't been aware he'd supported his mom so much, but it made sense. Family had always been Jesse's priority. I'd set my parents up as well.

"He invested in a lot of startups. Some have been successful and others have flopped." She traced a design on the palm of my hand as she thought, but I doubted she realized she was doing something so erotic to me.

To put a stop to it before my cock noticed, I grasped her hands in mine. "Brat, he left everything to you. He wanted to make sure you and Bailey never wanted for anything."

She rubbed the back of her hand on her forehead. "Dean, he didn't just look after me. He looked after all of you. Every time he invested in a startup, he put in small sums for you, David, Frankie, and his sisters. He managed the investments on his own. I don't know—

38

maybe he was going to give them as gifts eventually. I'm not going to do that. I'm going to give each of you the things that belong to you."

"Okay." I hadn't known about the investments. I had plenty of my own, and it had never occurred to me to invest in anyone else's name. "That was thoughtful."

A line formed between her eyebrows. "Dean, they may have started out small, but they grew. Each of you now has a few hundred thousand to play with."

"Oh." I hadn't known any of this, and now I felt like even more of a dick because I hadn't done anything nearly as thoughtful for my friends. "Wow."

Angry tears glistened in her eyes, rendering them even brighter. "You're all fucking morons."

"You don't mean that." My inner Dom was coming to the fore. While I tended toward being firm, I was also gentle. I preferred praise to punishment, but that didn't mean I avoided it.

"Yes, I do. You're each wealthy enough to walk away from this life and never look back. You don't have to go out there and put your life on the line every week. You don't need the money." She swiped at her eyes as if they'd disobeyed by crying. "When he bought that house, I was shocked he'd spend so much. I mean, I thought he was going back to work to pay for the fucking house, but it turns out he bought it with cash."

I felt I had to defend his memory. "Jessica, he loved you."

"He loved me so much he left me to put his life on the line for what? Nothing—that's what. He takes down someone in a cartel, and five more pop up to take their place. I've been on that side of the law, and I know firsthand there is no shortage of people willing to do bad things in the name of money and power. I never thought Jesse was one of those people, but I guess I was wrong."

She was teetering close to the brink of losing her mind, and I had to pull her back.

"Brat, that's enough. Jesse didn't do this job for the money. None of us do. We do it because we know we make a positive difference in this world."

"Bullshit," she sneered. "You aren't fooling anyone." She slammed the heels of her palms into my chest.

This was different from when she'd slapped me before. She'd been stunned by her reaction as much as I had, and I saw immediately she hadn't meant to hit me as much as she'd wanted to smack away the information.

But now she was attacking me. She was in pain and lashing out.

With a neat twist of my arms, I captured her wrists and pinned them behind her back. "Brat, I know you're upset, so let's take a minute to calm down."

She struggled against my hold. "I don't want to calm down. I've been calm for months, and it hasn't helped. I'm tired of being rational and good. I'm tired of feeling all this pain, and no matter what I do, it doesn't go away. I'm tired of pretending for all of you that I'm fine when I feel like I died months ago."

My heart broke at the raw pain written on her features and trembling in her voice. Without further thought, I lifted her onto my lap and held her against me.

Her whole body softened, and she melted into me. I cradled her head, and she rested her cheek against my chest. Her hand grasped at my shirt.

Though the wrong circumstances had landed her in my arms, protectiveness and pure joy surged through me. After all this time, we finally had more than a surface-level connection.

I didn't know how long we stayed like that, but I wasn't going to move voluntarily.

After a long time, her body shuddered.

I kissed the top of her head. "Feel better, Brat?"

"Dean?"

"Yes?"

"Don't call me Brat."

I wanted to argue that it fit, but then it hit me that Jesse had called her by that nickname, and hearing it had to be too painful. "Sorry. I won't do it again unless you're being a brat."

She straightened up, and since she was on my lap, it put her face inches from mine. She looked from my mouth to my eyes and back again. Then she leaned forward, closing the gap and brushing her lips over mine.

It felt so fucking good. I'd wanted this for so long, and I'd all but given up on the idea she could ever love me back.

Moving slowly, I gradually increased my participation in the kiss. I cradled the back of her head and put my other hand on her hip. Tilting her head a little more, I deepened the kiss. She tasted like sunshine and warmth, with a hint of mocha and peppermint, and when she moaned, I reversed the possessiveness to claim her as mine.

Her hand, which had been gripping my shirt, slid along my neck and teased my earlobe. I groaned as she stumbled upon one of my most sensitive places.

She shifted to straddle me, and her hands were suddenly a flurry of activity. She loosened my tie and attacked the buttons on my shirt, all without breaking the kiss. The Dominant part of me wanted to take her in hand, restrain her passion until she couldn't contain it anymore, but the nurturing part of my Dom side understood she was already desperate and half out of her mind.

I slid my hands up her legs and grasped her luscious ass. She moaned loudly and ground her mound against my growing cock. She broke the kiss as she ripped my shirt open, and then her hot mouth was on my bare flesh. I let her explore until she bit my nipple.

With a grunt, I grasped a handful of her hair and jerked her head back. "Kitten, if you bite my nipples, I'll bite yours."

With her head tilted back and her neck exposed, she gasped. "If you bite my nipples, you're going to get a surprise you might not enjoy as much as you'd think you might."

I kneaded her left breast. "Do you like that, kitten?"

"Yes. I'm okay with rough nipple play, light spanking, and hair pulling."

"And bondage." I added that one because Jesse had confided in me how quickly she achieved subspace with bondage.

"No," she said. "No bondage."

I guessed she wasn't ready to cross that line with me yet. Baby steps, I cautioned myself. We were still in the wooing part of the process. Lifting her, I shifted us to put her underneath me.

She lifted a knee and rubbed her thigh against mine. "Are you okay with this? I kind of attacked you."

Her too-large shirt had slipped down to expose one shoulder. I pressed a line of kisses along her collarbone. "Yes, kitten. I would have stopped you if I wasn't. If we're going to list preferences, I like that thing you did to my earlobe, I prefer to take charge, and I like scratching, so don't sheathe your claws."

She gazed up at me, her soul bared in her eyes. I saw trust and affection, pain and yearning. It was enough for now. I kissed her again, devouring her mouth as she tangled her tongue with mine. Jessica was no pillow princess.

I lifted her shirt to expose her breasts, which were extra large and doubly tempting. I closed my hand over one delightful globe to find it was more than handful. I broke the kiss and regarded her chest thoughtfully. I'd never made love to a woman who had recently given birth. Should I keep my hands off the food bags?

"If you're afraid of accidentally nursing, don't suck on them. They may leak, but it's not poisonous if you happen to come into contact with the milk."

I decided to leave them contained for the time being. I kneaded them through the bra before venturing out to caress the rest of her soft skin. While I explored, she finished removing my shirt and tie, and then she went for the fastener on my pants.

My hands were around her wrists before I remembered her prohibition against bondage. I moved her hands to my torso. "Not yet, kitten. I want to taste you."

And taste her, I did. I licked and sucked my way down her body. As I peeled away her leggings, I worshipped her thighs and calves. By the time I reversed course, she was a quivering mass of need.

She spread her legs, welcoming my kisses on her dripping pussy. I played with her, caressing my knuckle over her slit to elicit gasps and those kittenish noises begging for more. By the time I swiped my tongue over her clit, she was thoroughly primed. She tasted like a slice of paradise, and I eagerly licked and sucked at her essence. Her hips thrust, seeking control of her pleasure, so I threw an arm over her pelvis to hold her down.

With a small mew, she submitted to my dominance.

All too soon, she stiffened and cried out Jesse's name.

I guided her through the orgasm, and as she came down, I laid my head on her stomach in an attempt to gather my wits.

Never in my life had a woman cried out another man's name in bed. However this was different. She was still mourning him. Perhaps I had moved too soon, but wasn't that exactly what he'd done originally—moved on her before she was ready?

Did that justify my actions now? After all, she'd kissed me. I hadn't made the first move. I'd been there for her as a friend.

I soothed my damaged ego with the thought that if she'd loved him this deeply, then she would eventually love me even more. It was proof she had come a long way in her therapy.

She ran her fingers through my hair, lightly scratching my head. "Dean? I'm sorry. It's just—I haven't been with anyone else in more than five years."

"I know." I lifted my head. "I've never been called by another man's name before."

"I guess that's one argument in favor of a gag." She grinned to show she was teasing. "I'll understand if you want to stop and forget this ever happened."

I sat up and pulled her with me. "I think putting the brakes on this for now is a good idea, but I'm against forgetting it happened."

She got dressed while I fixed my shirt and tie, and then she sat back down on the sofa. "I don't want to go home tonight. I was going to sleep here."

"On my sofa?"

"Yeah. I don't want to be in Jesse's office, and David's couch has to be covered in fluids I'd rather not touch. Same with Brea's. And Frankie doesn't have a sofa."

I laughed softly at her rejection of David and Brea's sofas. The pair of them often had sex in their offices even though we'd repeatedly informed them it was not proper workplace behavior.

"Why don't you want to go home?"

"It's lonely, and Jesse is everywhere I look."

She was asking as a friend. I couldn't turn her down, but staying here wasn't what she needed either. "How about you stay the night with me?" I closed down my laptop for the night.

"Okay."

I stuck my hand in my pocket, looking for my keys, and I came up empty.

Jessica held them out to me. "Sorry. Hard habit to break."

I was aware of her difficulty. "It's good you keep trying."

Fifteen minutes later, we'd made it to my foyer, and Jessica looked around. "Is Mr. Whitley here?"

"He's in bed. I let him know earlier I planned to work late." I motioned for her to follow me up the stairs. I led her down the main hall and stopped in front of an open door. "There's a robe in the bathroom closet, and the bathroom is fully stocked with anything you'll need. If you check the drawers in the bureau, you should find a selection of night shirts."

She chewed her bottom lip and peered into the room. "Can't I sleep with you?"

I frowned. Had she attempted to seduce me in order to find an alternate place to spend the night? "What are you asking?"

"I don't want to sleep alone."

Time to take the plunge. "Did you kiss me tonight because wanted a place to sleep?"

Buying time to think, she pushed her hair back out of her face, but the wild curls sprang back where they wanted to be. "Yes and no." Anguish twisted her features as her gaze met mine. "I'm tired of being empty and alone. I'm tired of the ache in my chest that won't go away. I want to feel something, Dean. When you look at me, I see that you have feelings for me, and tonight when you kissed me, for the first time in far too long, I felt something beautiful and sweet. I want that again. I want you to make my brain shut off so I can just feel the things you make me feel."

It wasn't a declaration of love, but it was progress. My touch chased away the pain, and she'd found bliss in my kisses. I led her across the hall to my room.

I switched on the light, and she looked around. I tried to see it through her eyes—the elegant yet understated furnishings and the exquisite paintings featured on the walls. As an artist, she had to appreciate fine art. She'd been to my home before, and she'd commented positively on several paintings downstairs.

But her gaze barely skated over the furniture. She zeroed in on the pajamas Whitley had laid out for me. "Does he tell you what to do, since he's known you since you were seven, or do you tell him what to do?"

"I ask for the things I want, and Whitley does his job."

She turned to me. "You can't honestly tell me he's been in your life for almost thirty years, and he's just a servant."

"Butler is the term for which you're searching. He takes care of me and my home. He's my friend and, in some ways, my mentor. I value his service and his opinion, which he doesn't offer unless I ask."

She set her bag on an ottoman. "He's the perfect submissive."

I hadn't thought about it that way, but it made sense on some level. "Not the way you're thinking." I lifted my chin in the direction of her bag. "Is that an overnight bag?"

"I wish." She sat next to it and lifted out a contraption I recognized as a breast pump.

"I'm going to shower and change. I'll give you some privacy."

She grinned. "I never thought I'd see the day when the great connoisseur of women, Dean Alloway, was afraid of boobs."

"Those aren't boobs," I said. "Not while they're a feed station for a baby."

I took my time in the bathroom, and I masturbated to the image of her in my bedroom. When I returned to the bedroom, I found her in my bed—wearing one of the nightshirts from the guest room across the hall. She looked so perfect there, a fantasy come to life.

She looked up from the book she'd been reading, a teasing lilt to her lips. "When you have women over, do you make them sleep across the hall?"

I'd never kept my peccadilloes secret from Jessica. "That's where I have sex with them."

Her eyebrows lifted. "You don't bring women into your bedroom?"

I turned on the lamp next to the bed and doused the room lights. Then I climbed under the covers, keeping a good bit of distance between us in my king-sized bed. "No, Jessica. I don't let women I bring home sleep in my bed. You're special."

Before she could say more, I turned off the lamp. As I adjusted my pillow, she sighed and moved closer. I felt her soft body against my side, and I turned toward her, intending to offer her the comfort of a warm embrace, but she had other ideas. Our lips met in violent clash, and her hands were everywhere. Before I knew what she was about, she'd divested me of my shirt. Her nails traced light trails down my arms and across my back.

I chuckled. "Damn, kitten. I knew you had a light touch, but I wasn't prepared for this."

She pushed me onto my back and straddled my midsection. "Do you have condoms?"

"Yes."

"Then you're prepared enough." With a swish of cloth, she tossed the nightshirt aside. The room was dark, lit only by ambient light from nightlights in the hall.

She lifted my hands from where they rested on her thighs and placed them on her breasts. Through my hands, she cupped and kneaded her breasts. Once I asserted my understanding of what she wanted, she let go, arching into my touch. I traced my fingertips around her areolas and teased her nipples to sharp points.

She undulated, grinding her pussy against my stomach, and when I pinched her nipples and twisted them viciously, she cried out and gripped my arms.

I flipped us so that she was underneath me, and I pinned her down with my larger body. "Let's get one thing straight, kitten. In this bed, I'm in charge."

She ran a light caress over my shoulders and up my neck. "If you say so."

"That's, 'Yes, Sir.'" Using my knee, I spread her legs and settled against her warmth.

Beneath me, she stiffened. "Dean, I'm not submissive. I'm okay with you being dominant and bossy, but I'm not okay with titles and submission."

I'd slept with women who didn't identify as submissive before, and Jessica did not fall into that category. She could be strong and assertive when she needed to be, but the whole time I'd known her, she'd bloomed under the tender care of a Dominant—specifically Jesse and me. We'd spent a lot of time visiting her in rehab, and we'd dominated her every single time.

We'd groomed her for this, and she'd submitted with a smile. Her assertion shed new light on the things Jesse had confided in me about how she didn't understand submission. But I would have thought she'd been with Jesse long enough to learn to embrace her true nature.

This was not an occasion where I was prepared to withdraw to help her get in touch with her inner submissive. I'd wanted her for far too long to let that get in my way. She needed to be loved and cherished, and I was prepared to give of myself to her.

I ran my palm down from her shoulder, lifting my body so I could feel the whole length of her silky skin. I worshipped her slowly, with reverent caresses and murmured praise, memorizing every inch of her delectable body. I drank every sigh and moan, and I luxuriated in the firm caresses and light scratches she used to explore my body.

When she slid her hand down my sleep pants and gripped my cock, I shuddered.

"Condoms?"

Her nimble fingers worked magic on my cock, and I thrust into her hold. "Not if you keep touching me like this."

She circled her thumb along the underside of the crown. "Is this what you want?"

I wanted her. I'd wanted her for so long—too long. I wasn't going to orgasm in her hand, not until later and under other circumstances. I pressed a kiss to her forehead. "Wait here."

Since I wasn't in the habit of having lovers in my bed, I padded across the hall to where I kept my condoms. When I returned, I found her where I'd left her. Though she hadn't moved, the hand that had been wrapped around my cock was now between her legs.

As I approached, I considered turning on the lights so I could better watch the show, but then I rejected the thought. Tonight was steeped in darkness because I sensed she needed it as a layer of protection. She wasn't mine yet. It would take time before she would allow me to claim her in all the ways I wanted.

I utilized the teasing tone she liked. "Impatient, I see."

"Mmmm. Just keeping it warm for you."

She sat up as I came closer, kneeling up on the edge of the bed to greet me. Our lips met. I kissed her thoroughly, and she clung to me. Somehow she also managed to rid me of my sleep pants and underwear. Truly, she had a skilled touch.

I lifted her, repositioning her in the center of the bed. I knelt between her legs and rolled the condom over my cock as she scratched caresses along my thighs.

"Kitten, I like your claws."

"I'll try not to break the skin."

Pressing her back, I aligned my cock with her opening. "Don't constrain yourself. I'm okay with broken skin."

With that, I sank into her waiting warmth. Satin fire enveloped my manhood, sucking me balls-deep. She felt so fucking good—better even than I'd imagined, and I had a pretty spectacular imagination.

"Jessica." I exhaled her name on a reverent breath.

"Oh, God." She canted her hips and planted her feet on the mattress. "Oh, yes."

She held onto me, clutching at my shoulders and digging her nails into my flesh. Pleasure, borne on waves of pain, streamed through me, and I increased my pace. She met every thrust with a gasp or a moan. Soon she writhed beneath me, a trembling mass of wild energy.

I know she'd prohibited bondage, but she seemed to need more in the way of an anchor, so I hiked her leg up and held it with my arm wrapped behind her knee to limit her movement.

Suddenly she cried out and stiffened. Her pussy clamped down on my cock with manic undulations that drove me over the cliff and milked a climax from me. I rolled, taking her with me so I could hold her to me without crushing her.

The day had been long and tiring, and I'm ashamed to say I promptly fell asleep.

Chapter 5

Jessica

Nestled in Dean's arms, I listened to his breathing even out as he fell asleep. I wasn't upset that he did a typical male thing; I was relieved. I didn't want to stay up talking about what I'd done and the implications of my actions.

The emptiness he'd chased away for a few moments came crashing back, only this time it was larger and more painful. I felt like a spiked mace had slammed into my gut, punishment for betraying Jesse.

I waited until I was sure he was out, and then I disengaged myself from his arms. I found the nightgown I'd cast aside, and slipped it over my head. Then I tiptoed to the sex bedroom across the hall and broke down.

It wasn't pretty. Great, hiccupping sobs tore from me, ripping the scars off my wounds and making them bleed fresh. What kind of person slept with her husband's best friend only three months after his death?

To make matters worse, in the darkness, I'd closed my eyes and pretended Dean was Jesse. What I'd done was beyond wrong. There was no coming back from this.

I cried until I was sick, and I spent the next hour on the floor of the guest bathroom, mired in guilt and hiding from Dean.

In the predawn hours, I cleaned myself up as best I could. When I'd changed into this nightgown, I'd had the sense to leave my things in the sex bedroom. Maybe I knew the whole time I wouldn't make it through the night in Dean's bed.

One thing was for certain: I had no business being here. I should never had kissed him or led him on. I had no excuse for my behavior except I was lonely and hurting, and for a little while, he'd made me forget pieces of me were missing.

Dean didn't live far from the house Jesse had bought for us, about a half mile. I walked home, the longest walk of shame in my history, and I showered the scent of Dean off me before I crawled into the bed I'd shared with Jesse.

I cried until I fell into a deep, dreamless sleep.

"Jessica?"

The sound of my name called to me, pulling me from the seductive embrace of nothingness. I opened my eyes to find Sylvia sitting on my bed with Bailey in her arms.

Immediately I sat up and looked around. Bright sunlight streamed through the windows. The clock on the mantle above the fireplace indicated it was almost two in the afternoon.

"I overslept."

Sylvia's eyes softened with sympathy. "Honey, you've been sleeping poorly for months. You needed this." She handed Bailey to me and got up. "I'm going to get you a cold cloth for your eyes."

They must have looked really bad for her to say something. Sylvia usually didn't comment on the signs of my grief. She was a hugger, not a pointer-outer.

I kissed Bailey's cheeks. She smiled and grabbed a handful of my hair. The girl had a strong grip. With difficulty, I disengaged and wrapped her fists around my fingers. We chatted until Sylvia returned with a damp towel.

She handed it over and took Bailey. "Dean called to see if you'd got home okay. He said you were at SAFE Security last night?"

The way she phrased it, I knew she wanted an explanation. I'd told her I was meeting Brea for drinks.

"I was going to clean out Jesse's office." I wasn't sorry for lying, but I knew I owed Sylvia an explanation. "I wanted to do it alone."

"Jessica, you don't have to lie to me. I would have understood."

While she might have understood, she would have offered to go with me, and then she would have been hurt when I turned her down. My actions were mostly about avoiding unpleasant conversations with a mother who was as stubborn and opinionated as me. I loved her, and the more I got to know her, the more sympathy I had for Jesse and Warren. We were high-maintenance and hard to handle.

"Sometimes I just want to get out without telling anyone where I'm going or why I'm going there. I know I shouldn't lie, but it's what seems to come out of my mouth."

"Maybe, when you lie, you should try retracting the statement. You can practice on Warren and me. We're a safe audience. We love you, and we want to help you however we can. We missed the years where we got to ground you for lying. And trust me, Jessica, the day is going to come when Bailey lies to you, and you'll have no one to blame but yourself because that's the example you're setting for her."

With that, she set Bailey on my stomach and left me alone to ponder her words of wisdom.

I took the towel off my eyes and spent some quality time with my baby. I did take time out to text Dean.

Sorry. I should have left a note. I didn't mean to worry you.

His answer came immediately. *A note would have been lovely. Dinner tonight?*

My stomach sank. I didn't want to date Dean. I wasn't ready to date anyone, and I still felt like a shitty person every time I thought about last night. I thought about what my mother had said, and I decided to be honest with Dean.

I'm not ready. Sorry.

I was sorry for leading him on. I didn't know if Dean had slept with me because he had feelings for me or because I was a connection to Jesse, a way to assuage the pain of loss, and a huge part of me was too chicken-shit to find out. I put off reading his reply until the next afternoon.

When I did, I cried.

I understand. This is difficult for both of us. I'm here as a friend if that's what you need. I care about you, kitten.

Brea and David came over for dinner that night. After we ate, I left David with my parents and Bailey, and I dragged Brea up to my room where I closed the door.

The master suite consisted of a large room that had a bedroom part and a living room part. Jesse had arranged the furniture similar to the way he had in his loft, with the couch and chairs in front of the fire and on the other side of the private balcony outside. The bed was set against an interior wall, and on the other side of it were two closets the size of regular rooms, and a shared bathroom.

My parents, in their master suite on the other side of the house, had separate bathrooms. My mom greatly enjoyed not having to share with my dad. She said after a few years of marriage, men stopped being careful in the bathroom and went back to being gross.

Since we had a housekeeper who kept all the bathrooms clean, I hadn't thought it would ever become an issue between Jesse and me. I'd already known he tended to be a slob, and I'd accepted it about him the same way he'd accepted I was a pickpocket and a liar.

Brea stood a few feet from the door, watching me lock it. "This looks serious."

My sister was my rock, but more than that, she was my moral compass. Okay, maybe that wasn't quite true. Together, we had planned and executed some very unscrupulous activities. Some of the directions on our combined moral compass were problematic at best. Still, we knew this, and awareness of the problem often meant we discussed what routes might be more moral than the ones we were inclined to take.

Birds of a feather, then. I needed my flock.

I flung myself on the sofa and sighed dramatically. "I slept with Dean."

She perched on the other end of the sofa, lines of confusion wrinkling her forehead and chin. "Are you in love with him?"

"No." I sat up and put my head in my hands. "I don't know what the hell I was doing. I went to clean out Jesse's office. It was late, and when I got there, I found all his stuff boxed up. His personal things weren't there anymore."

"Oh," Brea's face fell. "I'm sorry, Jessica. I didn't think you'd want to do that on top of everything here. David, Dean, and Frankie cleaned it out. They each took the personal things that had meaning for them. David has been drinking his coffee out of Jesse's mug, and Frankie took a set of pens they'd bought during a mission in Vancouver."

I waved a hand. "They're welcome to those things. I was blindsided, I think. It was late, and Dean's office was the only one with the light on. I went there, and he offered comfort. The next thing I knew, I was kissing him."

Brea scooted closer and rubbed little circles on my back.

"He went down on me, and I called him by Jesse's name." Tears stung my eyes. My story only got worse from there. "He took me back to his place, and he was going to have me sleep in the sex bedroom—"

"The sex bedroom?" She sounded equal parts amused and baffled.

I wiped my nose on my sleeve. "Apparently, when he brings home a woman for the night, he has sex with them in a room across the hall from his bedroom. He keeps pretty nightgowns in the dresser and feminine products in the bathroom."

"And this is where you had sex with him?"

"No. He wasn't going to come into the room with me. It was a real blow to his ego when I called him by another name. He said it had never happened to him before."

"Jeez, Jessica. I wasn't sure he was straight before now."

Given the sexual tales Dean had been sharing with me the entire time I'd known him, I knew he liked women, but that didn't preclude men. I shrugged. "Maybe he has a different room for when he brings home men?"

She giggled a moment before returning to the sobriety of the moment. "Go on."

"I..." I shook my head and squeezed my eyes shut. "I'm a horrible person. I didn't want to sleep alone. I just—I miss Jesse so much. I miss having him next to me at night. I miss—" A sharp spike of pain impaled my heart, and I lost it. I sobbed.

Brea kept her hand on my back, but she reached over and grabbed box of tissue from the table. "Use these instead of your sleeve."

I wiped and blew and confessed my sins to the only person I'd never lied to. "I wanted the ache inside to go away just for a little while. I was lonely. I asked Dean if I could sleep in his bed, and he said yes. He didn't try anything. It was all me. I seduced him. I attacked him. I used him."

"I'm sure he didn't mind." Brea pried wadded tissue from my grip and replaced it with fresh stuff. "He's proud of his reputation for playing the field."

"He didn't sleep with me in the sex room. He did it in his bed, where he said he doesn't bring anybody. He told me I was special. Brea, he has feelings for me. He told me so months ago, right before I ended up in the hospital on bed rest. I knew this when I seduced him." I broke off to breathe through a wave of misery and anxiety.

"Jessica, I know you care about Dean. Maybe not romantically, but as a person."

"That doesn't make it better, Brea." I sprang to my feet, anger at myself seeping out. "I told him I was lonely and tired of hurting. I told him I felt empty and alone. I told him I wanted him to make me feel something sweet and beautiful. Everything I said was designed to make him amenable to having sex with me."

I ranted for a while longer, spilling every last detail in a way that revealed me as manipulative and conniving, utterly without conscience.

Finally Brea grabbed me by the shoulders. "Jessica, stop. You're not a bad person. You didn't do anything wrong." She cupped my face and forced me to look into her green eyes full of unshed tears. "You lost your husband. I can't imagine what I would do if I lost David. The fact that you can even get out of bed shows you have strength and resilience. That doesn't mean it's easy for you. Wanting to escape the pain—that's human nature. It means you're trying like hell to move forward with your life. Not only do you need to do this for you, but you need to do it so you can be here for Bailey."

"I used Dean. I closed my eyes and pretended he was Jesse. That's not fair to Dean."

"Or to you." Brea sealed her forehead to mine. "Jessica, Dean knows how deep your love for Jesse runs. He took advantage of you just as much as you did him, but that's not necessarily a bad thing.

You're both in pain. You're both mourning someone you loved beyond reason. Right now, everything you do is about grief and healing."

"How is what I did part of the healing process? Jesse's been gone for three months. His body is still in Honduras. There's been no memorial service. What would Jesse think of me if he knew what I did?"

"He's not here to have an opinion." She sat me back on the sofa. "I'm sorry, but he doesn't have a vote in what you do from now on. Jesse would absolutely hate it if you slept with anyone else because when he was alive, he wanted to be your one and only true love. But he's gone."

Jesse had succeeded in his quest to become my one and only true love, and then he'd left me—voluntarily. The anger I'd felt the other night returned with a manic vengeance. "Yeah. He didn't have to go on that mission. He chose to leave me. He chose to risk his life for something that isn't going to make a difference in the end. It's his fault I'm alone. He did this."

Brea's mouth fell open. "Jessica, I didn't mean—"

"No, I know what you meant. You meant he's gone and I have to grieve him and move on." My hands curled into fists. "But he didn't have to go." I faced her with fire in my stare. "None of you *have* to go. You don't need the money—you just want the adventure. You're addicted to the rush of danger, the thrill of pulling off a con job. You keep gambling with your life because you keep winning, and that makes you reckless and careless. I hate SAFE Security. I hate your job. I hate that you don't see the chances you're taking aren't worth it."

She got to her feet slowly, her skin ruddy with anger at my unexpected attack. "Jessica, I know you're upset, so I'm trying really hard to focus on that, but you need to remember I lost Jesse too. He was my friend. He was my teammate, and I was part of the team that failed to protect him. I've spent the past few months finding every point where I could have done something different, something that would have changed the outcome of that mission. I've berated myself over and over. I've broken down from the guilt and the pain of losing him—we all have. I know you loved him. I know what letting yourself take a chance on him meant. But you're not the only one who is in pain, and attacking what we do isn't going to make it better."

For the first time in my life, Brea walked out on me when I needed her. I sank down on the sofa and thought about the fact that I'd finally pushed away the one person I thought would never leave my side.

Did I not have one redeeming quality?

A knock sounded on my door, and some of my desolation eased. That would be Sylvia bringing Bailey to me for the night. I wiped my nose—on a tissue—and got up with my arms out to hug my baby.

53

Only it was David standing there. He grinned and opened his arms. Even though I stopped coming closer, he pulled me in for a big hug.

"I thought you would have left by now."

He released me, and then he closed the door and leaned against it. David was a tall man, about six feet, and he was very athletic, but next to Jesse—or even Dean—he looked thin. I guess I could say the same thing about Frankie, and she could kick all their asses.

Despite how he towered over me, I didn't find David threatening or imposing. He gazed at me sympathetically. "I'm sure Brea is going to tell me later why she's both crying and mad."

I waited, and when he didn't continue, I said, "But you're hoping I tell you first?"

"No. I know Brea has all night to rant and rave and cry to me. But you don't have anyone to hold you, and reel you in, and tell you it's going to be all right."

What a way to make me feel better—by reminding me of everything I no longer had. In defiance, I lifted my chin. "I'm strong. I don't need anybody."

"You're strong," he agreed. "But that doesn't mean you don't need a friend."

Brea was the person who was always supposed to be on my side. Even when Jesse and I had broken up and David wanted them to remain neutral, she'd been on my side. The problem with this situation was that Brea and I never fought. We disagreed about a lot, but we always ironed out all that pretty quickly. Our whole lives, it had been us against the world.

Now she had a new life, and I kept forgetting we didn't have to fend for ourselves anymore.

"It's fine," I lied. "I'll be fine."

"You used to be a much better liar," he said. "Look, sometimes it helps to talk to someone who is more objective than Brea, considering that she's not at all objective where you're concerned."

I met his assertion as if he'd issued a challenge. "My husband has only been dead for three months, and I've already betrayed his memory."

David's brow wrinkled in confusion. "How?"

"I had sex with his best friend."

To his credit, he contained his shock well. He ran a hand through his hair. "So, I guess what you're saying is you're human?"

I called his bluff. "So, if you died suddenly, you'd be fine with Brea running into the arms of your best friend? Or anyone, for that matter?"

He thought about it. "Well, I'm guessing you slept with Dean, where I'm about seventy percent certain Brea would sleep with Frankie, which is kind of hot."

"Let's keep it a sausage fest," I said. "For the sake of honest comparison."

"Okay, sure." He came into the room and settled on an occasional chair next to the window. "So, you slept with Dean?"

"Yes."

David nodded. "I've seen him work his magic, Jessica. Women are powerless when Dean dials up the charm." His eyes suddenly widened. "Oh, you're in love with Dean?"

"No."

His eyes returned to normal size. He tapped his hand on his thigh as he thought. "That's good because I'm not sure Dean has the desire to be anything other than a player. Any long-term relationship he's had has always been open. And short, maybe two months. He claims he gets bored."

I knew all of this about Dean. He'd been open and honest with me about his sex life and his attitude toward romantic relationships from the beginning.

"Maybe it's a good thing," he continued. "You and Dean can help each other through this, and then when you don't need each other anymore, you can part ways as friends. He's really good at maintaining friendships. It's one of his best qualities."

"You're saying it's okay for us to use each other."

"As long as you're both honest about what you're doing." He came to where I sat on the sofa and he took my hands in his. "My heart breaks every time I look at you and I see how much you're hurting. There's not a right or wrong way to grieve—there's only your way. You deserve an escape, something to help you move forward. Just be honest with Dean about your motives, and he'll be honest with you."

I was about to argue that Dean did have feelings for me that went beyond friendship, but when I thought over his texts, I realized that he'd only said he cared about me, not in what capacity. Even months ago, when he'd confessed to having feelings for me, he'd framed it as if winning me had been a competition between him and Jesse.

David mistook my silence. "I know he went after you pretty viciously before, but the two of you seemed to have moved past that?"

"Yeah. He explained his motives, and rather than apologize, tried to make a case for how what he'd done was in my best interest."

David laughed. "That's Dean—never admits he's wrong and rationalizes his mistakes instead of admitting he was wrong. Look, I'm not saying you should try for a relationship with Dean, but maybe don't beat yourself up for being human, and maybe don't hate yourself because you found a few moments of peace. And maybe revisit some of the ways BDSM can help you deal with your emotions. I know you don't go for the submissive stuff, but impact play helps Brea a lot. I wouldn't be surprised if she asks for some tonight. And I know you like bondage too. Dean is good at both of those things."

Somehow, the idea of letting Dean tie me up seemed a worse betrayal of Jesse than having sex. In retrospect, I really hated that he'd kept a bondage submissive at the beginning of our relationship. I hadn't realized how much I still resented Wendy.

David put his arm around me and kissed my forehead. "Or don't. Bottom line is it's okay for you to have needs."

He was telling me the same things Brea had, and the anger I felt at her for needlessly putting her life in danger also applied to David. Rather than go off on him, I picked up on the one question he hadn't addressed. "You never said what you'd want Brea to do if she was in my situation."

"Because I don't have an objective opinion. The possessive part of me wouldn't want her to move on and get over me, but the rational part of me knows that's an unfair perspective. Though it stings to think of her without me, I'd want her to be happy—whatever that means for her."

I disentangled from his hold and scooted to sit on the edge of the cushion. "Jesse was mad at Dean because Dean told him he'd kissed me. He might see this as a slap in the face."

"The Jesse I know would still come out on the side of you being happy." David got to his feet. "My phone is vibrating something fierce, which means that Brea wants to go home. She'll most likely be over in the morning so the two of you can kiss and make up."

He was at the door when I called his name.

"David? Thank you."

Smiling over his shoulder, he waved. "Anytime."

Chapter 6

Dean

My phone buzzed with Jessica's ringtone as I poured myself a second glass of Scotch. Given that she had yet to text me again after last night, I hadn't expected to hear from her. The lax way Jessica had of returning calls and responding to texts—especially when she was avoiding someone—had driven Jesse crazy. I missed listening to him bitch about it.

"Jessica, how are you?"

"Can we talk?"

I smiled. "That would be one of the implicit permissions that come with the answering of a phone."

"I mean, can you come here?"

"Of course. Give me a half hour." I lived a two-minute drive away, but as it was late, I'd thrown caution to the wind tonight, and I needed to shave. I also needed to find something appropriate to wear. Was this a casual visit, or should I wear a suit?

"Sure. Don't knock on the door, though. Come around back, and be quiet. I'll be on my bedroom balcony."

This sounded suspiciously covert, which wasn't her usual style. Jessica tended toward brash actions unless she was picking a pocket.

For this, I selected casual pants, dark gray, and I paired them with a white, long-sleeved linen shirt. It wrinkled fairly easily, but it hung on me in a very flattering manner. I arrived on time, parked in the driveway, and went around back.

The balcony faced the side of the house and overlooked a manicured garden. I found Jessica standing next to the railing. She wore a colorful, striped dress that clung to her body and fell to her ankles. In deference to the cooler fall weather, she hugged a sweater around her body. She smiled when she saw me. "I'll be down in a minute."

"Don't bother." The railing was metal and wood. Jumping up, I grasped a post and pulled myself up.

"Wow," she laughed as I climbed over the railing. "You dress like a man of leisure, so I forget that you're also a commando."

It was great to hear her laugh, but when I took a closer look, I noted the puffiness around her eyes—evidence she'd been crying recently. I wanted to take her in my arms, but after the way she'd fled my bed in the middle of the night, I questioned whether she'd be receptive to an embrace.

"Yes, well, I'm here. Are you going to offer me a drink?"

"No."

Though her directness didn't surprise me, her refusal to observe the niceties did. "Really?"

She arched an eyebrow. "Are you thirsty?"

"Not particularly."

"Okay, so then I'm not going to offer you a drink." She laughed again. "But I will invite you inside. It's getting a little chilly out."

In point of fact, her nipples were erect, a salute to the dropping temperature and an advertisement of her lack of bra. My pants had been comfortable when I'd put them on, but now they were a little tight.

She took my hand and pulled me after her and into the house.

"You're in a very good mood," I observed. "Maybe you've already had a few drinks?"

"Two glasses of wine with dinner, but that was hours ago. In the meantime I've had a huge fight with Brea and a good talk with David." She stopped abruptly and faced me. "I'm going to choose not to dwell on the idea that you think I can only be in a good mood after a few drinks."

My brain scrambled for something to save face. "I only meant that it's been a long time since I've seen you smile for real."

She inclined her head and regarded me somberly. "I could say the same thing about you."

Yes, well, life had sucked a lot lately. "Okay, Jessica. What was so important I had to come over to discuss it in person?"

She sat on one half of a loveseat and patted the opposite cushion. "I wanted to explain why I left the other night."

I knew why she'd left. She'd come to me for comfort and affection. I'd given the comfort, but I'd fallen asleep before I could give her the affection she needed. But far be it for me to mansplain her actions. "I'm listening."

"I felt like I had been unfaithful to Jesse."

That was not what I'd been expecting. I leaned forward and closed my hand over hers. "Kitten, you weren't. Neither of us would have done any of that if Jesse was still here."

"Yeah, well, Nikki likes to tell me emotions don't always follow the rules we'd like them to. I've spent the last two days crying and hating myself."

Her agony tore at me. I wanted to fix it. "I wish you'd awakened me."

She shook her head. "I was ashamed of the way I manipulated and used you. I... I wanted to lose myself, and I felt safe with you. It's no excuse for—"

"Jessica, don't do this." I knew I should listen to everything she had to say before responding, but she'd spent two days beating herself up emotionally, and I wasn't going to let her continue. "You didn't manipulate or use me. You were very clear about what you were feeling and what you wanted from me, and I wanted to give you the balm you sought. I regret that I failed."

She chewed her bottom lip. "David thought you would feel that way."

Caught off guard, I swallowed wrong and ended up having a coughing fit.

Jessica went to the mini-bar and got a bottle of water from the fridge. She held it out to me.

I strove to restore some of the lightheartedness of our usual interactions. "Ah, that's what it takes to get a drink around here."

"In these parts, it's water or breast milk."

A swig soothed my throat. "So, you told David we slept together?"

"Yes. And I told Brea about your sex bedroom. She wants to know if you have one for male guests."

Due to my fastidious nature, my love of fashion, and my appreciation of elegance, my friends had long questioned the direction of my sexuality. As I enjoyed the air of mystery this gave me, I was happy to let them keep questioning. Passing this opportunity to clear the air, I grinned. "I expected you would confide in Brea. The two of you keep few secrets from each other."

She resumed her seat next to me. "David said we should continue to sleep together."

I capped the water and set it on a coaster on the coffee table. Then I faced the lovely woman in front of me. "Setting aside other people's opinions for the moment, let's talk about what you want. Jessica, I don't want to push you to do something you're not ready to do. It's okay to take as long as you need to mourn Jesse."

Not a day went by that I didn't miss him, and waves of grief often struck me at unexpected times. He'd been like an older brother to me since I was twenty years old and we were paired for our first covert mission together.

"I think I'm always going to mourn him." She ran a finger along the seam in her dress. "But I can't let that mean I'm going to stop living." Her gaze lifted, meeting mine with bold intent. "I think we can help each other heal."

My heart fell a bit. She was looking for solace, not love. I reminded myself it was going to take her a while to arrive at the point where she was ready for that, and if I wanted her to fall for me, then I needed to be the one here for her the whole time. I affected a flirtatious smirk. "Sexual healing?"

A beautiful blush spread above the scooped neckline of her dress. "If you want. Mini-golf is also on the table."

I loved her sense of humor, and I missed bantering with her. Jessica was one of the wittiest women I'd ever met. There was no verbal challenge she didn't meet with intelligence and panache.

"Mini-golf?" I pretended to consider it. "I am partial to a hole-in-one."

She laughed. "Look, I know how you operate. We'll always use condoms, and I'll never show up at your house without an invitation."

I understood the need for condoms, though I knew we were both clean. She didn't want to risk another pregnancy because there was a very real chance it would kill her. But I wanted to disabuse her of the other notion.

"Kitten, I know you're not the kind of woman who sleeps around. I'm willing to pledge fidelity."

She didn't appear at all impressed, which dealt a blow to my ego. "That's not necessary. I was thinking this would be therapeutic and fun. I'm not asking for more than that, nor do I expect it."

I wanted to rail at her that she absolutely should expect any man who wanted to be with her to be faithful, but I knew that wasn't what she wanted to hear right now. Rather than discuss it further, I said, "Are we keeping this secret? David and Brea already know."

"My parents don't, and I'd rather not have to face them right now. For the time being, I'm going to have to ask you to sneak in and out, or we can meet at your place." She glanced toward a baby monitor. "In some respects, it's easier if you come here. I won't have to get a babysitter, but there may be interruptions. She's a solid sleeper most of the time lately."

"Okay, secret therapeutic affair. This is not something I've knowingly done before." Some of the partners I'd been with had been fresh from breakups, so I knew all about angry, revenge sex. I wasn't sure about the kind that healed, but I knew empathy was involved.

"Me, neither." She set her hand lightly on my thigh. "I know you're hurting too. The therapy part should go both ways."

I agreed. "Share one memory of Jesse, and I will too."

"No. If we do that, then at least one of us is going to end up in tears, and the therapeutic sex will not happen."

"Perhaps, but then it's just sex instead of therapy."

She opened her mouth to disagree, so I launched into a story.

"One time in Afghanistan, I was providing support for Jesse's unit as they raided a Taliban compound, and through my scope, I watched him confront a man who was using a frightened woman as a human shield. He didn't know my position, but he knew I could make the shot, so he maneuvered the guy in a circle until I had a clear shot. It was genius, really, the way he got the guy to give up his secure position. Once the guy went down, he continued the raid. We took down a major stronghold that day, and by the next day, the Taliban were forced out of the city."

I omitted the gruesome and the classified details, and I thought the story would inspire pride in remembering Jesse, but I was wrong, and she was right.

She buried her face in her hands and sobbed. These were not little tears, and they bore no relation to the kind of crying one might do when they felt joyous. I lifted her and set her on my lap, and I held her until she brought herself under control.

I kissed her forehead. "Your turn."

She used tissue from the table to wipe her face. "No."

"It's part of the therapy."

"It's not, and just because you get off on torturing me doesn't make it therapeutic."

"Kitten, while torturing you would get me off, this isn't the kind of thing that does it for me. The more you talk about Jesse, the more you embrace and celebrate your memories of him, the easier it will be to live each day without him." I hated having to be so fucking reasonable. She was right that this probably wasn't going to get me laid, but right now, she needed coping mechanisms. She needed to face her loss and use it to make her stronger. Too many people around her let her wallow in pain when she could be reclaiming her life. She needed a strong hand to guide her through this, and the task fell to me.

"Is that why you keep coming over and telling me about things you and Jesse did?"

I'd made a point to visit her at least twice each week—more, when I wasn't working. "Yes."

She turned her face away, and I let her have a moment to gather her wits and her thoughts. When she brought her attention back to me, she said, "What kind of torture gets you off?"

That wasn't where I'd expected her to go, but it was the reason she'd called for me to come over, so I followed her lead. "Sexual torture—forced climax, orgasm denial, keeping you on edge for hours, ramming my dick down your throat. I like to use toys such as vibrators and dildos in all orifices."

Sitting up straight put distance between us. She pursed her lips. "I don't do anal."

"Pity. You're missing out."

Her emerald gaze fell and rose again. "Do you like anal?"

"I love anal. It's especially good when you also have a vibrator in your pussy."

"I meant receiving anal. Do you like that?"

I grinned at her cheekiness and the clever way she brought the conversation back to a topic I'd sidestepped. "You'll never have the occasion to find out."

"Dean."

"Jessica."

"You're impossible."

Laughing, I closed my hand over her breast and teased her nipple through the thin fabric. "So, you're not submissive, but I am Dominant. I'll honor any refusal you give in any form, and you're going to have to put up with me being authoritative."

"That kind of negates the whole idea of sexual torture," she said. "If I tell you to stop it, you'll stop. That's not what you like."

I heartily disagreed. "You're a competitive woman, so I'll just issue a challenge. It'll be a contest of wills. We both like that."

"What about things like spanking, rough sex, or impact play?"

"Well, I'm not against impact play, but it doesn't turn me on." I slid a hand under her dress. The stretchy material didn't provide much resistance. "If you ask for it, you might have to use persuasive techniques. Erotic spankings could be fun, provided it's part of a challenge. Do you like to be spanked, Kitten?"

"During sex, yes."

"That leaves rough sex. I tend toward being a gentle lover with a firm command of the pleasure given and received. I'm sorry, Kitten, but I'm not inclined to leave bruises or mar your skin." My hand brushed her sex, which was unobstructed because she'd foregone panties. I slid a finger through her wetness and directly into her vagina.

She gasped, but she didn't protest. "You—you like having your skin marred."

I arched an inquiring brow and inserted a second finger.

"Scratching. It—it—you really liked it."

Pumping my fingers into her, I found her sweet spot. "Yes, well scratches tend to fade after a day or two. I'll ask you not to get fake nails because I prefer the natural feel."

"Okay." Her head fell back, and her chest rose and fell rapidly.

I circled her clit with my thumb and massaged her vaginal tissues. My endgame wasn't an orgasm. I wanted to drive her out of her mind, which was what she needed.

"But manicures are fine. I'm partial to nail polish colors in shades of red or pink, some purples. No blue, green, orange, or yellow. All your nails should be one color, and you should avoid glitter."

Her eyelashes fluttered as she struggled to open her eyes. "You have awfully specific tastes in women's fingernails."

"True."

"I noticed you aren't giving orders."

"You're not a submissive. If you were, I'd phrase it as an order." I licked the column of her neck. "Tonight's challenge is for you to not climax until I tell you to."

Her breath caught as I found a particularly delightful rhythm. "But you're doing such wonderful things to me."

"Yes, and once you climax, we'll be finished for the night. I'd hate to have to leave earlier than I'd intended."

"You play dirty," she accused.

"I'm fond of debauchery," I admitted. "But this is not news to you."

Her head rolled on my shoulder, and before I knew what she was about, she grazed her teeth along the shell of my ear. Shivers raced down my spine, and my cock responded with enthusiastic approval.

She attacked my shirt next, her fleet fingers dancing down the row of buttons. I was going to wear button-down shirts from now on just so I could witness this graceful show again and again.

I withdrew my fingers from her pussy and set her on her feet. "Remove the dress. Let me look at you."

In one move, she lifted it over her head and tossed it onto the table behind her. Hands at her sides, she stood before me in all her naked glory. I noted she had opted not to play up the sensuality of the striptease. Instead, she'd followed my order exactly.

Not submissive, my ass. One day she would embrace the truth of what she was, but she had to arrive at that destination of her own accord.

I took my time drinking in her singular beauty. Dark hair, neglected these past months, fell to her shoulders in a riot of curls. Visually, I caressed the smooth skin of her shoulders, skated over the globes of her breasts, and noted I could count her ribs. The generous curves of her hips were still present, though bones protruded there as well. Even her legs were thinner. I knew she worked out religiously and did her physical therapy, but this wasn't the result of healthy physical activity.

Commenting on a woman's weight was verboten, but because I cared about her, I had to say something about her health. "Jessica, you haven't been eating."

"I just had dinner."

I suppressed the urge to call her out on how much she'd eaten. "Kitten, you're still eating for two. From now on, you'll have three meals a day and two snacks. You can space them out however you see fit."

She scowled. "You can't tell me what to eat. For fuck's sake, Dean, if you're not attracted to me, just say so."

Before I'd traveled this road, I'd known it would be a bumpy ride. "Oh, but I am very attracted to you. That doesn't mean I'm not concerned about your health. Even if you're not feeling hungry, you will eat. This is advice I'm following myself as well."

With a mulish slant to her mouth, that scowl turned downright pouty. "This is not sexy. I'm finding it very easy not to climax right now, and if you don't stop talking about how I'm too skinny, nobody is going to climax here tonight."

"Sore spot. Noted." I crooked a finger. "Come here, Kitten. Show me how you've sharpened your claws."

As she straddled me, she slid her hands up my chest and over my shoulders, ridding me of my shirt. "Didn't anybody ever tell you it was rude to give your opinion on a woman's weight, especially after she's had a baby?"

I caressed her thighs and squeezed her ass. "I like a little meat on a body." Closing my mouth over hers, I captured her for a kiss so deep and passionate that we both moaned. "You're going to need to keep up your stamina if you're ever going to beat me in a challenge."

Reaching between us, she cupped the bulge in my pants. "It's on, Scratching Post. I'm going to make you blow your wad like a twenty-year-old virgin."

As I processed the idea that she'd just relegated me to the status of furniture, I let her wrestle my pants and underwear over my ass and down my thighs. Though she was surprisingly strong, she was no match for me. Grinning at her buoyant spirits, I lounged back and let her remove my pants from my legs. I even admired the way she looked kneeling on the floor between my legs.

Then she pounced. Before I guessed her intent, her lips closed around the head of my cock. She worked it into her mouth, wetting it as she set a leisurely pace. Every time she came up, she ran her tongue along the sensitive ridge in a way that sent electric tingles all the way to my toes. My heartbeat sped up as delicious tendrils of pleasure radiated from my cock to spread everywhere.

When the tip of my cock bumped the back of her throat, I thought she'd wrap her hand around the base, but she swallowed and took my whole length.

My hips shot off the sofa. "Holy shit, kitten. This is supposed to be how I torture you."

I had failed to anticipate the underhanded lengths to which she would go to win. She took me deep a few more times before I ripped her sweet mouth away from my manhood.

She wiped her lips on the back of her hand and grinned. "Chicken."

Hauling her to her feet, I kissed her hard, and then I guided her to kneel on the sofa with her hands braced on the back of it.

"Condoms are in the left drawer of the coffee table."

I grabbed one. A small pang of loss hit me as I realized I was using Jesse's condom, but I pushed it aside to focus on the woman who needed me.

The way I'd positioned her meant the angle was a little off. It was perfect for teasing and drawing out the experience. I slid the head of my sheathed cock through her wetness, playing it against her clit until she whimpered. Only then did I drive it into her dripping pussy.

When I was inside her, I paused to make sure she wasn't having second thoughts. "Kitten, give me your color."

"Green." She gasped the word.

I grasped her hips firmly, holding them in place as I fucked her hot tunnel. She pushed against me, fighting for control until I slapped her ass. With a cry of pleasure, she arched her back and settled down.

The arching let me deeper inside, and her moans progressed to cries so loud she snatched a throw pillow from the sofa and buried her face in it. I hit her ass again and again. Each time her pussy clenched tighter. Soon it pulsed with the kind of slow, rolling orgasm that would go on for a long time if I didn't mess up.

I closed my eyes, timing my thrusts with the pulses in her pussy, and I ran through a laundry list of not sexy things to stave off the inevitable. Eventually I reached the end of my list, and the sweet siren's call of her incoherent pleasure combined with the insistent throbbing of her vagina. With a mighty roar, my orgasm detonated. It started in my dick, but it traveled up my spine in delicious sparks that rendered every bone in my body useless.

Collapsing forward, I landed on Jessica. She grunted, possibly because the back of the sofa jabbed her in the stomach, and pushed me to the side. I fell in a blissful stupor, but this time I had the mental wherewithal to bring her with me. She lay on top of me, as boneless and spent as I was. Her heartbeat thundered against my chest, and I held her tightly.

If she was going to cry, she was going to do it in my arms. She nestled her head against my shoulder, and I felt the flutter of her lashes as she blinked.

"How are you doing, Kitten?"

"Good." Her voice was hoarse. "And you?"

"Excellent. You did well tonight. I'm proud of you."

She smacked my chest lightly. "Don't be an ass, Dean."

My lips curved in response to her fighting attitude. "You dislike praise?"

"I dislike condescension."

"Ah, I see. You're a sore loser."

"You cheated." She smiled. I felt the stretching of her lips against my chest.

"All's fair, kitten."

"Dean?"

"Yes?"

"Thank you for this."

I held her even tighter.

Chapter 7

Jessica

"Tell me how you're doing." Nikki set a bottle of water in front of me and sat back.

I stared at the water and gave some thought to how to phrase what was on my mind. "I'm having an affair."

If my therapist was surprised, she hid it well. Nikki Eliachevsky was a petite woman with a huge, comforting presence. She was beautiful even though she tried to play down her looks with garish lipstick and plain clothes.

"Well, not an affair. He's not married. And, I guess I'm not either." I rubbed the heel of my hand over my forehead.

"What's bothering you about your relationship with this man?"

"It's not a relationship, and he's one of Jesse's best friends." Five weeks after my first encounter with Dean, I revealed the details of our sexual therapy deal to my actual therapist.

"You know, Jessica, everybody deals with grief differently, and there's no timeline for when you should move on. The only signpost is whether you're ready or not."

"That's where I'm having a problem. I'm not sure I'm ready. I feel guilty. We get together a few times each week unless he's on assignment. It's easier each time, but there's always a sense I'm betraying Jesse." I closed my eyes as heat rose in my cheeks. Yeah, I was blushing at my therapist's office. "Sometimes I pretend he's Jesse. Okay, it's more than sometimes. It's most of the time."

"So, you have two sources of guilt—one stemming from feeling like you're being unfaithful and one from feeling you're not being fair to your new lover."

"I don't miss Jesse as much as I used to, and thinking about him doesn't bring crippling agony and emptiness with it." I took the water bottle and twisted the cap open and closed.

"That's good. It's progress."

"It's never going to stop hurting completely. I've started working in my studio again, and sometimes in the middle of a project, things get really bad. It creeps up and strikes me without warning, battering me with waves of debilitating grief. My knees give out, and I find myself on the floor, trying to catch my breath. I'm not even crying at this point, but it feels like someone is sitting on my chest or an iron band is squeezing my heart. Once it eases, the tears come, and I sob like it's the first time they told me he was gone."

Nikki handed me the box of tissue, and I realized I was crying. I did it so often now I didn't always notice when it was happening.

"How often is that happening?"

I shrugged. "Less often now than before I started sleeping with Dean."

"It sounds like you needed the physical connection. It's okay to not feel guilty about that, or about the thoughts you have while you're with Dean. Many people fantasize during sex, and from what you've told me, you've been honest with him about your conflicted feelings."

"I think he has, you know, *actual* feelings for me."

"He may, but it also sounds like he understands where you're coming from and he's not pushing you."

This was true. Dean was unfailingly attentive and charming. He brought his sense of humor, and he didn't always tell me stories about Jesse. Sometimes he came for regular visits, where he had dinner with my parents and played with Bailey, and he would tell her stories about her father.

I realized something in that moment. "I'm not crying as much. I used to hold Bailey and just cry, and now I talk to her and laugh with her. I've been taking her for walks in the stroller. Sometimes it's just us, and sometimes my mom or dad comes with me. Last weekend, I went to an art show with Frankie."

"You're leaving the house voluntarily for more than doctor's appointments," she said. "Jessica, that's huge!"

She was right. In the last five weeks, I'd been getting out of the house for normal activities. I went shopping with Brea, and we met David for lunch. Leon had taken me to a baseball game, and Dean took me mini-golfing. My mom and I had a spa day, and my dad and I shared a huge tub of popcorn at the movie theater. We'd engaged in a licorice fight that had garnered disapproving looks from the other patrons.

"I've started painting again." I sipped the water because my throat was suddenly dry. "I was messing around with a furniture piece—this table made from driftwood—and I started painting a landscape on it. It's really subtle. I used the grain of the wood in the actual painting.

After a while, I realized I was creating art as I see it in my head." Yep, I started back up with the waterworks. "My style is different, but it's good. It's more mature."

"That's excellent." Nikki took a tissue. She was also tearing up. "I'm so happy for you, Jessica."

I took a moment to brag about my other accomplishments. "I'm caught up on my online orders."

"From what I'm hearing, it sounds like you're having more good moments than bad moments?"

Now that I thought about it, she was right. "Yes, and I refuse to feel guilty about that."

"You shouldn't. It's perfectly fine for you to embrace life. You can't grieve forever, and Jesse wouldn't want you to anyway. He'd want you to be happy."

He'd always wanted me to be happy. He'd spent so much time and effort helping me find my way—there was no way he'd want me to wallow in misery. He'd want me to be healthy and happy and a good mom to our daughter.

I left therapy that day feeling better than I had in months. My chest still ached with a constant sense of loss, but now I felt like I could concentrate on celebrating Jesse's life rather than mourning his death.

On the street outside Nikki's office, I sat on the curb as one of those attacks washed over me. I sobbed in public, not caring who saw, until Warren lifted me up, hugged me to him, and took me home.

Dean

Thanksgiving brought us all to Jessica's house for a meal prepared by Sylvia, Warren, and Brea. I'd eaten more than my share, and then I'd indulged in several slim slices of Brea's incredible pies. In addition to the traditional pumpkin pie, she'd made an apple-walnut pie and a chocolate mousse.

Jessica held Bailey's hand and flapped it in the air. "Say bye-bye to Uncle Dean."

Warren paused in clearing plates from the dining room table. "Jessica, don't be one of those women who tells their kid to call their boyfriend 'uncle.' It's just not dignified."

Jessica froze, her wide eyes on me.

I shook my head. As per her request, I'd been discrete in entering and leaving her bedroom, often using the balcony as an entry and exit point. David, Brea, and Frankie knew Jessica and I were 'friends with benefits,' but they didn't openly discuss the matter.

David and Brea, who were finishing up a second piece of pie each, exchanged glances. Brea swallowed what was in her mouth. "I didn't say anything."

Warren snorted. "Only a moron would miss you coming and going at all hours of the night. Sylvia and I don't know why you feel like you need to hide it."

I hadn't felt any such need. Jesse would appreciate that I'd stepped up to be here for Jessica. In the past six weeks that we'd been seeing one another, she had begun to heal. She'd gained back some of the weight she'd lost. Her eyes sometimes sparkled, and she smiled more often. Laughter was still rare, but that, too, was making a comeback.

"Yes." Sylvia sailed back into the dining room with Frankie on her heels, each bearing more ice cream. "We could take Bailey for the night, and you don't have to pretend to leave just to sneak back in later."

Though I had done that a few times, tonight it wasn't in the cards. "Sorry, but I have plans tonight. My old Marine buddy, Joss Blaese is in town. We're going out for drinks."

Frankie sat down and put her napkin in her lap. Physically, she had healed, but her emotional scars were far from gone. She had yet to go on another mission, and we weren't going to push her until we thought she was ready. She spooned the ice cream onto her pie. "It's a job interview. Dean is going to take him out, get him wasted, and then David will show up later so they can throw him off a building or something equally as stupid."

We'd never throw anyone off a building on purpose, and David had no plans to join us. I responded to her hostility with dryness. "Rappelling is a necessary skill, and we don't know if he can do it with one arm."

"He has two arms," Frankie pointed out. "But one hand. If he wants to rappel, he can rappel. He's a freaking pilot, for crissakes, and former Special Forces. He's helped us out a dozen times over the past year."

I waited patiently for her to finish. "Your point?"

"That's hazing," Jessica gasped. "You think it builds unity when really it's just emotional and physical abuse."

I sighed. "The rappelling thing was a joke. We're having drinks and discussing terms of employment. You're all welcome to come along."

"No thanks," Brea said. "Jessica, Frankie, and I are going to have a sleepover. We're going to braid our hair and do each other's nails."

70

Since I'd mentioned my nail fetish to Jessica, she hadn't done anything to them. I was a fan of regular manicures for all genders, and I was itching to take her to my spa for a full body treatment. She'd gone with her mom for what she called a spa day, but she'd only had a facial and massage. When it came to pampering herself, Jessica was still in the minor leagues.

"Huh," I said thoughtfully. "Joss is staying at my place tonight. David, since you're not doing anything tonight, you're welcome to join us."

David looked around the table as if he suddenly realized he was outnumbered by women. He looked to Warren. "Want to come? Dean's buying, and he always orders the good stuff."

Warren got to his feet. "I'd love to."

And so I found myself in a wine bar with David, Warren, and Joss.

Warren took in the private tables and the long-legged women all over the place. "This is an interesting place for a guy who isn't single to come."

David leaned back against the padded seat and sipped from his glass. "Joss is single, and Dean shies away from commitment. Warren, you and I are casual observers tonight."

While that may have been true in the past, it wasn't quite the case now. "I am committed to Jessica. She's just not on board with the plan."

"She's not seeing anyone else," Warren offered.

"Neither am I." I refilled my glass and topped off Joss's.

Joss eyed me doubtfully. "Sounds like a commitment."

"It's complicated," I said. "She's not over her husband."

At that, Warren stared at his empty wine glass, lost in thought. I knew what he was feeling—helplessness. He wanted to protect his little girl, but there was nothing he could do to make the hurt go away. Similarly, I was wrestling with some deep and momentous feelings she wasn't ready to hear about.

I squeezed his shoulder. "It'll take time. I'm a patient man." Before the night could take a maudlin turn—it was supposed to be about welcoming Joss to the team—I smiled at Joss. "Tell David about the time you rescued four troops from a downed helicopter, and two of them strapped themselves to the skids of your chopper to return fire as you got everyone to safety."

He grinned, his dark eyes sparkling with reflected candlelight— this place was big on fireless candles—and a little too much alcohol. "Besides the fact that it was my first mission after flight school, you kind of said it all. It was crazy, but it goes to show you what a well-trained team can accomplish together."

Warren motioned to Joss's hand. "How did you lose it?"

"IED. I was on the ground. Transport was taking me to my new deployment—it was my fourth tour—and the bomb went off under our car. Shrapnel mangled my hand beyond repair." He shrugged. "I used to be right-handed, but now I'm pretty good with my left. I have prosthetics, and I'm looking to design one to better help me with flight controls."

"Still a hell of a pilot," I said, clapping him on the back.

Later, after we dropped Warren back at home, David and I took Joss to SAFE Security Headquarters. We'd done some moving of equipment, and for now, the newer team members were being housed in the conference room. With a little remodeling, we hoped to have an open area where crew could share space so we could regain use of the conference room. Right now, none of us could bring ourselves to reassign Jesse's office. We'd packed up his stuff, but we'd left the boxes in the room because we weren't ready to see it gone.

I grabbed the mail from the first floor boxes, and one envelope caught my gaze. It was plain and white, but it bore the seal of the Honduras government. David punched in his code for the elevator, and I ripped open the letter. I scanned the contents, and feeling left my extremities.

"Fuck, no."

David glanced over at me. "What is it?"

My lungs suddenly didn't work right. "Jesse—those remains aren't a DNA match. None of them are. David—he's still out there."

"How is that possible?" David crowded closer to see the letter. "He hasn't contacted us. It's been almost five months. There's no way he's still alive."

"Even so," I said. "We failed to find him."

My mind raced with all the terrible possibilities. What if he'd been there, injured and suffering, and he'd died because we'd given up the search? Or maybe his body had been left out, exposed to the elements and scavengers? No matter what scenario presented itself, we'd failed Jesse even worse than I'd thought.

"I'll call Frankie." The elevator doors opened to the lobby of the office where Jessica had painted the SAFE Security logo on the wall and Brea had set up two chairs and a tall table where we kept a bowl of mints next to our business cards. For the first time, seeing that mural made an acid pool of dread form in my stomach.

"No." David said. "She's been through enough. Let's research the hell out of this."

Joss looked from David to me. "Look, I'm new around here and all, but from what I know about Frankie, she's going to kick both of your asses for treating her like a porcelain doll, and then she'll finish the job because she's tough as nails."

I appealed to David. "He's not wrong."

"Okay, but don't say a word to Brea or Jessica." David pinched the bridge of his nose. "Not until we know something for sure. Jessica has been through enough, and Brea sucks at keeping secrets from her, especially anything big like this."

Ten hours later, we were on a private plane headed to Honduras.

Frankie sat next to me, and I put my hand on her leg. I meant to be supportive, and she took it that way. She looked at my hand, lifted it up, and dropped it on my thigh. "I'm fine," she said. "Pissed off at myself, but fine."

Fine was the word women used when they weren't fine. It was one of those words that meant the exact opposite from the dictionary definition, which is the one men went by when they were ignorant in the ways of the woman.

"Let it out, Frankie. Yell, scream, say mean things you'll regret later, but let it out now."

The whole time I'd known Frankie, she'd always been outgoing and friendly. She talked a million miles an hour, sharing anything on her mind and inviting whomever she was with to confide in her. She was easy to talk to, and I often took her effusive nature for granted. Ever since this last mission, she'd been quiet and closed-off. We'd begged her to see a therapist, but she refused, saying she didn't need a head shrinker to tell her what she already knew. After that, she'd head to the gym and take it out on the practice mannequins and other equipment.

David and Joss sat across from us. David had been brooding while staring out the window, but now his attention was on Frankie and me. "It's not your fault, Frankie. You were injured. We sent you back, and we promised to find him. We're the ones who fucked up, not you."

"I know," she said softly. "I've never been so incredibly angry at two people in my whole life, and I hate feeling this way. The thoughts in my head are mean and hateful, and they're better left unsaid because I don't know how much of it I actually mean."

"Safe space," I said, circling my finger in the air so she'd know I referred to the here and now. "It's better to let it out than to keep it inside."

We needed her to be clear-headed and focused, and that wasn't going to happen if she was trying to contain an emotional volcanic explosion. In the past few months, I'd spent a lot of time drunk, and being with Jessica had helped tremendously. She'd loved him as much as I did—probably more—and as much as they made her cry, my tales captivated her. And they helped keep him close to me.

Frankie frowned, her whole face conveying severe disapproval. "Okay, fine—but don't say I didn't warn you." She exhaled hard. "I'm pissed at you both because I believed the proof too. I looked at those bloody and torn clothes and that wedding ring, and I assumed it was enough proof that he was buried in one of those graves. I was too wrapped up in my own problems to question it, but I should have known it wasn't enough—that picture of Jessica and Bailey wasn't there. He would never let anyone take that from him. He might give up his clothes, his wedding ring, and everything else he had with him, but there's no way he was letting that picture get away from him."

"You don't get to blame yourself," David interjected.

"Fuck you, David. Don't fucking tell me how to feel." Frankie's eyes flashed with unrestrained vehemence.

David was unfazed. "You almost died, Frankie. You were fighting for your life, and you were in no condition for that to occur to you. Even if it had, it's scant proof. It's paper—it could have burned in the fuselage or been lost along the way."

If we'd been in a gym, Frankie would have taken a swing at him. Since we were in a plane, she settled for, "Fuck you, anyway."

I hazarded a glance at Joss to find him watching quietly. He'd lost more than just his hand in combat, so I knew he understood the stakes and the guilt we all felt.

"I keep thinking maybe you didn't want to find him so you could take a run at Jessica." Frankie uttered that quietly.

Hearing that accusation hit hard, mostly because I'd wondered it myself. Had I given up prematurely because, with him out of the way, I had a fifty-fifty chance with her?

"Dean would never do that." David defended me. "And I sure as hell wouldn't let that happen even if he was so inclined. We're heading back to that village, and we're going to find out how they had his personal items. We're going to retrace his steps, and we're not giving up until we find him—dead or alive, Jesse is coming home with us."

Joss leaned forward and took Frankie's hand in his. "No matter what's gone on in the past, you have the future to make it right."

She looked from the tender way he held her hand to the empathy in his dark brown eyes, and she said, "Men who touch me without my permission are taking their lives in their hands."

He lifted her hand to his lips and kissed the backs of her knuckles. "You, *princesa hermosa*, are worth the risk."

She eased her hand away and sat back, shooting a severe frown in his direction. "When we get back, I'm going to show you how close you came to dying just now."

He put his hand over his heart. "Francesca, I am looking forward to our date."

In my whole life, I'd never seen anyone flirt with Frankie for more than two seconds. One look usually shut them down. At any rate, I wasn't going to let this go on. As leader of this team, I issued a warning. "Joss, back off. We're professionals, and sexually aggressive or flirtatious behavior is against our company policy."

Regarding me with the same arrogant grin, he said, "David and Brea are married. That didn't happen without sexual aggression or flirtatious behavior."

"Sure," I conceded, "but that happened before she joined our team. Frankie is off-limits." She'd parted ways with her boyfriend after she'd been released from the hospital, but that didn't mean she welcomed uninvited attention.

"I can take care of myself," she muttered. "I don't need you to defend me."

From the moment she said she was fine, I knew I was damned. "I'm just trying to keep him alive."

She let loose with some rapid-fire Hindi and sprinkled in a smattering of Persian curses I recognized from my time in the Marines. I wasn't sure if she was directing it at Joss or me, but I waited until she'd said her piece.

Joss regarded her with a stupid grin.

I sighed. "Feel better?"

"Yes," she admitted. "This time around, I don't want to take a translator. I don't want anyone on our team we haven't vetted."

David scratched his unshaven chin. "You think our translator lied to us last time?"

"I don't know, and I'm not taking a chance." She gestured to Joss. "He speaks fluent Spanish. Most of the villages down there, even the ones who speak indigenous dialects, have adopted at least a pidgin Spanish."

"No problema," Joss said. "I stand willing to translate."

Without a guide, we relied on GPS to get us to where we needed to go. Also without a guide, we moved more quickly. With his military background, Joss easily fell into our system. He was mindful and observant.

At one point, he crouched low, signaling for the rest of us to freeze. Then he pointed to a spotted leopard monitoring our progress from the underbrush nearby. "She is hungry," he said. "She has been stalking us for the past half mile. Stay close to one another so that we look like bigger prey."

I'd been stalked before, but never by a jungle cat. She was majestic and beautiful and all that, but I didn't care to be regarded as a meal. Of course, my brain jumped to an image of Jessica and the way she'd looked at me before taking my whole cock in her mouth. She'd had a predatory air similar to the she-cat intently watching us navigate the jungle.

There was a road to the village, but in order to use it, we'd have to pass through government checkpoints, and we risked exposure to at least one of the cartels we'd hit in the past. Combine that with my dislike of the Honduras government—it shouldn't have taken so long for the results of the DNA test—and Frankie's strategy of sneaking up on the village, and we were in for some serious mountain hiking. We purchased a vehicle in Guatemala and drove it as far as we could.

We parked it off the road and camouflaged it with the area's flora, and then we began the long, dangerous trek into Honduras.

At the crest of the mountain, I pointed out the faint outline of the scar left by the cargo plane that had gone down.

Joss surveyed it with a practiced eye. "The pilot controlled the landing enough so that it didn't crash nose first. Were the drugs still in the plane?"

While I thought about that, David frowned. "There were some melted bricks stuck to the fuselage, but I'd say most of it was gone. We'd assumed it scattered in the crash because there was powder residue around the crash site.

Frankie said, "There were two full pallets of drugs stacked almost the entire height of the cargo bay. That wouldn't be residue—that would be snow."

This new information would have been helpful before, not that Frankie had been in any condition to relay every little detail.

"Okay, so somebody took the drugs."

We all whipped out high-powered binoculars to surveil the village. I noted the structures from before—houses scattered along the stream. Across the way, fields of coffee were being harvested. The rounded bushes were higher than they'd been five months ago, but they looked a bit scraggly.

"That's a lot of women." Joss's observation had a side of bafflement.

I'd been counting bodies, not so much noting gender. Given Joss's statement, I studied that peculiarity. Women of all ages were around, which wasn't the case when we'd visited before, but the males tended to be smaller children or older men. Several younger men were congregated in the village around a long structure made of metal that I'd taken for community storage. It was the kind of building suitable for storing food and medical supplies.

"I count seven armed men," David said. "But the opening to the building is on the far side. I can't see what they're guarding. Eight, nine—I can't see all the guards."

"Drugs," Joss said. "It's harvest time."

I closed my eyes. "That's not coffee?"

Joss chuckled. "From this distance, I can see how you would confuse the two, but no, that's not all coffee. Although, that is coffee lining the fields. The larger, fuller plants are coffee. The smaller ones in the interior are the coca plants. I used to fly international scouting missions for the DEA in Columbia, so I'm very familiar with the aerial view."

This underscored how much we needed team members with more diverse experiences. David and I had always concentrated on apprehending specific individuals, so we didn't have much experience with plant identification.

"This changes the narrative." Disgusted, I set down my binoculars and rubbed my eyes.

David sighed. "They had Jesse's clothes. According to the Honduras government, they buried five bodies, all of which we had tested for a DNA match. That leaves two unaccounted for—Jesse and one of the Magas cartel members."

"We're going to find out what happened," Frankie said. "Even if I have to sacrifice you two to do it."

Though I knew she wouldn't, it was a testament to where she placed the blame that she was threatening us at all. Frankie wasn't given to reckless statements or behavior. I squeezed her shoulder, and she didn't shrug me off. That was a good sign.

Joss peered at her. "Working for the local cartel is a way of life in these places. Villages are often conscripted into forced labor. If they refuse, the cartels visit horrors upon them. Even those who comply are often at risk from competing cartels. This is a dangerous place to live, and every person's life is consumed with day-to-day survival."

"That's no excuse," Frankie said. "Let's get closer so we can see what we're up against. We'll pick them off, one by one, for questioning, until we find what we need."

A few hours later, we were closer and on the other side of the village. We'd gone through the site of the wreckage and found all the cocaine gone, even the melted bricks, and there was still no evidence of what happened to Jesse. At least David and I hadn't fucked up that part of the search.

As the sharpshooter in the bunch, I knew how to belly-crawl through anything and disguise my presence. I inched closer to the storage building, looking for a place with clear sightlines. Once I found it, I settled down and used the familiar lens of my spotting scope to check it all out.

From this vantage point, I counted twelve men armed with assault rifles guarding the place. Six were positioned on the perimeter, and six were clustered on the end with wide, loading-bay doors. There was an awning over that end, and two unarmed men sat at a card table. Their clothes were threadbare and torn. Stains from sweat and dirt darkened their shirts and pants, and neither of them wore shoes. Their backs were to me. Electronics were scattered on the table, and the men were fiddling with them.

Now that I had a count and knew their positions, I took a closer look. Four of the guards were familiar. They'd been with Fernando as he provided us with the possessions belonging to the remains. I recognized Father Juan in the shade of the patio, cradling an AR-15 like it was relic of the cross. Fucking hypocrite.

Fernando emerged from the storage facility with a thin man relying heavily on a crutch. Another fucking hypocrite. I wanted to capture him because I knew he was the leader. It was in his bearing and the deference of the guards. His lips moved, and he gestured to the table. The man with him nodded, which drew my attention to him.

His blond hair stood out in contrast to the darker colors found in this region, and it fell to his shoulders. Unlike most of the other men, he didn't tie it back. His beard, thick stubble on the lower half of his face, was darker, though it was only light brown. The eyes were what hit me in the gut—clear, crystal blue.

Jesse was alive.

My heart raced, and I spent a moment getting it under control. I wanted to race into the valley and rescue him, but I knew doing so could cost both our lives.

He was injured, and he'd lost a ton of weight, but that was my Jesse. Our Jesse. I watched for a few more minutes, taking stock of his shocking physical appearance. When I returned to my crew, I shared the grim news.

"Jesse is alive, but not for long."

Frankie's fist flexed, and I knew she wanted to punch something—probably David or me. Or both. Her eyes flashed, and anguish made her voice husky. "We left him here for five months."

Joss closed his one hand over hers. "Francesca, we will rescue him first. There is no time for guilt or blame right now."

She shook off his hand, but she didn't glare at him for using her full name. "What's the plan?"

"Twelve armed guards, including four of the ones who gave us Jesse's personal effects and Father Juan." I shot a look to David.

"Praise the Lord and pass the ammunition," he muttered.

I continued, giving details about their formation. "We'll need to watch for a while to monitor their rotation schedule, check for weaknesses."

Storming into a stronghold wasn't a small undertaking. The element of surprise wouldn't work. We were four against twelve, not including Fernando and the two men at the card table. Then there was the entire rest of the village to consider. This was a community operation, and so they were all a threat.

We couldn't take on two hundred people, so we needed to sneak in there and get him out.

"He's not moving too well," I said. "He's leaning heavily on a crutch."

"What do you mean by saying he's not alive for long?" Joss asked. "It's likely he broke his ankle in the crash and it didn't heal correctly. That's not a life-threatening injury."

"He's turning yellow. Liver damage, probably from internal injuries sustained in the crash or through repeated beatings." I wiped a hand across my brow. "He wouldn't cooperate willingly, not unless he's posing as a member of the cartel, which I doubt. Someone would have exposed him by now, and if not, he would have found a way to get a message to us."

Frankie took my spotting scope and crept closer. David covered her six.

Joss and I stayed put to cover both of them.

"You got a signal for situations like this?" Joss kept his gaze glued to the situation at hand. "Like a bird call or frog noise or something?"

"No."

"The longer we stay here to watch, the more chances we take that we'll be noticed. If we're still here tomorrow, we're pushing our luck."

"You have an idea for a plan of attack?"

"You said they eat dinner, and then they all go to sleep. Stands to reason they'll leave guards on the goods, but out here, the wilderness makes the prison. They'll take minimal precautions with a prisoner."

For the rest of the afternoon, we watched Jesse sit at the table with the two other prisoners. It looked like he was teaching them to repair radios.

At dinner time, the trio was led to a small hut next to the storage facility, and they were locked inside. One guard remained on duty at the door. He settled on a wooden chair, and when a woman brought a plate of food, no guard replaced him as he chowed down.

David motioned us forward. This was our chance.

Before we left the cover of the forest, a woman approached. She smiled at the guard and pointed at to the door.

I signaled for my team to lay low as she went inside. Through a window, we saw their silhouettes. Talking happened.

When the door opened again, Jesse hobbled next to the woman all the way down the path in front of numerous huts. She slowed her walk, but she swept past people like some kind of queen with Jesse trailing in her wake.

Moving with them, we changed our trajectory of attack. I hated impromptu plans because they had a much higher potential for things going wrong, but I didn't see where we had much choice. Joss was correct in his observation that the longer we remained in the area, the higher our risk for discovery and capture.

The hut where she stopped was past Fernando's hut where six of the guards sat at a wooden table outside and gobbled down a spread that looked fairly tasty. Instead of turning him over to them, she led him past that hut. Two more huts down, she led him to the back, which faced the woods. If he had been able to run, this would have been the perfect time.

He leaned against the back of the hut and closed his eyes. From here, I could tell he was exhausted and in pain, but his training had not deserted him. He still looked strong and able-bodied to someone who hadn't known him before.

Next to him was a high table where I spied a basin and a mug.

She disappeared through a door. Few of the huts had doors on the back, and those that did were a little larger than the rest of them. In seconds, she returned with a straight-backed chair. Painted blue with a woven seat and back, it was nicer than anything I'd seen laying around outside.

Without being told, Jesse sat and stared straight ahead. His entire body was tense, and he took several deep breaths to force himself to relax.

She lifted a rag from the basin, and she squeezed the water out. She straddled his lap and washed his face. Her lilting voice carried to our hiding place, as did his murmured responses, but we couldn't make out what they said.

I looked to Joss, and he shrugged, indicating that he wasn't catching anything either.

When she finished, she rose and got the mug. Using her fingers, she smeared shaving cream on his stubble, and then she proceeded to shave him with a straight razor. The shaving of a prisoner wasn't something I'd expected to see, and it threw me off. I frowned, flashing Frankie a WTF look because maybe a woman would better understand the actions of a woman.

Rather than kill me for covert sexism, she whispered, "She's seducing him."

David and I both looked at her curiously.

"Interesting theory," David muttered.

"Whiskers are scratchy. She's getting rid of them first." Frankie indicated the careful way the guards remained vigilant without looking at the tableau unfolding below. "She's important in the village..." Her voice trailed off. "Oh."

Glancing back, I saw that Frankie had been right. The woman was back on Jesse's lap, kissing him as her hand worked its way down his pants.

There's no way Jesse was on board with that, but he didn't appear to have options. My stomach turned. There was no fucking way he'd want us to see this.

Chapter 8

Jesse

Breathing a silent apology to Jessica, I put myself on autopilot and sent my mind elsewhere.

The sound of the engines screamed in my ears, and altitude dropped much too quickly. I'd shot the merc, and when he'd fallen toward me, I head-butted him in the face hard, knocking him out. Then I'd wrapped my legs around him and flung us both out of the airplane.

With my hands still zip-tied behind my back, pulling the ripcord was impossible. It had been years since I'd prayed, and I did so now. I also used all my strength to jerk on the plastic tie. The progress I'd made in cutting it with the sharp piece of metal bore fruit. Suddenly my wrists were free. I pulled the ripcord on the guy's chute and clung to him with my arms and legs.

The chute tangled in the trees, and we hit hard.

I'd been shot twice and had jumped out of a plane without adequate time for the parachute to slow us down. The last thing I remembered was a branch slamming into my back.

The next month or so passed in a feverish haze of me floating in and out of consciousness.

When I woke one day, I found myself on the dirt floor of a small hut. It felt like I was naked under a scratchy blanket. A man bent over me, peering into my eyes, and I tried to move away.

"Do not try to move. You are very ill."

I tried to ask where I was, but my throat was on fire. The man was older, silver threads making up half of his dark hair, and he was painfully thin.

He was a doctor, he'd explained, and he was caring for me.

"What are my injuries?"

"Right ankle is broken. It is in a splint, but it is not healing correctly. You were shot on the left side, and that is where your infection was the worst. But your fever broke. You may live a few more days." He helped me sit up, and he poured some water into my mouth.

The burning in my throat eased. "Who are you? Where am I?"

"I am Jorge. This village is called Rio Escondido, which means hidden river, but you will not find it on a map."

Over the next few days, as Jorge nursed me back to some semblance of health, he filled me in about the village. Terrorized by the Magas cartel and forgotten by the government, they'd turned over most of their farming to growing coca for the cartel. In a matter-of-fact tone, he told me about how the Magas cartel would send soldiers into the village to rape the women as they worked in the fields or string up a young man and cut him thousands of times until the ground could not soak up more of his blood.

I knew things like this happened. It was one of the reasons we took these risks. While we knew full well that other cartels could move in, we also knew we made a difference. We'd crippled several major organizations and sharply curtailed the flow of drugs into the U.S. through the use of strategic operations. We often worked in conjunction with the DEA or CIA, though they would neither confirm nor deny our involvement.

Once the village acquiesced, the cartel had installed people loyal to them in positions of power to keep everyone in line. Protected by the cartel that had terrorized them, the village had lived in relative peace for the past six years.

Of course, most of their able-bodied men had been conscripted into service for the cartel, but they were allowed to visit their loved ones on a regular basis.

Though I saw armed guards outside whenever the door opened, Jorge was the only person allowed in the hut where I was kept. Every morning, the guards came and got him, and they brought him back every few hours to tend to me. That gave me a lot of alone time, but I could barely move. There was no way I was going to survive a trek through the jungle. I spent a lot of time wondering about Frankie. Had she survived the jump? Was she safe, or was she a prisoner like me?

I trusted that my friends would mount a search for us both. Though my friendship with Dean was tenuous at best, I knew that would all fall away. There was no resource they wouldn't expend to find me.

While I waited, my mind always went to Jessica and Bailey. Did they think I was dead? Jessica had been through so much already. She was a strong woman, and I knew she could survive without me, but it killed me to think of the anguish this would cause her. Whenever I closed my eyes, I saw her face, the way she smiled whenever she saw me or the intense concentration she affected when she worked on a piece. I'd lost my picture of them, so I closed my eyes a lot.

When I was strong enough to finally get up, I found out my ankle was worse off than I'd hoped. The constant pain meant shards of bone were free-floating, and I knew this situation could become deadly if one moved.

"I'm going to need crutches," I said.

Jorge considered this. "Probably not. I think they will execute you today.

This news did not surprise me. "Why did they bother making me well if they were just going to kill me?"

"It is less that they wanted to heal you and more that they didn't want to outright kill you. I tell them you are part of Magas. They will be rewarded if they give you back to them."

In all my time with Jorge, I'd never asked him where his loyalties lay. I had no reason to expect he might be on my side, because he was as much a prisoner as I was. I wasn't going to deny being part of the cartel until I knew whether it mattered.

That day, Jorge was allowed to take me outside and give me a bath. As the sun beat down on me, I shivered under the cold water he poured over my head. He handed me a sliver of lye soap, and I washed as much grime from my skin as I could.

Less dirty than before, I donned a worn out shirt and a pair of pants that were too short and too loose. It was good to have actual clothes. I'd been getting around with a blanket tied around my waist for so long that I got used to wearing a skirt.

The sound of a woman's voice had me turning. She approached, speaking in rapid Spanish. I picked out a few nouns and articles, but that was all. I looked to Jorge for a translation.

"This is Magdalena. She is the sister of Fernando, the man who controls the village."

I inclined my head. *"Hola, senorita."* My lack of Spanish-speaking ability was sure to out me as not a member of the Magas.

She came closer, a flirtatious smile on her round face. Her long black hair had been corralled into a braid that fell down her back, and she wore a shirt and skirt that flattered her figure. The confident way she moved told me, more than anything, this was a woman who got what she wanted.

She ran a hand over my biceps before moving to feel my chest and thighs. I let her do this, though I kept an eye on where her hand wandered. When she went to feel my package, I put a restraining hand on her wrist.

The two guards who'd been lazily supervising stepped forward.

Ignoring them, I kept my gaze locked to Magdalena's. "Most people offer dinner and some wine before making a move."

Peals of laughter stopped the nearest goon from shoving the business end of his rifle into my face. She said something more and eased her hand from my grip. Then she walked away.

I turned to Jorge. "My Spanish sucks, but did she just say I had a nice ass and something about killing me?"

"Yes," Jorge said. "The cartel will visit today, and your fate will be decided."

I contemplated running, but I couldn't put weight on my ankle without excruciating pain making me almost pass out.

Jorge read my thoughts. "They will kill you before you make take two steps."

"Jorge, they have to know I'm not part of the cartel. I mean, I don't exactly look like I'm from around here, I don't speak much Spanish, and they're keeping me under guard."

"Yes, well, I am the village doctor, and I am also a prisoner."

The guards motioned with their guns, so we walked in the direction they indicated.

I hobbled along beside Jorge, my energy flagging as sharp pain from my ankle shot up my leg. "Now, why is that, exactly? You'd think they'd celebrate a doctor."

"I'm not here by choice. I came a little over a year ago as part of an international relief effort. I staffed a clinic in a large city near the coast that was filled with such poverty as you will not believe. One day, the clinic was raided, and I was carried off. I have been here for over a year."

That was a terrible story. "Where are you from, originally?"

"I was born here, in Honduras, but I went to the U.S. when I was fifteen. I went to high school and college to be a doctor. Then I came back here to try to make a difference."

The U.S. didn't let their doctors disappear like that. A recovery effort, overt and covert, should have been underway. "It's weird that nobody has come for you."

"I was illegal in the U.S. so they won't miss me." He shrugged. "And here, the Magas cartel has an arrangement with the government. They probably took me because I do not have legal status anywhere anymore. They are not stupid. Nobody will come for you either."

My faith in Dean, David, and Frankie remained strong; however, I knew I needed to get word to them. With this amount of time passing, they had no idea where I was. I had no idea where I was.

The guards led us to a small gathering. In front of the milling crowd was a table where four men sat. Armed commandos swarmed the area. I counted too many to take down even if I was in good physical condition.

A man with a round face and a passing resemblance to Magdalena rose. He grinned. "I am Fernando. What is your name?"

I narrowed my eyes, calculating the value of giving my real name.

"He is Jesse Foraker." A big man with blond hair and an imposing manner sat at the table. He cut a piece of mango with a knife and ate it. "Mercenary."

I knew this man because he was the very person Frankie and I had been dispatched to snatch and transport. He went by the unassuming name of Jack Smith, though his given name was John. Born and raised in Macon, Georgia, he actually had a lot in common with me. We had two sisters, a brother who'd been killed in Afghanistan, and we'd left the military as decorated heroes.

Frankie and I had formed a meticulous plan to capture Smith. We'd intended to grab him en route to a theater show. Our plan had been solid until we found ourselves surrounded by three times the force we'd anticipated.

Normally I objected to being called by that title, but right now, it was probably in my best interest to cultivate it. I pretended ignorance. "Have we met?"

"You were hired to bring me to the good old U.S. of A. for prosecution." He grinned, revealing a row of even, white teeth. "Let's not play games."

If that's the way he wanted it, fine. "What are you planning to do with me?"

His grin was more like a dog baring its teeth than an expression of happiness. "I'm not planning on doing anything with you that you weren't gonna do with me. You'll stay here. Fernando will use you as he sees fit. You can work the fields." He gestured to Fernando. "Our friend has a reputation for being good with electronics. Keep him away from anything he can use to communicate. Shoot him if he tries anything or pisses you off. Fernando, this is your reward for a job well done—slave labor."

To me, Smith said, "Welcome to twenty years at hard labor, Foraker. It's been a pleasure."

He lifted his chin in the direction of one of his minions, and I was taken back to the prison hut where I'd recuperated.

A loud moan snapped my brain back to the present. Magdalena dug her nails into my chest and moved her hips faster. She was close to finishing. I grasped her hips, helping her move on top of me.

I fucking hated this woman more than I'd ever thought it possible to hate a woman.

After Jack Smith had passed sentence, it hadn't taken Magdalena long to stake her claim. During the day, I worked in the fields or in the village—wherever Fernando decided I was needed. After the evening meal, I often belonged to her.

My ankle had never healed, and I relied heavily on a crutch to get around, and so I'd never found a way to break out of here. As much as Jorge was my companion, he was also a man who looked out for himself. The moment I made a move, he would raise an alarm.

I wouldn't get far on foot, so I kept my eyes peeled for any opportunity to get a message out.

Lately, Fernando had been using me to repair electronics, but he kept a close watch over everything I did, and he forced me to explain my actions and to teach my skills to Jorge and Carlos, a boy from the village who I thought was his son, but I wasn't sure.

With a cry, she collapsed against me, and I embraced her. I'd learned early on that pleasing Magdalena was the difference between being beaten by multiple guards and enduring three days on tortilla and water rations, and preserving my strength while looking for a way to escape.

After a few moments, she laughed. "We will go to my bed. I have a treat for you."

Unless that treat was an unattended cell phone, I had no interest in anything she offered. "Then let's go inside."

The treat turned out to be tequila, which I enjoyed. Getting blitzed out of my mind was the only way to ease the pain in my ankle, but it wasn't a good strategy for keeping Magdalena's temper in check. She was likely to start asking questions about if I loved her, and she didn't want to hear the truth. Telling her that my hatred for her was the strongest emotion I felt could cost my life.

So I downed two shots, and then I faked drinking the rest. It wasn't too hard. I distracted her by pulling her onto my lap so that she faced away from me, and I played with her tits. Every time she called for us to drink a shot, I made sure she didn't see me pour mine under the chair and into the hard-packed dirt floor.

"You think I could run this village?"

I'd been planting seeds like that in her head for a while. Pumping her up meant she placed trust in me, and that put me one step closer to opportunities for escape. "You could run this village better than anyone. Now that you can process the coca leaves yourselves, why do you need the Magas? They take most of your profit."

Magdalena liked the idea of profit. Jumping to her feet, she whirled and threw her arms in the air, and then she drank more, bolstered by talk of striking out on her own.

I'd shown them how to process the leaves, something they hadn't know how to do. In the storehouse, I'd taught them how to dry the leaves, mulch them, and use cement as a binding agent. Then they mixed in some gasoline to form the yellow paste that could be further processed into cocaine powder. I even counseled them to wear respirators when mixing the paste to counter the effects of the noxious fumes.

In Columbia, where I'd spent some significant time, this paste was often used in place of money. Farmers used it to barter with local stores for food goods. I told her about how she could use it to bring better supplies to the village, including building materials, food, and clothes. She liked the idea that being the person to rain riches on her fellow villagers would bring her more power and prestige. I played to her vanity. I liked to think it was a strategy Jessica would have used to manipulate her way into control of a situation.

When she was so tipsy she forgot the little bits of English I'd taught her, she took off her clothes and dragged me toward the bed. I got away with fingering her to orgasm, and she promptly passed out.

If I could have left, I would have, but the guards outside wouldn't let me leave without Magdalena's permission.

On the plus side, I got to sleep on an actual mattress instead of on a dirt floor.

I closed my eyes and thought about Jessica. This was my one respite. No matter how shitty things were every single day, remembering our time together was my single refuge.

A soft sound brought me from a light sleep to full awareness. Quickly I took stock of the hut. Magdalena was asleep beside me. The front door was closed, and the dim light the guards kept out front showed their shadows in place on the front porch.

It was also enough light for me to make out shadows inside the hut.

"Jesse?"

I recognized David's voice and immediately I clamped a hand over Magdalena's mouth. She struggled against me, so I rolled to pin her down.

"David, I have a hostile here."

A second shadow loomed over the bed. "We know."

Dean. I'd never been so happy to hear his voice.

Tape ripped, and I moved my hand long enough for Dean to slap it over her mouth. She made angry, protesting noises.

A light knock came from the front door, the guards not wanting to disturb her while also making sure they did their job. "Senorita?"

Before I could call out, a woman moaned and made sex noises. David took over restraining Magdalena, and I turned to find Frankie standing guard in the back door.

The knock came again. "Magdalena?"

"Mas rapido," Frankie moaned loudly, really playing it up. *"Mas rapido!"*

The guards' footsteps showed they were beating a retreat.

Magdalena resisted, but David and Dean got her tied up tightly. She was a fighter, so she wasn't giving up, and I knew that as soon as we were gone, she'd do something to raise the alarm.

I took David's pistol and hit her hard on the temple. I honestly didn't care if it cracked her skull or killed her.

Dean hoisted me onto his back, and we retreated into the forest. We traveled in silence all night, my crew pausing a few times to transfer my carcass to a fresh back. There was no way in hell I could have kept up with them.

When dawn broke, we were miles away.

Now that we could see where danger might be coming from, Dean called for our party to stop. David set me on my feet and hugged me tightly.

Another set of arms came around me from the back and side as Dean and Frankie joined in.

I'm not going to admit we were all crying like babies.

When they stepped back to let me breathe, I gestured toward the fourth man. "Hi. We haven't met. I'm Jesse."

"Joss Blaese. It's good to meet the legend in person."

"Joss, it's a real pleasure." I didn't feel like a fucking legend, but I focused on the matter at hand. "If we can build a crutch from some sticks, I can walk for a bit, give y'all a break."

Frankie handed me a stick of beef jerky. "We're going to eat something, and then we're going to keep moving. They have vehicles, and we're parked on the other side of the Guatemalan border."

"I am so fucking happy to see you," I said. "I was worried that something bad had happened."

A big, fat tear lodged in her eyelash, and she blinked it away. "Don't, Jesse. I can't hold it together if we debrief now."

"Jessica?" I asked the question that had been burning a hole in my tongue.

Dean said, "She'll be okay."

Already exhausted, I didn't want vague platitudes. "Meaning she's not now? What aren't you telling me?"

David set a hand on my shoulder. "She's had a tough time, but she's dealing."

I studied his face and tried to read his mind. "She thinks I'm dead."

"We all did." He opened his mouth to say more, but Dean motioned for us to be silent.

On high alert, we all froze and studied our surroundings. From a distance, we heard the crash of something through the underbrush. A wildcat emerged with a furry, rodent-looking thing in its mouth.

We all exhaled at the same time.

Dean motioned for everyone to get moving. "We'll talk once we're out of danger."

It took the rest of the day for us to make it to the car. There was no way I would have been able to make this trek on my own. Frankie, who'd been carrying me this stretch, set me down next to a tree. She rubbed her leg.

"You were shot there," I said.

"I carried your ass for the last two miles," she countered with a grin I'd sorely missed. "I ache all over."

"I can help with that," Joss said as he headed over to help Dean and David uncover the car.

I grabbed Frankie's wrist to prevent her from killing a man who'd risked his life to save my ass. "Really—what happened?"

"I was shot in the leg. It got infected. They flew me home where I had a couple surgeries over a couple months. A little rehab, a little PT, and I'm good as new." She waved away any concern I might have.

"How long before they got to you?"

Her gaze dropped. "Two days. They sent me back, and David and Dean went after your GPS signal. They found the wreckage, and when they went to that village, the priest there said they'd buried you."

I wasn't surprised by Father Juan's lie, but I was a little confounded by the fact that Dean and David had bought it without proof. "And they didn't insist on digging me up?"

"We did, but when we took a break, they filled in the graves." Dean's voice came from behind me. "They gave us your personal effects—remnants of your clothes that were burned and bloody, your boots, and your wedding ring."

That explained what had happened to my things, but I didn't understand why that had been enough proof. "Still not a body."

"They had photos," David said. "It was enough to convince us, but Dean still insisted all the bodies be dug up and DNA tests run. He had to go through official channels. When we got the results a few nights ago, we chartered a private plane and came right down. I'm so sorry, Jesse." He shook his head, his words breaking off as his eyes filled with liquid anguish.

I knew this had been hard on them, but a huge part of me was pissed that they hadn't pushed harder for proof—because I hadn't been dead.

I climbed into the backseat and lost myself in brooding thoughts.

Chapter 9

Dean

Joss drove, his firm hand on the wheel putting significant distance between us and the Magas cartel. Adding him to the team had proven to be a good decision. Except that he seemed to have a crush on Frankie, he fit in seamlessly.

Jesse sat between me and Frankie, resting his head against the back of the seat. I knew he was tired, but I wanted to debrief. I wanted to know how the hell he'd survived.

"Jesse, can you tell us what happened after you pushed Frankie out of the plane?"

"Go fuck yourself, asshole."

The vehemence of his reply left no doubt he blamed me for months of imprisonment and abuse. I shared his sentiment. "I will, after you tell us what happened."

"You fucking left me stranded in Central-fucking-America." His fists clenched and unclenched.

David turned around. "Jesse, we know we fucked up. We know we let you down. Words can't express how badly we feel, and I don't blame you if you never forgive any of us."

"At least you understand my timeframe."

"But the least you owe us is a debrief, and we owe you one as well." David watched Jesse, but Jesse didn't move. He didn't lift his head and he didn't open his eyes.

Frankie twined her fingers with his, and he let her. At least it was something. After a few minutes, he fell asleep. It was likely the first real rest he'd allowed himself in months.

He woke with a start two hours later, lifting his head and looking around with bleary eyes.

When his gaze met mine, I smiled. "You snore."

"David, give me your phone."

David handed it over. I think we both expected him to check our position electronically, but he dialed Jessica.

From my position so close to him, I heard the greeting loud and clear. "Sir? Did you mean to call me?"

"Brea?" Jesse smiled. "It's Jesse. Where is Jessica?"

I read shock into the silence. We had not informed Brea or Jessica of Jesse's rescue because we wanted to get him out of the country first.

"Brea? Are you still there?"

"I'm here. Who did you say you were?"

Voices through cell phones didn't sound the same as they did in person, and I understood Brea's confusion. I reached over and pushed the button to put the call on speaker.

"Brea, this is Dean. We rescued Jesse. It turns out he wasn't dead after all."

"Oh. Holy shit. Jesse? Oh, my God. Jesse?"

"Yeah, Sugar. It's me, and I'm happy to hear your voice, but I really, really want to talk to Jessica."

Brea shrieked, reaching a pitch that hurt my ears. The projection of her voice turned away from the phone. "Jessica, get your ass in here. Guess what? Jesse's alive, and he's on the phone. Jessica? Jessica! Oh, crap. Dad!"

A clattering noise shook the speaker, and all the sounds muted.

We all leaned closer to the phone and watched as the call disconnected.

Jesse stared at the black screen for a second, and then he hit redial. It rang and rang, but nobody picked up.

My heart leaped to my throat, but I kept my wits about me and called Sylvia. "Hi, Sylvia, this is Dean. Is Jessica all right?"

"She fainted." Sylvia panted into the phone, likely having run to wherever Jessica and Brea were. "Brea was thinking she had a seizure, but she just fainted. Is it true, Dean? Is Jesse alive?"

"Yes, it's true. Is she awake now? He'd really like to talk to her." I tapped Jesse's arm and handed him my phone. "She's okay. She just fainted."

Jesse snatched it from me. "Sylvia? It's Jesse."

I didn't hear Sylvia's words, only her voice. Then I heard Jessica's tremulous tone.

"Darlin', I've been missing you."

Her sobs came through, loud and clear. I wanted to be there with her, holding her as she fell apart, but she wasn't mine anymore—not that she'd ever really been mine. While losing her stung, having Jesse back went a long way toward negating that loss, and that's when I realized Jesse had been right—I didn't love her the way he did. Mine

93

was a feeling, a yearning for companionship, a need for affection, but his was an all-consuming fire.

She deserved to have that fire, and so did he.

I'd been a shitty friend to both of them, and I'd let Jesse down in a way that, as David had indicated, had probably irreparably damaged our friendship. I'd gained so much in the last day, and I'd lost everything.

Jesse

Hearing her voice, even if it was sobs punctuated by words, was a salve my heart had long needed. I felt some of the sharp edges of the shrapnel inside me begin to blunt, and tears streamed from my eyes.

"You're coming home?"

"Yeah, darlin'. I'm coming home. Joss is driving us to the airport now."

"The new guy?" She sniffled and blew her nose.

"That's the one."

"This was his job interview?"

I laughed at that. "I have no idea. Tell me about you, darlin'. Tell me about Bailey."

"We're okay." Her voice cracked, and I knew she was lying for my benefit. "Bailey is so big now, Jesse. She's sitting up, and she's so curious about everything. She watches everything going on around her."

"Yeah? Does she still have blue eyes?"

"Yes. They're just like yours. Your mom came out a couple weeks ago, and she brought baby pictures. She looks so much like you."

It did my heart good to know that my mom was an active part of their lives. Jessica needed all the family she could get. "I'd rather she looked like you."

"Oh, shit—your mom. Jesse, you have to call your mom."

If my mom thought I was dead, she'd have a heart attack if I called her out of the blue. "How about you do it for me? I can see her when I get back."

"Okay. I'll call Mia and Olivia too. Do you know when you're getting back? They're all going to want to see you."

"Thanks, darlin'. I appreciate it, but I want to hear everything about you."

"Oh, Jesse." She broke down in sobs.

"Jesse? This is Warren."

"Hi, Warren." I liked my father-in-law quite a bit, and in the months we'd lived in the same house, we'd become friends. "It's great to hear your voice."

"Back at you. Listen, Jessica isn't doing really well right now." The sobs in the background quieted, and I realized he'd left the room. "She's had a really tough time since you've been gone. I'm sure you have as well. But when she fainted, she hit her head. I'd like to take her to the ER to get checked out. Her health hasn't been great lately."

My stomach dropped. When I'd left, she'd been fine. I hated that my absence exacted a toll from her. "Absolutely. You can reach me through David, Frankie, or Dean. Keep me posted, okay?"

"Sure thing. We can't wait to see you."

I handed Dean's phone back to him. He took it without comment, and I didn't say anything either. He messed with it, and then he handed it back to me. It was opened to a social media app. "Jessica has quite a following for her business."

Swiping through the feed, I saw images of furniture she'd repurposed and added her touch to, and I saw occasional images of Bailey. I spent a lot of time looking through that feed, seeing my baby grow through images.

In the afternoon, Joss stopped at a strip motel.

I scowled. "This isn't the airport."

"Observant," he said drily. "I'd heard that about you."

"We're going to get cleaned up, contact the pilot, and get a departure time." Frankie squeezed my hand, and I realized I'd been holding onto her for the entire ride. She looked down at my worn clothes, castoffs from the villagers. "We're burning your clothes."

David booked two rooms while Joss and Frankie did a perimeter check.

In the parking lot outside the rooms, Frankie did a happy dance, swinging her hips in wide circles as she spun around. "I finally get my own room!"

"No, you don't," David said. "Four beds, five people. Coin toss."

She moved closer to me. "I'll share a room with Jesse. We each get our own bed."

David stowed the coin he'd taken from his pocket, and he regarded me. "Tell me what you need."

I leaned against the car. "I need a long, hot shower, and I need to get home. I have a wife and daughter I haven't seen in months. I don't want to spend another night here."

David opened the door to a room. "I'll get in contact with the pilot. We'll go as soon as we can get a flight plan cleared."

"I don't have a passport," I said. "Getting through customs might be a problem."

David nodded. "I'm on it."

Dean put his arm around my waist to help me walk. "Let's get you inside. Frankie, you go with David. Joss, come with Jesse and me."

He had that tone he got when he wasn't going to listen to anyone who argued with him. I let him help me into the room. He let me go next to the bed nearest the door, which was a few feet into the room.

Joss checked out the room, searching for anything and everything. I hobbled toward the bathroom. I hadn't been in a place that had plumbing in months.

Dean blocked my way. "Jesse, I need to take a look at your injuries."

"I'm fine. Get out of my way unless you want me to piss on you."

He took a calming breath. "Jesse, I know you're angry with me, and you have every right to be, but you're yellow. That means liver damage. If you won't debrief, then you're going to have to let me check you over."

Joss coughed. "I can leave if you two want privacy."

"I want another set of eyes," Dean said. "David is making plans for our departure, and Frankie won't be able to handle this."

"She can't handle it?" Joss's brows lifted almost to his hairline. "I thought you said SAFE Security did not condone sexy stuff with its members?"

Dean's pained expression did not make me feel any sympathy. "Joss, Frankie was severely injured when David and I went looking for Jesse, and despite what she claims, she blames herself for our failure to find him."

Sitting heavily on the foot of the bed, I took the makeshift splint off my ankle. The swelling changed depending on how I used it, and right now it was on the tight side. The bones hadn't healed correctly, and my foot was turned inward as a result.

"Fragments are floating around in there. I can feel them."

Dean touched my skin lightly, pressing to gauge the extent of the swelling.

Joss took a position near my knee. "Can you rotate it?"

"No. It doesn't bend at all."

Next, Dean shined a flashlight light into my eyes and they both went on a scavenger hunt for who knew what.

"Definitely your liver. Is this recent?" Dean lifted my arms, looking at the skin there. "When we get back, you're going directly to the hospital. I'll call ahead and have an ambulance waiting at the airport."

I didn't know anything about problems with my liver, and I'd been feeling poorly the whole time I was there, so I didn't have any idea when problems may have started.

I took off my shirt, and let him see the scar from the bullet wound. "There was a doctor who was a fellow prisoner, but he didn't have surgical tools. He was never sure he got all the fragments. I was grazed, but it still took a chunk out of me."

He looked over every inch I'd let him see. When he tried to pull my pants down, I drew a line.

"I've seen you naked plenty of times." He scowled indignantly.

"I showed you my injuries, and now I'm going to take a shower. I'll be in there until the hot water is gone, maybe longer." With that, I got up and limped to the bathroom.

I washed myself over and over, especially my dick. I felt dirty and used, and I never wanted any of them to know the truth about what I'd done to survive—especially not Jessica. I never wanted her to look at me and see anything other than the man she fell in love with. As I shampooed my hair, I wondered if I should buzz it before she saw me again. I'd never had hair this long before, and it was kind of irritating. I think it was as long now as Jessica kept hers, and mine was bleached from long hours in the sun.

I emerged wearing a towel to find Dean and David waiting for me. They were both clean, evidence that my shower had indeed been long enough for them to each take one in the other room.

David handed me a stack of folded clothing. "The pants might be a little long, but the waist should fit." His gaze wandered down my exposed torso. "You've lost a lot of weight."

Hard work and stringent rations would do that to a person. I lifted the layers of fabric. "No underwear?"

Dean smirked. "You like going commando."

I lost the towel and got dressed. It felt good to have my uniform back on my body. Perching on the bed, I rolled up the legs. Normally I borrowed from Dean because we had a similar build, but since the waist fit my new, slim figure, I knew these were David's pants.

"Did Jessica call?"

David rubbed his jaw. "I talked to Brea. She's at home, resting. They gave her something to calm her nerves. No concussion, no seizure. The pilot is prepping for takeoff. We should be wheels up in four hours."

"Good, about the flight. Who's gonna give me their phone so I can call Jessica?"

Dean and David exchanged a glance.

Dean sighed. "Jesse, we watched you for about half a day before we found a window of opportunity to rescue you."

Dread twisted my stomach. If they'd been watching, then they'd seen some things. Hell, they'd rescued me from a hut where I was in bed with a naked woman. I nailed them both with one nasty glare. "You'd better not say one fucking word to Jessica—or to Brea because she'll tell Jessica. She doesn't need to know the details of what I did to survive."

Dean nodded, his lips pressed together so tight they were rimmed with white, and he held my gaze. "You did it to survive?"

I injected steel into my gaze. "The less said about that, the better. Look, you want to debrief, I'll debrief. I'll tell you about anything but that."

"Okay," David said. "Tell us what happened. You pushed Frankie out of the plane, and then what?"

I told them everything, every detail about what I remembered, including how Jack Smith had sentenced me to hard labor as the village slave. They listened intently, as they always did. When I finished, I prepared myself for their questions.

"Are you planning to go back to rescue the doctor?" David asked. He rubbed his hand on the back of his neck. "It doesn't sound like you really trusted him?"

"I didn't trust anybody," I admitted. "They didn't mistreat Jorge, though they did enjoy occasionally beating on me. He saved my life, but I don't feel an obligation to go back for him."

"What about this woman?" Dean very casually slid that question in. "What was her name?"

I didn't want to talk about her, but she was part of the power structure of the village. "Magdalena. Her brother, Fernando, was in charge of the village for the Magas cartel."

"She forced you to have sex with her." David didn't phrase it as a question.

Fucker was pushing where I'd told him not to push. I glared, hating him for judging me. "It was that, or she gave me to her four favorite goons for hand-to-hand combat practice, and they cut my rations to tortillas and water. I was weak enough before that. It nearly killed me." I leaned closer and lowered my voice to a growl. "If you say one fucking word to Jessica—"

His eyes widened. "You honestly think I'm angling to rat you out? I'm not going to tell Jessica or Brea, and neither will Dean, but you need to talk about it. And you have to know Jessica would understand."

I swung at David, connecting solidly with his jaw. "Jessica is never going to know about it." I lashed out again with my fist, but Dean intervened, catching me before I made contact again.

"Jesse, we know you're angry and traumatized. If you can't talk to us, and you won't talk to Jessica, then you need to find a therapist. This isn't going to just go away."

His arms tightened around me like iron bands around a barrel, and I didn't have the strength to counter his move. I relaxed until he let me go, and then I sat heavily on the bed.

"I fucking hate both of you. I wouldn't have had to endure any of that if you'd fucking cared enough to do your job right."

"I know," Dean said.

For the first time in my life, he looked utterly defeated, and so did David. I wanted to be understanding, but I didn't have the capacity just then.

A knock on the door brought a welcome reprieve. Frankie and Joss came in.

She looked from David to Dean to me, her face reflecting the anguish and helplessness we all felt. "Car is packed. Brea is working on your passport. They'll meet us at the airport."

Joss stood behind her, visible because he was about five inches taller than her, which was unusual. At 5'11, Frankie towered over most men, including me.

He smiled. "An ambulance will be waiting at the airport, and a team is standing by ready to treat Jesse. I hired an ankle surgeon, and I got a hepatologist."

I grimaced. "A person who studies reptiles? I managed to avoid snakebite."

"Hep-a-tol-o-gist," he repeated. "As in hepatic—of, or relating to the liver. You're yellow, buddy. That's liver. To be safe, I got a kidney guy, an autoimmune guy, and a neurologist. I watch a lot of medical shows, and Dean gave me an unlimited budget. The guys might be girls. I was only picky about whether they were tops in their field."

Frankie smiled, and that little bit of her effervescent personality peeking out made me feel like I was finally going home.

I hobbled over to her, and she offered her arm. "You're smelling a ton better," she observed. "If you want, I can cut your hair on the plane. I know you'll want to look your best for Jessica."

She helped me to the car.

"What you really mean is my appearance is so different, it'll shock Jessica into sobbing uncontrollably when she sees me?"

"She's going to do that anyway," Dean said. "Heck, she's probably crying right now."

"Don't be a dick," David said. "Leave her be."

Disgusted I scowled at Dean. "And here I thought you'd move right in after my death. What's wrong—did she not go for your suave sophistication and metrosexual charm?"

Dean's face lost color, and his gaze dropped. "I was there for her as a friend. She—she liked to hear stories about you. It made her feel better." He sighed. "And then she'd cry."

I laughed, not at the fact my wife had been bereft after losing me, but at Dean's hubris. "Aww—that's right. You dislike emotional women. It must have been a rude awakening for you to realize Jessica is one of them."

Frankie inhaled sharply. "Will you two stop it? This whole thing has been really hard for all of us. Jesse, what happened to you sucked, and I'm going to want you to debrief on the plane, but what we went through wasn't any better. We thought we'd lost you. We thought we'd never see you again. We thought you'd died because we fucked up a mission. We didn't have the intel or backup we needed, and that's on all of us, not just David or Dean. That's on you and me. And now, when we should be celebrating and rejoicing that we're back together, you and Dean are sniping at each other because he's had a crush on Jessica for as long as you have, only he hid it and you didn't. I fucking knew she was going to tear apart our team; I just didn't know how or when."

Shocked, I gaped at her like a boy whose mama had just discovered the stiff socks he'd been using to hide his secret masturbating in his bedroom.

Dean recovered first. "You knew? This whole time?"

"Yes, Dean, I knew." She looked from him to me and back. "I knew you both liked her. I know you two better than you know yourselves. I can tell when you're smitten. But I didn't know her, so I didn't know who she'd choose. Honestly I wasn't sure she'd go for either of you. Dean's a little too fussy to get serious with an artist, and Jesse, sometimes you're just a dick who finds a way to get what he wants no matter what she might want."

Frankie's observations were surprisingly accurate. Jessica and I had broken up over that exact thing.

David peered into the backseat. "So, this whole time, you knew what caused the rift between them, and you said nothing?"

Frankie crossed her arms and extended the scope of her scowl to include David. "David, don't turn this around to make me the bad guy, or I'll talk about all the ways you're a dick as well."

Joss chuckled. "Damn. I see what you mean about getting my balls handed to me on a silver platter."

"Monday at six, fly boy. Bring the platter."

"Yes, ma'am." He whispered to David in the passenger seat. "Six in the morning?"

"Yep. Frankie is all sunshine and smiles in the morning."

"Smart chicks are hot at any time of the day."

Ignoring him, I turned to Frankie. "I'm sorry, but Jessica didn't do anything to tear our team apart. That was all on Dean."

I dared Dean to disagree with me, but he only stared out the window with that defeated expression on his face.

Chapter 10

Jessica

The night passed in a surreal blur. Brea and Sylvia fixed my hair, taming the frizz so each lock was visible. Then they picked out an outfit for me to wear to the airport. While they discussed whether I should wear a dress or pants, my mind flittered through thoughts and images without landing on one.

As I stared off into the middle distance, Brea came and put her arm around me. "Hey, big sister. What are you thinking about?"

I answered honestly. "I don't know what to think."

"What do you mean? Jesse is coming home. You can think about that."

My gaze focused, and I looked at her. "Coming home—from where? Why was he gone for so long without a word? And how could they tell me he was dead when he wasn't?"

At that moment, I accessed my anger reserves. I shook off her hug and rocketed to my feet.

"How could Dean and David tell me he was dead when they obviously had no proof?"

She watched me carefully. "They thought they had proof. They had his wedding ring, his clothes and boots, and they saw a picture."

I exploded. "They saw a fucking picture, Brea. They didn't see his body. They left him down there—lost, injured, and who knows what else. They abandoned him when he needed them the most."

"I think you're being a little unfair. They had every reason to believe he was dead. You *know* David and Dean. You *know* they wouldn't believe just anything."

"Obviously, they did."

She stood and parked a hand on her hip. "Look, right now I'm sure David and Dean feel like shit. I'm sure they feel like utter failures for letting him down—if that makes you feel better."

"If it makes me feel better?" My mouth fell open because I couldn't believe she was being such a bitch. "If they'd done this to David, you'd be singing a whole different tune right now. I lost five months with my husband. When Jesse gets back, his own daughter won't know who the fuck he is. No, Brea, the fact they might be feeling guilty doesn't make a bit of difference."

Flipping her hair over her shoulder, she went full diva. "You know, a month ago, you were pissed at Jesse because you felt he made a choice that took him out of your life."

"Enough." Sylvia stepped between us. "Now is not the time for the two of you to argue. You're both tired, stressed, and elated—a confusing combination of emotions. Taking shots at each other isn't going to make either of you feel better. Jessica, Brea was trying to help. She's here to support you. However you also need to remember that Jesse is her friend. She was devastated by his loss, which you might not have noticed since you were wrapped up in your own grief."

"I can't believe you're taking her side." I was the one who'd embraced Sylvia as our mother long before Brea would even consent to meeting our parents.

"I'm not taking sides," Sylvia said. "I'm refereeing a discussion that needs to wait until you have all the facts."

What she said made sense. I backed down. "Sorry."

Brea slammed into me with a hug. "I'm sorry, too. I can only imagine what you're going through right now." She petted my hair. "You should wear a skirt to show off your legs."

"It's cold out tonight. I'm wearing pants." I didn't think Jesse would notice my outfit at all. He was going to be too busy looking into my eyes and kissing me.

Though their flight wouldn't land for a few more hours, and I'd been up all night, I wasn't tired. And then I got a series of texts from David letting me know Jesse wasn't in great shape, and Dean would have an ambulance waiting at the hospital to transport Jesse.

I would ride in the ambulance with him.

I stared at the texts, a million worries racing through my mind.

"What's wrong?" Brea spooned some yogurt into her mouth as she came into the kitchen where I'd been filling up a bottle with water to take with me.

"Jesse isn't coming home. David texted me. He's going straight to the hospital."

Brea and I stared at each other, and in the silence that followed, she solemnly swore to be by my side. Or, at least that's what I hoped the prolonged look had meant.

I threw some snacks in my purse, and then I went upstairs. In his closet was a set of matching luggage. I packed a small bag with underwear, socks, sweat pants, and a couple shirts of varying weights. Hospitals tended to be cold, and I didn't want him to catch a chill.

Brea came out of our bathroom with his toiletries bag and his electric shaver. "He's going to want to shave, whether it's his head or his face, he's going to need this."

Jesse had a few passports hidden away in his office. I grabbed one and threw it into my purse. "Let's go."

Sylvia and Warren were going to watch Bailey. Their flight was scheduled to land after midnight, and I didn't want to stress Bailey out by changing her schedule. She would be cranky all day if I carted her around a noisy airport tonight. I knew Jesse wanted to see her, but in light of where he was going, I stood by my decision to leave her at home.

We left quietly, Brea driving because I still wasn't cleared to drive, and I was too nervous to pay attention to the road anyway. At this rate, I might as well hire a driver. Jesse could afford to pay one.

Brea used valet parking, and she led me to the VIP section of the airport where things were so much more relaxed. All the tension in this terminal was being generated by me.

We waited for a long time.

David came out, and he beelined directly to us. I thought he'd go for Brea first, but he gathered both of us in a great, big hug. While I appreciated seeing him again, he wasn't the reason I was there.

"Jessica, I know you're only humoring me, but I wanted to prepare you." He kept an arm slung around my shoulders as he guided me toward a closed door. "He's different—thinner, ill, and his leg is messed up. We've been trying to keep his spirits up, but he's angry and hurt, and he's been through a lot."

Recalling Sylvia's admonition to get the whole story, I swallowed down the bitter bile of the recriminations threatening to vomit from my gut. Letting a stream of poison out of my mouth now wouldn't help Jesse.

"I'm taking you to the tarmac. They're going to take him directly from the plane to the ambulance. You brought his passport?" He nodded to a security guard who opened a locked door for us. "Dean can only charm the Customs officials for so long after not sleeping for two days."

I'd forgotten about Dean. In the past month, he'd become an escape, someone who helped me learn how to embrace the moments of peace between bouts of bone-crushing grief. What could I say to him?

David led us down stairs and across the part of the airport I'd only ever seen someone walk across in a Sixties movie.

Stairs led to the plane. Waiting at the bottom were a man and a woman wearing black nylon jackets emblazoned with 'EMT' in reflective green lettering. They had one of those stretchers on wheels, and other medical equipment hung in bags strapped to their bodies.

My mind put this together with the fact David had come to prepare me by describing Jesse's appearance, and my heart raced. "David? How bad is he?"

The arm around my shoulders tightened its hold. "He's awake and aware of what's going on, but he was badly injured at the same time Frankie was, and he's gone all this time without proper medical attention."

Dean came out first. When he was a few steps down, he turned back. Frankie appeared at the door with Jesse next to her. His arm was slung over her shoulders, and hers was around his waist. He paused at the threshold, his gaze searching until it landed on me. He smiled, easing some of the tightness and strain in his bearing, and started forward. My breath caught. Even after the phone call and all I'd done to prepare, part of me didn't believe Jesse was actually alive.

He leaned heavily on Frankie, and she helped him down the stairs. Vaguely I noted the addition of Joss Blaese, the newest member of the SAFE Security team.

I moved to the side so I could better see Jesse, sandwiched as he was between Dean and Frankie. David hadn't lied about how different Jesse looked. His bulky, muscular build had diminished. His shoulders had been broad and strong, but now they were thin and shaky, and that change had happened all over his body.

As he came down the stairs, he relied on Frankie instead of putting weight on his right foot. Something about his coloring was off. At first, I thought it was the brightness of the airport lights, but then I realized everyone else looked washed out, but only Jesse appeared sallow.

When he got to the last step, I broke away from David. I wanted to run to him, to launch myself into his arms, but I didn't think he could handle the force of impact. In a daze, I floated to him. People magically moved out of my way.

I stopped an arm's length away, and I forgot how to breathe as I looked into his crystal blue eyes. This was my Jesse, the man who'd patiently weathered all my storms. Right now he was looking at me as if he wasn't quite sure I was real. Closing the distance, I slipped my arms around his neck.

"Jesse, please tell me I'm not dreaming."

His arms came around me, holding me with familiar strength, and his chest rumbled against mine as his gruff voice responded. "If I'm dreaming, darlin', I never want to wake up."

With that, his mouth closed over mine. It was a slow, reverent kiss, reacquainting our lips and tongues with one another and reveling in the feel of us together. When it ended, tears leaked from my eyes. I opened them to find that he was similarly affected. I buried my face in his neck, and he did the same with me. We held each other for a long, long time.

"Jessica," Frankie's voice broke through the invisible barrier separating us from the crowd. "You need to let go. Jesse needs to get in the ambulance."

Reluctantly, I released my tight hold on my husband.

He slipped his hand in mine. "You're coming with me."

It was an order, issued in that bossy, Dom manner that was such an intrinsic part of who he was, and I didn't argue. "Wild horses couldn't rip me from your side."

Brea hugged him next. He returned her embrace without releasing his hold on me. "It's good to see you, Sugar."

She kissed his cheek. "I'm going to bake you a chocolate fudge cake with chocolate frosting."

He flashed a brief smile of acknowledgment, but his gaze roamed the area. "You didn't bring Bailey?"

"No," I said. "My parents will bring her to see you once she wakes up."

The two EMTs helped Jesse onto the gurney.

As he cooperated, he held tight to my hand. "They don't let babies inside hospitals as visitors."

Pulled by his grip on my hand, I followed along as they wheeled him toward the ambulance. "Jesse, it's like you've forgotten who I am."

"Ma'am, I'm going to need you to let go for a minute," said the EMT.

He released my hand so they could load him into the back of the ambulance.

I climbed in behind them, and I sat on a low bench where the guy pointed.

Jesse resumed holding my hand as soon as I was within reach. "You're still crying."

I'd long ago stopped noticing when my eyes had sprung a leak. I wiped moisture from my cheeks. "None of this seems real."

He closed his eyes and groaned. His features pinched in a grimace.

"He's in pain," I said to the EMT.

The name tape on the EMT's vest identified him as Jeremy Gauthier. He was about my height, but he had strong shoulders and muscular thighs. Everything else was covered by loose clothing, so that's all I had to go on. His dark brown eyes seemed warm and intelligent. "I'm taking his vitals now, and there's a whole team of doctors reading the results in real time."

While Jeremy did his job, I struggled to not say something rude about how he needed to fix Jesse. I reminded myself we did not know the extent of his injuries. So I focused on what he'd said. "A team of doctors?"

Jesse squeezed my hand. "It's nothing, darlin'. It's overkill. You know Dean—he can't do anything halfway."

My gaze roamed Jesse's body, cataloging everything that was different from before. His color was concerning, as was the loss of weight, but otherwise Jesse looked okay. I relaxed the tiniest bit at his assurance. Jesse had never lied to me, and I wanted desperately to believe him.

Jeremy listened to Jesse's heart, took his blood pressure, and looked into his eyeballs. When he pressed on Jesse's abdomen, Jesse grunted.

"On a scale of one-to-ten, how would you rate the pain?"

"Four." Jesse gave my hand a little squeeze, and I realized he was downplaying his pain for my benefit. My big, strong hero didn't want to appear weak in my eyes.

"Jesse, be honest. Jeremy can't do his job if you don't give accurate information."

He closed his eyes. "Fine. It's a four if you're not pushing on it. Seven if you are. My breathing is also tight."

Jeremy wrote some things on a clipboard, and then he got on his walkie-talkie. "Fever, abdominal pain, rapid heartbeat, elevated blood pressure, reduced O-2 stats."

We arrived at the hospital in record time, and they pried me from Jesse's side. I watched him disappear through the Emergency Room doors surrounded by medical personnel.

I stood outside, alone and afraid.

"Mrs. Foraker, let me show you to Mr. Foraker's room." A woman with cinnamon skin and a motherly air put her hand on my arm. She wore white scrubs with a hearts-and-balloons pattern, and her hair was slicked against her head all the way back to a small bun at her nape. "I'm Taniqua. I'll be taking care of Mr. Foraker while he's here."

She led me to a private room in a quiet wing, chatting the whole way about how he had the best doctors in the state working on him.

Somewhere along the way, we progressed to being on a first-name basis.

Looking around the room, I noted the similarities between it and the room I'd stayed in for six weeks when I was pregnant. Dean had spared no expense.

None of it mattered right now. This was window dressing, and it didn't mask the real reason we were there. I turned to Taniqua. "I don't know what's wrong with him. Why does he need the best doctors?"

She led me to a comfortable chair and sat on the one next to me. "Let's talk about the tests that have been ordered, okay?" Over the next little while, she led me through a long list of tests and what each test was designed to look for.

"Is this a private party?" Brea's cheerful question interrupted Taniqua's explanation on how long it would take to know the results of the scans.

I motioned for her to come in. "Taniqua, this is my sister, Brea, and her husband, David."

She rose and held out her hand. "It's a pleasure to meet you."

Brea's smile didn't quite reach her eyes, but Taniqua gave her a warm greeting just the same. "Have you heard anything yet?"

I shook my head.

Brea set the bag I'd packed for Jesse on the foot of the empty bed.

Taniqua clasped her hands together. "Now that your family is here, I'm going to go check on the status of the tests and get some things ready."

David sat heavily in the chair Taniqua had vacated, and he pulled Brea onto his lap. "Jessica, he's going to need you to help him adjust to being back."

"You said he was different." In my lifetime, I'd encountered all manner of people, and I'd learned their weaknesses in order to better exploit them for my gain. I didn't know how to be nurturing. "How can I help him adjust when we changed our whole lives just before he left? Nothing is the same."

"You're the same," he said. "He's not coming home to a house— he's coming home to you."

I'd mourned my husband, and grief had changed me. Right now, I wasn't sure about the ingredients in the kaleidoscope of emotions churning through me, and I didn't know what Jesse expected or needed.

"Listen, we all talked, and we think it's best if you don't mention anything that happened between you and Dean until he's physically better." David cleared his throat. "Or maybe not at all. Dean is with our lawyers right now. There are some issues with the way we went about extracting Jesse, and he'll make all the problems go away like he always does. That's why he's not here right now."

Thinking about Dean and our therapy was not even on my radar, and I felt a little bad about that for a variety of reasons. Other emotions included indignation and anger, but I didn't examine any of that.

Brea said, "You're worried it's going to be awkward."

A noise in the hall drew my attention because I was on the lookout for Jesse. When the talking people continued past the room, my shoulders slumped.

"He's going to be gone for another half hour," David said. "I saw the schedule for the MRI. They're doing a full-body scan."

Brea left David's lap and scooted onto the chair next to me. She put her arms around me and her head on my shoulder. "David is worried you're going to choose Dean over Jesse."

"No, never." I closed my eyes. "If you hadn't told me that Jesse was dead, I never would have—" Breaking off, I did my breathing exercises to stave off an anxiety attack.

Brea stroked my hair near my temple. "I know, Summer. I know."

David and I both started. It had been a long time since she'd slipped up and called me the name I'd chosen when we'd broken away from BS to live a crime-free life. It was also the name to which we had defaulted whenever we weren't living a con.

She straightened. "Sorry. I don't know why I said that."

I knew why. "You think I'm so traumatized by everything that's happened, it's going to send me into revenge mode."

"Revenge mode?" David frowned. "I've never seen you be vindictive."

"When she's good, she's very, very good, but when she's bad, she's rotten." Brea twined her hand with mine.

"I think the poem uses 'horrid,'" David said. "Not that it matters. Why do you think that, Sugar?"

"David, you and Dean told her that Jesse was dead, and she believed you. She mourned him, and she started seeing Dean. Everything she's thought, said, and done for the past five months has been based on a lie." Brea faced him, her eyes luminous.

He appealed to me. "I thought it was true. For Pete's sake, Jessica—he's my friend. As overjoyed as I am to have him back, all I can think about are the things I did wrong. Every mistake, every misstep is playing through my head in a loop, and believe me—that's what Jesse is already focusing on. We need you to be on our side."

"I'm on Jesse's side." Nothing about this situation didn't suck, but the question of where my loyalties lay was not in doubt. I loved my sister, and I owed my life to David's intervention in my treatment when I was in a coma, but somewhere along the line, Jesse had become the most important person in my life.

"I know," David said. "So are we."

If Jesse was even angrier with them than I was, it wouldn't matter what side David or Dean was on. Jesse could put the dividing line between them.

Except the Jesse I knew wouldn't do that. He understood loyalty and forgiveness were key parts of maintaining a successful unit. He'd overlooked and forgiven so many things I'd said and done, and I'd done the same with him. That was what people who loved one another and who were committed to having a lasting relationship did.

What if Jesse was no longer committed to his friends or to SAFE Security?

Did I care? I mean, yeah, it would suck for him to lose those friends, but if he left SAFE Security, it meant I wouldn't have to go through this ever again.

Rather than issue platitudes or make promises I wasn't sure I could keep, I leaned back in the chair.

Brea came with me, as glued to my side as she'd always been. I wondered, when all was said and done, if this would damage our relationship, too.

Chapter 11

Jesse

They wheeled me back into the room without telling me anything significant. I'd been poked, prodded, and scanned. Four different doctors had asked endless questions about everything that had happened, wanting details down to how the villagers made the corn tortillas that were a staple at every meal.

I told them, in clinical terms, about my initial injuries and anything sustained during my time spent as a prisoner of the drug war. Before they could leave, I snagged the arm of the immunologist.

She was a small Indian woman with the same no-nonsense attitude as Frankie, yet she somehow projected an air of compassion and caring. I'd forgotten her name, so I looked at her badge.

"Doctor Laghari, I'd like tests for every STD."

She'd been about to follow the others out, but she inclined her head. "I'll order them. Do you suspect anything specific?"

I shook my head. "Just test for everything, and if anything comes back positive, don't give me the results in front of my wife."

"Okay, but if you have something that can be transmitted, we're required by law to notify her that she's at risk."

"She's not at risk." Thinking about how Dean and David had dragged details from me about things I'd rather not divulge, I shuttered my expression so this doctor wouldn't get ideas.

"Jesse, I'm going to remind you about doctor-patient confidentiality, and then I'm going to ask if you need me to run a sexual assault kit, or if you just want the STI tests?"

Since she hadn't brought it up already, I knew David and Dean hadn't disclosed things I'd asked them to keep confidential. Doctor Laghari's assurance helped me to avoid denying it. "I've already showered and discarded the clothes. You've scanned me for injuries. The person responsible lives in a remote Central American village. It's safe to say prosecution isn't going to happen. Just test for STD's so that I can kiss my wife without worrying I'm going to give her a disease."

"Sure thing. I'm going to have a psychologist stop by as well to examine your mental state."

I glared. "My mental state is fine."

"Just the same, it's best if you talk to someone about your ordeal. If you're worried your wife won't understand, we'll make sure she's out of the room when the doctor visits."

My wife was a huge proponent of talk therapy and would probably agree with Doctor Laghari. I'd seen firsthand how much it had helped Jessica heal her emotional scars and transition to living a normal life, and I envied her courage.

"Yeah, whatever."

A male orderly wheeled me to the private wing of the hospital where I'd placed Jessica when she'd been on bed rest. The room was down a different hall at the opposite end of the same floor.

Jessica rose as soon as I came in, anxiety and fatigue drawing lines around her mouth and eyes. Or maybe that was the result of months of grief? Brea stood next to her, close enough so I could tell they'd been sitting in the same chair. David occupied the other chair. Though he was wearing different clothes, I could tell he hadn't been resting either. He was slower in getting to his feet.

The orderly parked my bed in the middle of a bank of hookups for various machines. "Your nurse is Taniqua. She'll be along shortly."

Jessica watched him go, and then her gaze snapped to me.

"They don't have test results yet." I scooted over and patted the space beside me. "How about you come over here and warm me up?"

She perched on the edge of the bed and touched my face. "You're already really warm."

"It's the fever," David said. "Infection."

"Thanks, Doctor Eastridge. Whatever would we do without you?" Sarcasm slipped out, and I wasn't sure if it was because I didn't want him there, or if I was upset Dean and Frankie were missing.

Jessica's gaze dropped, and I realized she was on the verge of tears.

"Hey." I circled my hands around her wrists and tugged her closer until she fell against my chest. Hugging her to me, I angled my face to breathe in the scent of her hair. "I'm okay, darlin'."

David took Brea's hand. "Sugar, it's time to go."

She didn't look like she wanted to leave, but she let him move her a few steps toward the door. "Jesse, we'll be back this afternoon. I know you're going to want to rest and be with Jessica. Um, my parents

112

are on their way with Bailey. I'll tell them to make sure to give you guys time alone."

"Thanks," I said. "I appreciate it."

David stopped at the foot of the bed. "Frankie is handling transport for your mom and sisters. Your mom's flight is due to land any minute, and your sisters will be here by this afternoon. Dean is..."

He trailed off, nodding at Brea who closed the door.

"The village of Rio Escondido filed a complaint with the Honduran government alleging they were raided by an American cartel that set fire to their crops and assaulted four men and a woman." His gaze momentarily slipped to Jessica before returning to meet mine. "Dean is dealing with the CIA. They aren't happy we failed to go through proper channels."

It wasn't like them to plan a mission sloppily. Every time I got pissed at Dean for failing to file mission reports, I reminded myself that his excruciating attention to detail was largely responsible for our success stats. "That's unusual," I allowed.

David shrugged. "When we found out you might be alive, we didn't wait on clearance, and we didn't look to see if we were stepping on toes."

While we didn't work for the CIA or any governmental agency, we frequently worked in conjunction with them, and so we were in the habit of checking to see if we needed to watch out for any active missions when we visited foreign countries.

"Set fire to their crops?" Jessica sat up partway, putting distance between us without leaving my embrace. "Sounds like a cartel town that's trying to go into business for themselves. That never ends well."

I knew what she meant—they were using a cover story of destruction to hide their cocaine haul. Once the cartel moved on, the town would try their hand at refining and selling the drug. Rio Escondido wasn't ready to strike out on their own with any degree of success. I wouldn't be surprised if the Magas cartel went in and cleaned house.

Somehow it made me feel better to know Frankie and Dean weren't home resting up after a mission. I stroked a caress along Jessica's spine. "Karma's a bitch."

Brea kissed my cheek, and David hugged me, and then they left.

Jessica settled back into the crook of my arm. "Promise you'll never leave again."

She'd never before asked me for anything she knew I couldn't give. Then I considered the state of my ankle. The surgeon hadn't made any promises other than to assure me I'd regain some mobility

113

after surgery. He'd wanted to study the scans and x-rays before he presented a plan of care.

I kissed her forehead. "I'm not planning to go anywhere for a long time."

My evasion wasn't lost on her. She lifted her head and looked into my eyes. "We'll talk about it later."

The nurse came in and wagged her finger at us. "Jessica, I'm going to have to ask you to get out of the bed so I can check vitals and get this IV going. If you want to rest, I can have a cot brought in, or that wide chair folds out into a bed."

Jessica eased from my arms. "Taniqua, this is my husband, Jesse. He's going to give you a hard time."

Taniqua was a mite of a woman who made up for her lack of stature with a big smile and an authoritative air. "Oh, I'm sure he'll be fine." To me, she said, "It's a pleasure to meet you, Jesse. You have quite a lady there."

I liked people who recognized how wonderful Jessica was. "I know. She's lucky to have me."

My joke fell flat because Jessica burst into tears. Immediately I was up, swinging my legs out of bed and gathering her into my arms. I balanced on my good leg while soothing my woman.

"Darlin', I'm sorry. My comic timing sucks, which is nothing new, right? So at least that's not broken."

"I'm sorry," she sobbed, her fists grasping my shirt. "I thought I'd lost you, and it was horrible. I can't—I'm not—"

"I know." I said that over and over until the crying tapered off. Then I kissed her forehead and pushed her toward a chair. "Let's let Taniqua do her job, and then you and I will talk about everything, okay?"

She nodded, but she didn't sit down. Instead she took the tissue box into the bathroom.

When she was gone, I apologized to Taniqua. "She's had a tough time lately."

"I know," she said. "Your friend, Dean Alloway, was here earlier. He briefed me on the situation."

With great efficiency, she started an IV and got things going.

"I recognize saline, but what's the other thing?"

"Antibiotics."

"Are the test results back?" I hadn't anticipated anything happening so quickly.

"Not yet." She smiled. "You have a fever, and given your recent accommodations, antibiotics are a no-brainer."

"What if it's not an infection?" I pushed because it was in my nature to do so.

"Let's take it one step at a time," she said. "Right now, you can spend some time with your wife or get some rest. The doctors will be here as soon as they know something."

She left, and I was finally alone with Jessica.

Once again I scooted to one side of the bed. "Come back over. You're the only medicine I really need."

Jessica slid back into bed, careful not to jar my IV. I put my free arm around her and tucked her to my side.

"I want to ask what happened," she said. "But I always hated it when people tried to make me talk. So I'm just going to say I'm here for you when you're ready."

I loved this woman with my whole heart and soul. I hugged her tighter. "Thinking about you is what got me through every day. When things got tough, I'd close my eyes and think about how I used to visit you at rehab when I knew you'd be in the hot tub. I'd sneak peeks at your cleavage while we talked, and then I'd towel you off afterward."

She laughed. "You didn't fool me. I knew why you timed your visits to coincide with the end of PT. I had Brea get me a bathing suit with a more flattering cut."

"The blue one with the wave pattern?" The sides had been cut high, showing off her thighs.

"Yep."

"I liked that one. Whatever happened to it?"

"Chlorine kills bathing suits. It eventually fell apart."

"Actually, washing them in a washing machine kills them. You should rinse them in the shower and lay flat to dry."

Once again, she giggled. "I love that you're such a good homemaker."

Having moved around from hovel to hovel as a child, Jessica wasn't well-versed in a lot of household skills I took for granted. I kissed her forehead. "I'm sure you've come a long way in the past few months."

"Well, you're wrong," she said. "If my parents weren't around, Bailey might have fled in search of a better life by now."

"How is she doing?" Having been born eleven weeks early, Bailey had spent her first seven weeks in the NICU. I expected her to be behind in growth and development, and we hoped to avoid long-term issues with her eyes and lungs.

"She's good, no crossing of the eyes since the surgery. She's sitting up and reaching for things. She rolls over, and she does upward-facing dog really well. When I do my PT, she lays on the floor next to me, and I swear she's trying to mimic my movements."

"Does she talk yet?"

"Not words. It's still early for that. She's vocal. She babbles, and she has some fairly serious facial expressions."

A powerful wave of longing took me by surprise. I missed her so badly. More than that, I'd missed out on five-eighths of her short little life. I'd only meant to be gone for a few days, a week tops. "She doesn't know who I am."

Jessica's fingertips wandered over my chest. "No, she doesn't. I talk about you all the time, and I show her pictures, but she's a baby. Pictures are things to grab and put in her mouth."

I played with her curls. I'd missed twisting a lock around my finger. It drove Jessica nuts, but it calmed me. "Okay, truth time—did you get rid of all my stuff?"

"No."

If she'd thought I was dead, there was no way some things weren't missing. In particular, I wondered about the fate of my tech stuff. "Seriously. I can take it."

"No, Jesse. I didn't get rid of anything. I didn't even pack anything away or rearrange the furniture. I tried a few times, but every time, I'd just break down sobbing." She turned into me, inhaling deeply.

I knew what she was doing. I'd missed her scent as well.

"I did go through your personal papers, though. Your mother said you had a will, and she thought you had a lawyer who was the executor, but she didn't have the contact information."

My mother was concerned that the allowance I put into her account every month didn't dry up. I sighed. "Sorry about that. I do have a will, and SAFE Security's lawyers have a copy. I changed it after we got back from Florida and I found out we were married."

"I know." Her voice was soft and low. "Dean told me. He wanted to make sure Bailey and I were taken care of."

At her mention of Dean, I stiffened. Though he'd been there for my wife and child, his upset over the unfairness of the way I'd pursued Jessica still haunted me. It wasn't fair, but a niggling, dark voice in the back of my head questioned whether Dean had really looked for me. With me out of the way...

It didn't seem to have mattered. Jessica hadn't packed up my stuff. She hadn't executed the terms of my will. I hadn't been gone long enough to lose her.

"Jesse, I have a confession to make."

I wasn't ready for this.

"Your mom—she was really insistent that I carry out the terms of your will, and I got really mad at her. I vented to my mom, and I said some really not nice things, and now my mom doesn't have a very high opinion of your mom." She looked up at me. "I'm sorry, Jesse. I didn't say anything mean directly to your mom. I—I know how close you are, but she—it was like she wanted to push me to do the will, and I didn't want to. It seemed so final, like if I did that, then you were really gone."

I thought about what Jessica had said on the phone. "You said my mom came to stay with you a few times."

"Yes—to see Bailey. She absolutely adores Bailey, but she doesn't like me so much anymore."

I pressed a kiss to Jessica's lips. "Well, I like you just fine, so she'll have to get over it. Plus, my mom was worried her bingo money would dry up. She was probably more worried she wouldn't have her money than she was upset about my death. She's a gambling addict. She's burned through everything my dad left her. I bought her condo, and it's in my name so she can't borrow against it. She has a pension, which comes to me because I had her declared incompetent, and I autopay her bills from that account. I give her a monthly allowance for incidentals, which includes bingo. My sisters don't know the extent to which I manage her gambling addiction."

Jessica relaxed as I explained. "Well, I didn't change anything you had set up. But I did bring you a new toothbrush. Your old one is at home. I couldn't get rid of it, but it seemed like it was time for a new one."

I kissed her again, long and deep. It went a little way toward filling the vast chasm inside me. "When we get home, I'm going to make love to you."

Her lips curved in a sinful smile, but she reined in her femme fatale instincts. "Jesse, what happened to your leg?"

"My leg is fine. It's my ankle." I told her about being shot and parachuting in a last-ditch effort to save my life. After I explained my daring feat, she didn't look as impressed as I thought she would.

Sitting halfway up, Jessica gaped at me, her incredulous expression edging closer to horror. "Why didn't you jump with Frankie?"

That was the million-dollar question. Laying in that prison hut all those nights—or in worse places—I'd asked myself that over and over. I didn't have an answer for her that was any better than the ones I'd given myself. "I didn't think of it."

"Knock, knock." Sylvia's voice carried into the room.

Jessica sprang up out of bed. "Come in." She met Sylvia at the opening where the small hallway past the bathroom opened up into the room.

Sylvia looked the same, as did Warren, who entered on her heels, but Bailey looked completely different. I'd left a tiny, sleepy-eyed baby, and this one was twice the size.

Alert and awake, Bailey squealed and kicked her legs when she recognized Jessica.

Jessica took Bailey from Sylvia, hugging and kissing her. "I missed you, sweetie."

Bailey grabbed for Jessica's hair, but Jessica skillfully dodged the attempt.

"Come on, baby. It's time to say hello to your Daddy." She brought Bailey to the side of the bed.

She checked me out, and I checked her out. She'd grown quite a bit. Her eyes were the same shade of blue as mine, and her hair was coming in thick and dark, like her mama's. She gazed at me with those baby blues, unconsciously making sure I was tightly wrapped around her finger. Jessica had been correct when she'd said Bailey looked a lot like me, but I'd been wrong in thinking it was an unfortunate occurrence. She was fricking adorable.

I held out my arms. "Hi, Bailey. Can I hold you?"

Bailey looked at Jessica as if asking permission. Jessica set her on my legs. "She's not picky about laps."

Before she could keel over, I supported her with my hands on her waist. On her new perch, Bailey checked out her surroundings, and then she zeroed in on me. Slowly a smile spread over her face, and just like that, she stole my heart all over again.

Before the moment was quite over, Sylvia threw her arms around my neck. "Oh, Jesse, it's so good to have you back."

With one arm, I hugged her, but most of my attention was on my daughter, who watched this development with intense scrutiny.

Warren greeted me next, but he kept it to a warm handshake.

"I see what you mean," I said to Jessica. "She watches everything."

"Yeah," Warren said. "She's started imitating as well."

I tossed a small, sly grin to Jessica. "If my wallet disappears, I'll know she's been watching her mother."

"Actually," Jessica said. "I've only stolen one thing since you're been gone, and even that was half-hearted, and they were only Dean's keys. It looks like it's more of a flirty thing between you and me and less of a compulsive problem. Of course, you're not even wearing pants, so there's nothing to steal."

Sylvia looked at her as if she'd lost her mind.

"It's okay, Mom. When I take Jesse's stuff, it's like telling him that I love him."

Warren put a hand on Sylvia's shoulder. "Let's give these crazy kids some time alone. There will be plenty of opportunity later to coach her on better flirting techniques."

After my in-laws left, I said, "I'm wearing pants. They gave them back after the MRI."

She sighed, but it was negated by the huge smile on her face. "Don't ruin my fantasies."

I chuckled. "I am not, however, wearing underwear."

Bailey's eyes got bigger.

"Shh," I said. "You're not supposed to be listening to stuff like that."

Bailey pointed at me and sounds streamed out of her mouth.

"Oh, yeah. You are your mother's child. She gets the upper hand in every conversation."

By the afternoon, I was exhausted. A steady stream of well-wishers filled my room, and my mother had taken up residence on the fold-out chair meant for my wife.

When two doctors appeared toward evening, I used the opportunity to shoo everyone out except for Jessica. One was Doctor Laghari, the immunologist I'd asked to run STD tests. The other was Doctor Sertain, whose name caused Jessica some difficulty. I knew she wanted to let loose with some jokes, but she didn't want to piss off my doctor. He was a regular-looking guy with a goatee and a bald head that reflected the florescent lights.

Jessica stood nearby as they palpated my abdomen and listened to my heart and lungs.

Doctor Laghari covered me back up. "We discovered abscesses on the liver, and you have a pleural effusion."

"That sounds serious." I frowned. While I felt fatigued and crappy, I didn't feel like I was near death.

She inclined her head. "It can be, if left untreated. Yours is a moderate case, and you're already responding to antibiotics."

"What's a pleural effusion?" Jessica asked. I was glad she spoke up, because it would save me from having to search for it on the Internet.

"It's when fluid collects in the sac surrounding the lungs. It's a side-effect of the infection in his liver." Doctor Laghari motioned to my midsection. "He'll need to be on IV antibiotics for a few days, and then he'll take them orally for the next couple of weeks."

Jessica seemed to like the idea I'd get better with medicine as much as I did. "How long will he be in the hospital?"

119

"Four or five more days. I want to monitor his heart, lungs, and liver. Once his levels are back to normal, he'll be able to go home. I'll need to do a follow-up in a couple of weeks, and I'll want to see him back periodically after that, depending on what I hear and see." She smiled. "Do you have any more questions?"

Jessica looked to me, and I had none.

"Great. I'll send a nurse in to deliver another course of medication."

Doctor Sertain stepped up to fill the void. "My turn. I specialize in ankles. I went over your scans, and I'm going to tell you what I can and can't do.

This did not bode well. Jessica slipped her hand into mine.

"Once your other problems clear up, and by that, I mean once Doctor Laghari gives the green light, we can schedule surgery. I can remove the bone fragments, which should eliminate most of the pain. With regard to your ankle, I can repair or rebuild most of it, which will give you back some of your mobility. I'm going to have to replace some bones with metal, and you'll need a graft for the ligaments you've lost. I like to use a tendon, and I typically take it from your hamstring."

"When you say 'some mobility,' what does that mean?"

"It means you'll walk without assistance, but you won't be winning any footraces. You'll be able to participate in everyday activities, but no extreme sports. Given the damage and the fact I'm going to have to rebreak the bone to straighten out the foot, you're definitely looking at arthritis. After surgery, it's going to take about six months of physical therapy. Even with all that, there's a good chance you'll walk with a slight limp."

Jessica made a sound that let me know she thought I was getting off easy. Her PT had been ongoing for about two years. "Your right side and my left side can go on a gimpy date."

Looking up at her, I grinned. "As long as you wear something pretty."

A light blush crept up her neck. "I think I can arrange that."

Two days later, Doctor Laghari found a quiet moment to let me know that my STD tests had come back negative. Knowing that lifted a huge burden from my shoulders. Just to be safe, I asked to have a second series of tests run.

Chapter 12

Jessica

"I think this would look great on you." Frankie held up a white nightie. The design was like a long tank top that had an actual shape to it, but it was longer and made of silk. The neckline plunged deep, and the bottom had lace that would spill across my upper thighs.

In the past two weeks, our house had been full of Jesse's family and friends. To be fair, some of my family lived there, and some of them counted as his friends, so it was also full of my family and friends as well.

Jesse came home from the hospital after three days with admonishments to take it easy. He'd insisted on having scans earlier than Doctor Laghari wanted, and he'd used the results to convince her to release him earlier than she'd wanted. Doctor Sertain also wanted Jesse to stay off his ankle as much as possible. To that end, Jesse had consented to crutches when Doctor Sertain had wanted him to use a wheelchair.

He really wasn't a very good patient.

Frankie had come by that morning, taken one look at me, and dragged me out of the house.

"You need some peace and quiet, and you're not getting it around here."

I eyed the sexy nightie. Jesse hadn't touched me since he'd been back. He kissed me a lot, but they tended to be light pecks or a firm press—nothing with tongue or an intention to get into my pants.

My pants missed him.

With a sigh, I shook my head. "I'm more of an old T-shirt kind of gal."

Frankie looked me up and down. "Is that because you want to be or because it's habit?"

I'd always been this way, but maybe I should take a chance with something out of my comfort zone. Maybe it would make Jesse look at me with hunger and heat like he used to?

Frankie pushed her way into the dressing room with me. The fabric was soft, whispering over my skin like a lover's caress.

Frankie whistled. "I was right. Get this in two colors, and let's get some new bras and panties. Not many people know this, but I have an underwear fetish. Whenever I'm not working, I'm wearing lace." She peeled down the waist of her pants to show me a pair of lacy black panties.

"If Brea was here, she might interpret this as a come-on."

Rolling her eyes, Frankie fixed her pants. "Your sister only says the things she does because it shocks David."

I disagreed. Brea wasn't one who went in for shock when there wasn't a strategic need. She honestly thought Frankie was the most beautiful woman she'd ever met. I got dressed. "I wish I could shock Jesse, but I think he's immune."

"He's not immune."

Back on the sales floor, I picked through a display of panties. "I've told him a lot of stuff most people would find shocking, and he's never had much of a reaction."

"He has a reaction. He just decides if it's going to upset you before he shows it. When he doesn't want to upset you, he'll work through it by putting in an extra hard training session, or we'll get a drink and talk. Sometimes both." She held up a pair of mossy green lace panties. "You have to get these. They match your eyes."

Remembering how Jesse had wanted to get rope to match my eyes, I nodded. He'd like those. "He told you about stuff I said?"

"Some. It depends." She glanced up. "He didn't betray any confidences, and it's not like I'm going to blab about it anyway. If you want to talk about him with me, you can, and I'll keep your confidence as well."

It would be nice to have someone other than Brea to talk to. She was wonderful, of course, but lately we'd been arguing more and more. I think she was tired of always taking care of me and dealing with my crap. I think she needed a break from me.

Later, when we were having dinner and throwing back a few drinks, I gave it a whirl. "Jesse hasn't touched me since he's been back."

Frankie's brows shot into her hairline. "I'm a little surprised. Is he on a medication that interferes with his ability to function?"

"He finished the antibiotics two days ago." I ate a little more. It was nice to eat a meal without having a dozen guests whose meals I had to see to first, or a baby in my lap, grabbing at my fork or the food on my plate. "It's something else. He still hasn't told me what happened down there. I'm sure everyone knows but me."

"We debriefed," Frankie confirmed. "He hasn't said anything at all?"

"No. I told him I was here for when he wanted to talk, but I kind of expected we would have talked by now." I thought of the way he avoided being alone with me until it was time for bed, and then he'd go directly to sleep. "He told me about parachuting with the enemy, but that was all."

"Are you asking me to fill you in? I can, if you want."

I needed to know something. "Yeah. I'd like that."

"Well, after that, he was captured. He had an infection from being shot. There was a doctor imprisoned there, and the doctor did his best to remove the fragments, but there were no real surgical tools. They splinted his ankle, which caused it to heal wrong."

Frankie paused, studying my reaction as she let me digest that part. "Despite the odds, he got better. It was a cartel town, which you already know, and the guy we were supposed to snatch and bring back for prosecution gave Jesse to the village to use as slave labor. He worked in the fields, harvesting cocaine, and he sometimes fixed their technology. They never turned their backs long enough for Jesse to get a message out electronically." She grimaced. "It wasn't pretty, Jessica. He wasn't treated well, and if he resisted, they beat him and restricted his food rations."

My imagination could fill in the rest, and this explained why he'd lost so much weight.

"You know," she observed. "You're a lot like Jesse. You both hide your feelings. Maybe stop doing that with each other."

"I'm not hiding my feelings," I sputtered. I was sure my face reflected the horror and sorrow I felt about what Jesse had endured.

"You're angry with him."

Sure, but there was a time and place for that. "I'm happier he's home than mad at him for leaving."

"You're going to need to have some hard conversations." Frankie buttered a warm roll. "I know, you're wondering where I get off giving you relationship advice when I haven't yet had a successful relationship."

It had occurred to me.

"Well," she continued, "I tend to date men who end up being insecure about the fact I can kick their asses and not break a sweat. Or they think being with them will make me want to settle down and assume a more traditional female role. Wrong." She devoured the roll, moaning over how good it was.

I was beginning to see why Brea thought she was so hot.

As I watched her, I thought about what she'd said. "I guess I did expect him to settle down once we had a family."

"It's not in his DNA," Frankie said. "He's wired for action and adventure."

If that was the case, were we doomed? I wanted a husband I could count on to be there for me and our daughter. I knew it wasn't fair—I'd known full well who Jesse was when I'd married him—but it didn't make it less true.

The next day, I wanted time alone with my thoughts, but it wasn't in the cards. Harper, Landon, and Lilias, Jesse's nieces and nephew, followed me to my studio. I set them to work stripping, staining, and sanding. They chatted amiably, and they told me stories about themselves and Jesse that only required me to passively participate in the conversation. Harper, at sixteen, was great about watching over her brother and sister to make sure they were doing quality work.

While they carried out their tasks, I uncovered a canvas I'd begun working on a few weeks before Jesse came home. It was of the view from Jesse's loft, a cityscape instead of a landscape. This was the first major piece I'd worked on where I felt like my hands were cooperating with my brain.

The chaos of my home fell away as I lost myself in art. This was my bliss, a bit of respite from the tumult of emotions and the many, disparate demands on my attention. Nobody wanted to bother Jesse, but they were all here to see him. Managing all of that fell on my shoulders.

"Jessica? What are you doing out here? You've been gone for hours."

Snapping out of my creative daze, I focused on the voice. Jesse stood on the other side of my canvas, his weight resting on crutches. He wore his usual nylon sweats and black T-shirt. The black expression on his face matched his shirt.

By contrast, I wore jeans and a smock splattered with paint and other substances.

"She's painting, Uncle Jesse." Landon spoke from behind me. "It's really cool."

I turned to find Landon and Harper sitting on folding chairs.

"Yeah," Harper said. "It's like watching one of those amazing artist videos, only it's in slow motion instead of fast-forward."

Jesse didn't come closer. "Do you know where your baby is?"

From the hostility in his tone, I gathered that he knew full well where she was. His objective was to make me feel bad for abandoning my child, which I had not done.

From the set of his jaw, I knew this wasn't going to end well. I turned to Harper and Landon. "How about you two find something else to do, and close the door on your way out?"

Harper got up, dragging Landon with her. She stopped in front of Jesse and parked her hands on her hips. "You know, Bailey is your baby, too."

His expression didn't crack in the face of a challenge from his favorite niece, and as she left, I girded my loins for the fight Frankie thought needed to happen. I took my paintbrushes to the sink and started the careful process of cleaning them.

I heard the telltale clicking of his crutches as he followed me.

"You can't hole up in here for hours and hours. You have a child who needs you."

Rather than respond, I washed my hands. If I said some of the things to him that I was thinking right now, we might never recover from the fallout. I got a clean cloth from the shelf and dried my hands. When I faced him, I found his glare hadn't abated.

Channeling my inner Nikki, I groped for a productive way to respond to his ire. "I was working. I get lost in my work, just like you do. This isn't new. What's really bothering you?"

"Lilias came to hang out with me. She said that you made them sand wood and work with chemicals."

Lilias was six. I hadn't given her a hard task, and Harper had been watching her. I addressed the things he wasn't actually concerned about. "Lilias worked with a piece of sandpaper. Landon put down a base coat of paint on a piece, and Harper stripped the finish off the legs of a dresser. She wore a mask, and there is plenty of airflow in here because you designed it that way. Mostly, they chatted with me."

"You can't talk to them like a normal person? You have to put them to work?"

I exhaled hard. This wasn't the first time he'd come after me since he'd been back, and it was getting more and more difficult to talk him through his anger. "I didn't ask them to come here. They came to see you, Jesse. They're all here to see you, but they settle for me when you're tired or busy or whatever reason you feel like you need to spend so much time in the bathroom. They asked if they could do something to help me, so I gave them small tasks that didn't matter too much if they messed them up."

"Fine." He abandoned that line of reasoning because it really led nowhere that would fuel his anger. "What about your own child? You've been here for hours. Who is taking care of Bailey?"

"Well," I parked my hands on my hips because I refused to cross them over my chest in a defensive gesture. Jesse was in full alpha-hole

125

mode, and he'd pounce on any weakness. "I would imagine she's being spoiled rotten by my parents and your mother. Then there's Mia and Griffin, who are apparently in love with babies and want Bailey to come stay with them while we go away for a romantic weekend."

I leaned closer and whispered conspiratorially. "You know who else might take responsibility for her for a few hours? Her father. I heard he was around all day, sitting on his ass and watching TV."

With the tables turned, Jesse narrowed his eyes. "I was not watching TV. I was playing with her and spending time with my mother, and as I fed her yet another bottle, it struck me that she was eating formula. You're supposed to be breast feeding. We talked about this. You were going to breastfeed for at least the first year."

Fucker hit me where it hurt. "My milk dried up."

"Because you haven't been feeding her. You spend hours out here instead of with your daughter."

Last straw. I threw the clean rag at him. "Don't fucking talk to me about where I spend my time. I've spent the last two weeks taking care of you and catering to everyone who is happy you aren't dead. This is the first time I've even been in here since before you came home. You, on the other hand, have been gone for five fucking months. Where were you when she got up in the middle of the night? Where were you when she caught a cold and had to be rocked or held all the time? Where were you when she spiked a fever and fussed until her tooth came in?"

"That's a low blow." His lips thinned, and his eyes flashed. "Brat, you know full well where I was. You know I would have been here if I had a choice, which is why I'm mad at you right now. You have a choice to be with your daughter and your family right now, and you're choosing to hide in your studio, making furniture to sell when you have a husband who is providing for you."

"Oh, I have a husband who is providing for me? Wow, well then I guess I don't have to do anything productive with my life. I'm so fucking lucky to have found a sugar daddy. Now I can get my nails done and work on my tan." I stalked past him, but he grabbed my arm.

"That's not what I'm saying, and this isn't the art you want to do anyway."

"You're saying I should get in the house and be a better mother to my baby."

His eyes flashed. "Don't put words in my mouth. I'm saying you need to make her a priority. You need to spend time with her."

"Make her a priority? Like you did?" I jerked my arm from his hold.

He was asking for it now, and the words tumbled out.

"You fucking left us, Jesse. You went off to Central America to get some fucking drug guy because you are more committed to making the world a safer place than you are to being a father to your daughter or a husband to me. When you left, I told myself it would be like all the other missions. You'd come home in a few days, sleep for a while, and then things would go back to the way they'd been for three months."

"I had every intention of coming home." Pain darkened his eyes, a thunderstorm of emotion that warned me to back down.

Perhaps because Frankie urged me to be honest, or maybe because I was so heartsick and broken from everything that had happened, I ignored his warning. "But you didn't. Dean and David came instead, and they gave me your wedding ring and their condolences. It wrecked me, Jesse. I didn't want to get out of bed. I only did it because my mom made me feed Bailey. That became what I did—I woke up and cried. I went into the bathroom and saw your things, and I cried. I fed Bailey and cried. Breastfeeding is supposed to be about bonding and hormones that make you feel good, but I didn't feel anything except a suffocating grief. When I tried to stop crying, it stockpiled in my chest, and then I couldn't breathe. Then I went to bed and cried into your pillow until I fell asleep. In the morning, I got up and did the same thing all over again."

The shock on his face was a welcome relief from the dark anger that had been there, but now the floodgates were open, and I was going to storm until I dried up.

"I found out my parents had been feeding Bailey formula because they didn't think I ate enough for my milk to have the nutrients Bailey needed. She wanted to feed from me less and less, but I pumped anyway because I was on autopilot, and I didn't know what else to do."

Water splashed onto my arms, and I realized I was crying. But these were angry tears, so hot with fury they boiled out of my tear ducts.

"So when I was spending my days and nights with you in the hospital, I forgot to pump, and she stopped wanting to feed from me at all."

"Jessica, I didn't know." He held up a hand to try to stem the tide, but he was too late. "You can't be mad at me for being gone. It wasn't my choice."

"It *was* your choice." Vehemence colored my words with vibrant red. "About a month before you returned, I forced myself to go through your financials because your mom was bothering me about her inheritance. You know what I found? You're a fucking millionaire. Here I was, thinking you had to go back to work because you'd bought this incredibly expensive house and you had to pay for it. But that's not true. You have more money than you'll ever need, and you chose to leave us. You chose to put your life at risk. You chose to put yourself in a position to not return to us, and you did it because you wanted to, not because you needed to."

"Darlin'—"

"Don't, Jesse. I'm so fucking pissed at you. I'm trying to be understanding, and the last thing I need is for you to come out here and tell me that my art is pointless and I should be in the house tending to the daughter you abandoned. She's fine. No matter what, I always made sure someone was looking out for her."

I finished with my brushes, and then I took them to the back counter so they could dry. This ritual also served to calm my racing heart and stave off the voice telling me I shouldn't have said those things to Jesse because he was in a delicate emotional state.

I knew he had PTSD. I knew he needed time and understanding.

I had not given it to him today.

When I turned around, I found him staring at the painting I had been working on. Rather than stick around and hear what he had to say, I left. I went inside and washed my face. Then I took Bailey from Sheila, explaining that it was time for her bath.

I spent the rest of the evening in Bailey's room. After her bath, we played, and she chewed on a cloth book as I read to her.

The next day, people left our house. Sheila went first, and Mia and Olivia's crews followed close behind. I hadn't meant to chase them out, but I was happy to see them go.

Warren found me in the studio working on a piece that had been ordered online. He set the baby monitor on the counter near me. "I put Bailey down for a nap."

"Thanks." I used a rag to massage dark stain onto a driftwood table. It had a deep split in it I planned to fill with seashells floating in resin.

"It's been crazy around here lately."

"Yeah. When someone returns from the dead, it's bound to get a little hectic." Last night, I hadn't said an unnecessary word to Jesse as we got ready for bed, and he hadn't pushed the matter.

Warren dragged over a folding chair and sat down across from me. "Harper told me that you and Jesse had a fight."

No sense in denying it. "We did."

"And then today, he booked flights for all his relatives and took them to the airport."

I wasn't sure what Warren was angling for. "I didn't tell him to do that. We didn't fight about having people here."

"What did you fight about?"

I stopped and lifted my gaze to meet my father's. "Do you really want to know? It's probably better if you stay out of our tiffs."

He crossed his arms. "Sweetheart, I'm your father. I'm here for you—to vent, to talk to, whatever you need. I like Jesse, and I know how much you both love each other. But you've been through a lot in the past year, and I just want you to know I'm here for you."

My heart swelled with love, and I hugged Warren. "I love you, too, Dad. I'll be okay. It's a fight we needed to have."

"About?"

"About how I was mad at him for leaving us. It's selfish, I know, but he made a crack about how I was neglecting Bailey, and I came back swinging."

"Did you clear the air?" The question contained no judgment, which I liked.

Had we cleared the air? I didn't know. Something had changed, but I didn't know what.

Chapter 13

Jesse

The canvas in her studio contained an amazing piece of art. On the surface, she'd captured the view from the bedroom window of my loft. Looking closer, it evoked feelings of wonder and excitement. It took my breath away, and it wasn't even finished.

I hadn't realized she'd begun painting again.

She hadn't said a word about the return of her talent.

Poking through her things, I found an image of the kind of rope design I liked to weave up her legs. She'd even drawn the delicate curve of the leg, and in the place where the line fell away, she'd depicted the textured imprint on the skin. It was utterly beautiful.

Why hadn't she shared this with me?

Last night I got into bed first and waited for her to emerge from the bathroom and turn off the lights. I wanted to say something, but I didn't know how to bring it up. For the first time, I realized how much had changed in the five months I'd been gone.

Tonight, she came into the room, distracting me from my thoughts. She went about her ritual, dousing the room lights and checking the baby monitor, and I stared.

Jessica had always been a sexy woman with lush, full curves, a round bottom, and generous breasts. In the time I'd been gone, most of that had vanished as well. Proportionally she'd lost as much body mass as I had. That wasn't healthy.

But there were signs it was returning. Thanks to Sylvia and Brea's constant cooking, we were both eating regular meals and partaking in Brea's baked treats.

When Jessica came to the bed, she shrugged out of her robe and set it on the settee at the foot of our bed.

I gaped. Instead of her usual oversized T-shirt, she wore a short, white silk nightgown that emphasized the curve of her breasts and the sexy length of her legs.

"That's new."

She paused, biting her lip in a surprise moment of uncertainty. "Frankie and I went shopping a couple of days ago." She tugged at the hem.

"It's pretty." Sitting up, I held out a hand to her. "Come here, darlin', and let me look at you."

Another area where I'd fallen short was in the sex department. For some reason, I couldn't bring myself to touch my wife.

She approached, her gaze pinned to my face.

I let mine drop, roaming her body as if it was the first time I'd seen it. Despite the weight loss, she was a vision. Beautiful and utterly sexy, this was the woman who'd promised to love and honor me, and she'd bore my child. I wanted to lick her pussy and kiss her stretch marks, but I wasn't sure I could worship her the way she deserved.

Something was holding me back, and I hated it. I hated everything that had kept me from her—that still kept me a stranger in her bed.

She brushed her fingertips across my cheek. "Jesse, if you're not ready, I'll understand."

I wanted her with a desire that humbled me, but I couldn't seem to harness that energy. Plus I knew she didn't understand why I hadn't fallen on her the moment we were reunited. How could she, when I didn't understand myself?

"How about a blowjob?" I wanted more, but perhaps this would be a good start?

A knowing grin lifted the corners of her mouth. She peeled back the covers and helped me shimmy out of my pajama pants. That was another thing I'd started doing—sleeping with clothes on.

She started with my lips, kissing me softly and inviting me to take control.

Perhaps that's what did it for me. It had been so long since I'd been in control, and here my sweet, bratty, submissive-who-wasn't-a-submissive needed me to dominate her.

Tangling my fist in her hair, I took over, kissing her savagely, and she responded with a moan. That was all I needed. I dragged her beneath me and touched her body, reacquainting myself with the taste and feel of her silky skin.

I reached between her legs and found her pussy drenched. "I see you missed me."

"Oh, God. So much, Jesse. So much."

I worked my fingers into her. She thrust her hips and gripped my arms.

My mind went to a dark place, a place I didn't want it to go when I was making love to my wife. I struggled against the tide.

"Darlin', put your hands above your head and keep them there."

Her eyes flew open. "You want to do Dom stuff?"

"Yes." I needed it.

She lifted her hands above her head and gripped the spindles on the headboard. "Okay, Jesse. I—I'll call red or yellow if I need to."

My brave woman. I knew what it meant for her to knowingly consent to something that may well force her submission. This had chased her out of my life once before, and I didn't want it to happen again.

"Promise," I said. "Promise to use your safewords if you need them, Jessica. Don't let me do anything you don't want, okay?"

Regarding me with a wealth of understanding in her somber green eyes, she said, "Yes, Jesse. I promise."

I left her for a moment to get a condom from the drawer in the bedside table. Opening it, I found a brand new package. Since the baby had been born, we'd been careful, and I was glad for that. It would take six months for the HIV test to show a result. I distinctly remembered the box in the night stand being half empty.

Perhaps my memory wasn't as good as it used to be? Tearing open the box, I tried harder to remember, using memory techniques I'd learned in covert ops.

"Jesse? Are you okay?"

"Yeah. I thought the box in here was open already. I remember leaving a half-empty box. My memory is usually pretty good." I extracted a condom, and then I looked at her.

Blood had drained from her face. She sat up. "It's a new box. I—I just bought it."

Understanding dawned. She had cleaned out some things, like old medications. She'd obviously disposed of the condoms because the reminder was a little too much. "Thanks," I said. "The other ones were probably expired."

I put it on, and she resumed the position in which I'd left her. Kneeling over her, I grazed my fingertips over her flesh. I started at her abdomen, and I blazed a path up to her fingers and down to her toes. This was my wife, the woman I loved and who loved me, and she was mine.

Settling between her legs, I positioned the tip of my cock at her entrance, and I kissed her deeply. She sighed, and her body melted against mine. Surging forward, I buried myself deep. Then I shifted my legs to outside of hers.

"Close your legs."

She obeyed. This position let me pin her with my weight. Completely at my mercy, she couldn't move. As I thrust into her tightness, I threaded my fingers in hers, holding her hands and restraining her at the same time. This was what I needed—evidence of her trust and devotion, proof she loved me and she was still my submissive, albeit a closeted one.

We'd been apart for far too long, and I was even more primed than I'd thought. I came much too quickly and long before she was ready. My climax hit hard. With a cry, I collapsed on top of Jessica.

After a moment, she disentangled our hands, and she wrapped her arms around me. She held me in silence, stroking a tender caress on the back of my neck.

"Sorry," I said.

"It's okay." She shushed me. "I just needed to know you still wanted me."

Jessica

His body trembled in my arms. I'd seen Jesse happy, angry, and worried, but no matter what, he'd always been strong, playing off anything that might be construed as "weak" with a calm stoicism.

But now he lay on top of me, shaking with the aftermath of something that had split him wide open. Having been in that position, I knew he needed to be held and soothed. He needed to know I could handle whatever he was going through.

He needed to know I could be his rock the same way he'd always been mine.

For the first time, I understood why he liked the D/s dynamic. In this honored and trusted position, I felt closer to him than I'd ever felt before. This is what he'd sought to have with me all along.

"I love you, Jesse."

He lifted his face from where he'd buried it in my neck, and he looked at me. His gaze roamed my features, and I knew he was memorizing every nuance of my expression. "How come you didn't tell me that you started painting again?"

I tried to lift a shoulder, but his weight didn't allow me to move. "We've been busy, and it seemed selfish in light of everything that's happened the last two weeks."

"Selfish?" He stroked his thumb along my hairline. "Jessica, this is huge. It's one of the most important things in your life. I want to know about everything in your life, big or small, especially something so momentous. When did you start?"

Oh, boy. This wasn't where I wanted a post-coital conversation to go. "About six weeks ago. I was working on a corner shelf, and I just started painting on it. The next thing I knew, it was exactly what I'd seen in my mind. So I got out a canvas and started painting. It took a few tries. I whited-out at least ten drafts before I got something I liked."

"That's incredible. I'm so happy for you, Jessica. I know how badly you wanted this, and I know what it means to you. I'm sorry I was an ass yesterday."

It meant a lot that he was apologizing, but it didn't erase my anger. However it made me feel like maybe the gulf between us wasn't so huge and our problems weren't insurmountable.

I played with the spot on the back of his neck that usually drove him crazy. "Thank you, Jesse."

He kissed me. Then he disposed of the condom. When he rejoined me in bed, he snuggled against me, and he fell asleep with me in his arms.

I'd missed this.

In the morning, I awoke to kisses on the curve of my neck. Jesse's hand roamed my front, cupping a breast before squeezing tenderly. His chest pressed to my back, and his arousal nestled against my ass cheek.

His questing hand slid down, and he parted the lips of my pussy. I'd gone to sleep still wet from the night before, and so I was still kind of primed for seduction this morning. He played with my clit, masturbating me until a soft sigh fell from my lips.

"You awake yet, darlin'?"

"Yes, Jesse." I deliberately chose his name in lieu of a title because suddenly using a title would shock the shit out of him and also not ring true, and I infused my tone with a hint of submission.

Was this manipulation? I didn't know. Maybe, but didn't people who loved each other do this sort of thing—be the person your lover needed you to be? That's all I was doing, and I trusted Jesse to let me know if I came close to crossing a line.

"Last night was too quick."

I chuckled, my voice still heavy with sleep. "It was a little fast."

He guided my hand to my pussy. "Touch yourself. I want to feel you come on me, darlin'."

I pressed and rotated my clit, and when he entered me from behind, my body responded with a shudder. My back arched, giving him easier access, and he lazily thrust into me. The tightness in my core unfurled, loosened by his increasingly frantic thrusts. My orgasm washed over my in languorous waves, and he buried his cock deep, crying out his climax.

Like last night, he held me to him tightly, and his body shook with emotion. If he'd eased up a little, I would have turned in his arms, but he didn't, and so I reached back to lightly scratch a caress back from his temple.

"Jessica?"

"Yeah?" His need for my submission had dissipated, and so I reverted to my normal tone.

"I want to tie you up."

"Will that aggravate your ankle?"

"I know your mind usually takes flight when I bind you, but you may recall that I use my hands to tie the knots."

It had been so long since I'd been in subspace. I missed it, and I knew he needed to create his art to find the sense of peace that still eluded him. "Tonight, I have a class with Brea, and Frankie might come along, so how about afterward? I should be home by nine."

His head lifted from the pillow. "A class? What kind of class would you, Brea, and Frankie take together?"

"You think we have nothing in common?"

"I know Brea and Frankie aren't artists, and I know you and Frankie don't bake, and I know you and Brea aren't into advanced martial arts."

I scoffed at his observation, mostly because it was true. While Brea and I were learning self defense, our skills were nowhere near close to where Frankie had probably been as a teenager. And the baking thing? That was a low blow.

Making a sound of mock outrage, I slid from bed. "I think I'm going to make you wait until after I acquire the skills the class teaches, and then I'll taunt you with them."

He sat up and scratched his belly. "You're going to taunt me with—pole dancing? Oh, darlin', yes. I heartily approve. I'll even install a pole in here so you can do private shows."

His guess was too close to the mark. I donned my nightie from where he'd tossed it, and I rolled my eyes. "Do *not* put a pole in here."

He followed me into the bathroom, hopping on one crutch. "Two poles and a crossbar. I could use it for Shibari too."

"You're too excited by this idea. It's not a pole dancing class. My hip isn't going to bend like that—ever."

Leaning against the jamb, he thought. "It's a skill you can use to taunt me. Do they give classes in blowjobs? Wait—I don't want you taking a class like that without me there for you to practice on."

I got into the shower to rinse off. "Stop guessing. Even if you were close, I wouldn't tell you."

"I'm wounded. I'm your husband. You're supposed to tell me everything."

In the privacy afforded by the curtain, I closed my eyes. There were some things he never needed to know. In that sense, I planned to keep a secret from him for the rest of my life.

Rather than respond, I misdirected. "You might not remember, because it's been so long, but I give great head. I resent your implication that I need a class. The only method I haven't used on you is to stimulate your prostate, but that's because I respect your preference to not have a finger in your ass."

He opened the shower curtain and joined me under the spray, his hand cupping my bottom. "I'll do butt stuff if you will."

It looked like the pushy, dominant man I fell in love with was finally back. This reaffirmed the rightness of my decision to give him the submission he'd needed. I turned around and plastered my body to his. "God, Jesse. It's so good to have you back."

He wrapped his arms around me and didn't pretend to not know what I was talking about. Frankie had been right—fighting with Jesse had cleared the air. The edge was gone from my anger, and I felt like at least one huge barrier between us had been erased.

Chapter 14

Dean

"Mr. Eastridge is in the library." Whitley made his announcement and waited for my response.

In the past two weeks, I'd run myself ragged trying to make sure Jesse had the best medical care and putting out the fires we'd lit by rushing into a Honduras village that was a major supplier to the Magas cartel. The DEA and CIA had been covertly trying to eradicate that menace for the past fifteen years, and our operation had been designed to bring them closer to their goal. Instead we'd disrupted everything.

Within a day of our raid, the villagers had staged a rebellion. They'd burned their coca plants, including all the picked leaves, and blamed it on us so the Honduras government would turn their investigation in our direction.

Like us, the DEA and CIA had no illusion about what had actually happened. Someone in Rio Escondido had made a power grab. I suspected Fernando because he was already in charge, and he liked power. From Jesse's description, Fernando chaffed at being under Jack Smith's control.

Also from Jesse's debrief, I had reason to suspect Magdalena. It was a mistake to dismiss a power-hungry person just because she was a woman, as both U.S. agencies seemed to have done. If Jesse had primed the pump the way he'd described, then it was possible he'd set up Magdalena to take down Jack Smith, which had been one of the goals of his mission.

"Sir?"

I'd forgotten about Whitley and David. "Show him upstairs. Bring another glass."

Whitley went to follow my order, and I poured another finger of Scotch.

David appeared. He sat in the chair opposite mine.

"Drink?" I motioned for Whitley to fill David's glass.

"Just one." David swirled the liquid until Whitley left us alone. "Dean, I'm concerned about you."

"Because Grayson Cuyler is such a gigantic asshole? Don't be. I have it under control."

"Gray is on this?"

Grayson Cuyler was someone who'd trained David and me when we'd first been accepted into Special Forces. He'd taught us most of what we knew about covert operations. Recently, he'd resurfaced as a hostile liaison between us and the CIA. Instead of asking us to help out with missions, Gray was fond of twisting our arms, and we did not like to have our arms twisted, especially by a man who consistently used Brea and Jessica as pawns.

He'd put their lives into danger twice already. Objectively I understood his tactics. On a personal level, it did not help foster any kind of good will.

"Yeah. They think he has a special relationship with us. It doesn't bode well for our national security that they think we trust him in the least." I downed the last of my glass and poured another.

David watched me with a pensive expression on his face. "Why don't you update me on the ways Gray is being an asshole?"

"Excuse me, Mr. Alloway." Whitley stood unobtrusively in the doorway. He'd been worried about me lately, and he'd taken to hovering even when he wasn't supposed to be working. "Miss Sikara is here. Shall I show her up and bring another glass?"

Frankie was here, which meant they'd coordinated their attack. The conversation was certain to turn to topics I'd rather not discuss. "Sure."

When Frankie was situated on my sofa, she declined a drink. I noted the stylish, moisture-wicking shirt and yoga pants. "Did you have a date, or were you planning for a late-night workout?"

Her gaze flicked to David. "I have plans with Brea and Jessica tonight. It's a secret from David, otherwise I'd tell you."

Given her outfit, I figured they were going to do something physical. I was glad Frankie was hanging out with Brea and Jessica more. She was one of my best friends, but sometimes she grew tired of hanging out with men all the time. "So, you dropped by because you urgently needed an update on our relationship with the CIA before you could enjoy yourself with your friends?"

Frankie exchanged a glance with David. "We're here because we're worried about you."

"There's no cause for concern. As I was telling David, the situation is under control. Actually, thanks to Jesse, the village of Rio Escondido has cut off their supply of cocaine to the Magas cartel, effectively cutting about forty percent of their profits. They're crippled, and Cuyler is poised to move in. He anticipates having Jack Smith in custody within a week." I chuckled. "Of course, he thinks we destroyed their stores to keep them from coming after us."

David had a pained look on his face. "If Jesse hadn't been injured, we would have."

"Yes, well, that wasn't our intent. We just wanted to rescue Jesse."

Frankie leaned forward and folded her hands on her knees. "Dean, we know how you feel about Jessica. You both thought Jesse was gone, and you—"

"We had sex, nothing more. It was therapeutic for both of us."

"You're friends," David pointed out. "You have feelings for her."

I sipped more of my favorite liquid. I was already feeling its effects. "Friends with benefits. I noticed you're not concerned she had feelings for me. That's good. She never moved past Jesse. Even when she was with me, she wasn't with me, if you know what I mean."

"Doesn't change the fact you have feelings for her," Frankie said softly. "That's why you come home every night and drink yourself into oblivion."

"Do not." Some nights I worked until I was too exhausted to think. Three nights ago, I'd gone to a dance club and picked up a temporary guest for my sex bedroom.

"Dean, don't. We're your friends. We care about you." Frankie moved to sit on the ottoman where my feet rested. She took my hands in hers. "We want to help."

"I don't see how." I leaned forward, accepting Frankie's comfort and peering into her dark eyes. "Unless you're offering to take her place? We've never been friends with benefits, but I guess I could give it a shot."

Frankie brushed a lock of hair back from my eyes in a gentle caress. "Dean, I know you default to asshole when you're feeling threatened or defensive. If you need the benefits that come with our friendship to help you get over losing a woman you loved—whether or not you admit it—I don't have to wait until you're sober to clean up the floor with your ass."

The alcohol was definitely getting to me. I grinned in the face of her promise.

"I'm not going to sleep with you, either," David said. "Not only am I committed to my wife, but there's no way in hell I'd bottom for you."

He took the sting out of my next avenue of attack—deriding him because he occasionally bottomed for Brea when she was getting her

Domme on. Miffed, I sat back. "I didn't ask either of you to come over here. I quite distinctly told you I was fine."

"Have you talked to Jessica?" David asked.

"Wouldn't you know if I had?" I shot back. Nobody kept secrets anymore. All this honesty was mildly disheartening.

He shrugged. "I think you should talk to her."

"Why? Because I'm a selfish bastard hell-bent on destroying their happiness?" Disgusted, I downed my Scotch and got up. My brain buzzed pleasantly, and I used Frankie's head to steady myself.

"You know what? I am a selfish bastard. I've already tried to come between them. You want to know why Jesse wouldn't talk to me for the last few months before he disappeared? It's because I, in my bastardly glory, confronted him about how he hadn't played fair in pursuing Jessica. We met her together. We flirted with her together. I stupidly thought that meant we'd both wait until she was ready for more, and then we'd court her at the same time. Let the better man win, right? I knew, in a fair contest, it would be me. After all, I'm charming and refined, where Jesse is bull-headed and a slob."

The window wavered as I went to it, and I knew I was completely inebriated. It accounted for my inability to stop confessing my worst sins.

"Jesse didn't like that. He wasn't even pissed she'd married him without his knowledge or that she'd gotten pregnant on purpose. In his shoes, I would have been livid." I paused, gazing at the watery reflection of myself in the window. I didn't like what I saw—someone weak and pathetic who'd been a shitty friend to someone who'd always had his back—and I tortured myself by not looking away.

"You know who he was pissed at? Me. That's right. He didn't know we were in competition, and he thought I was out of line to even bring it up." My reflection mocked me. "He was right, of course. I've always been a selfish bastard. I've always toyed with women and their affection. I would have toyed with Jessica too."

When I finally faced my friends, I found them watching me without an ounce of compassion or surprise.

"But you didn't," David said. "I watched you put time, effort, and thought into your relationship. You saved her, Dean. She was wasting away, ready to follow Jesse into an early grave, and you helped her embrace life."

I begged to differ on his assertion I hadn't toyed with Jessica. I'd done some shitty things to her prior to Jesse's disappearance.

"She started eating food and enjoying her time with her daughter and her family and friends," Frankie said. "She returned my calls and hung out with me. I thought she blamed me for everything and we'd never be friends again. And then there's you. Dean, grief was doing a number on you too. When you started seeing her, it grounded you. It brought you back from the blackness."

I knew full well the effect Jessica had on me, and it was farther reaching and more profound than I was willing to put into words. "So, what? You think I should try to win her away from Jesse because we found a respite together for a few weeks?" I shook my head, and then I stopped because the room was spinning. "Unbelievable."

"We're not saying that," David said.

"Then what are you saying? Because I think I've done enough to damage my friendship with Jesse. I'd rather not fuck it up beyond all repair. And Jessica—she always loved him. Even when we were together, her heart and mind were with him."

"You need closure," he said.

I disagreed. "It's closed. It closed the moment I saw the DNA test wasn't a match for Jesse."

"Dean—"

Cutting Frankie off, I said, "I just want my friendship with Jesse back. I want to go back in time and not say the things I said." I drew the line at expressing regret for sleeping with Jessica. She would always have a special place in my heart. "Talking to Jessica to say the things we both already know won't undo the damage I've done."

"Then talk to Jesse," Frankie said. "He's hurting over this rift as much as you are."

I laughed. "Not only is Jesse still mad about what I said, he blames David and me for taking so long to rescue him. I'd be surprised if he ever returns to SAFE Security. I'll be surprised if he doesn't slowly fade from our lives."

Frankie got to her feet. "I think you're a drama queen. When you sober up, have a short conversation with Jessica about the state of your friendship." She flashed a regretful smile at David. "I have to go. Sorry, but you're on your own now. If it gets really bad, call me."

David waved her away. "I got this."

I watched her leave. "I noticed she didn't tell me to talk to Jesse."

"In your state, you might say too much, and then he'll punch your lights out."

"He punched me last time," I admitted. "Course, that could have been because I told him I kissed Jessica."

"Don't tell him you did more than kiss her," David said as he poured himself another Scotch.

An hour later, we found ourselves at Jesse's front door, incessantly pressing the buzzer.

The door flew open, and Jesse stood there, leaning on his crutches and glowering. "What is wrong with you two?"

"We're drunk," David said. He extracted the unopened bottle of Scotch we'd brought with us from the bag Whitley had insisted we put it into for the walk over. "And we missed you."

"I'm busy," he said. "Please tell me you didn't drive here."

"It's like a fifteen-minute walk," I said. "We're practically neighbors."

David pushed past Jesse. "Whatcha busy doing? The women are out at a mystery class."

Jesse inclined his head, inviting me in since David was already through. "Brea didn't tell you what the class was, either?"

"Nope. She said she brought muffins over here." David went deeper into the house and headed in the direction of the kitchen.

Jesse and I followed. His nose scrunched up like he smelled something bad. It might've been me.

He said, "You came all this way for your wife's muffins?"

"Came over to see you." David said.

Jesse stood in the threshold to the kitchen with his hands in the pockets of his sweats, eyeing us warily. "Stay here. I'll be right back."

David and I found some muffins, and we helped ourselves. We perched on the high stools at the counter and powered through the remainder of the goodies.

"I was tempted to tell Brea she could only continue to work for SAFE Security if she brings fresh muffins every week." I confessed this as I used my fingertip to consolidate the crumbs on my plate for easy consumption.

"Where'd you go?" David asked Jesse when he returned.

"Warren is watching Bailey tonight. Sylvia is at her sister's house this weekend. I think she needed a break from the craziness around here." Jesse snagged the last muffin. "Brea made these for me, not you."

"So, you'll take the muffins from my mouth, but that's it?" David glowered unsuccessfully.

Jesse spent a moment staring, and then he ate half his muffin in one bite. "You're wasted. You're not even close to making sense."

I knew what David meant, so I attempted to explain. "He's saying you avoid talking to him. And me."

"I talked to David two days ago when he was over here, and you were here three days ago." Jesse finished the muffin. "And right now, I have things to do, so do you need a ride back to Dean's so you don't get picked up for public intoxication?"

"What things?" I frowned, though it felt a lot like a pout.

"Checking my rope. Jessica and I are going to scene tonight."

That image slid into my head and cut some things with its sharp edges.

"When we were here, so was your family, and you avoided talking to us. We need to have a long talk about all the bad shit between us." I blurted that out before the microcuts combined to do worse damage.

Jesse nailed me with a gaze that let me know the politeness had been an act. "Right now, I'm getting ready to have the first scene with my wife in six months. I don't want to deal with either one of you."

I had to know. "Is our friendship over?"

His gaze slid away, and he swallowed hard. "I don't know, Dean. I honestly don't know."

Chapter 15

Jesse

I decided against mentioning Dean and David's visit to Jessica.

When I returned from driving them back to Dean's house, I had less than five minutes to prepare for the scene. I'd been playing with Bailey in the living room when our party had been crashed.

Jessica found me measuring out lengths of rope and checking them for frays. A small smile played around her mouth. "I'm going to rinse off in the shower real quick."

"Rinse off?" I watched her remove the tight workout shirt and leggings. Though she hadn't wanted to share the details of where she was going, I deduced from her outfit it was some kind of physical activity.

"Yeah. I'm a little sweaty, and I want to be fresh for you." She pinned her hair up. It had grown since I'd been gone, and now it was down to her shoulders. "I bought some sexy lingerie the other day. Did you want to pick out something, or do you want me naked?"

I wanted her submissive, and right now, she was not in that headspace. How would wearing lingerie affect her? Last night, it had been her way of inviting me to make a move. I wanted to know what it meant to her, so I made a decision. "It's up to you."

When she emerged, she wore a red lace thong and a matching bra that emphasized everything and left nothing to the imagination. My cock saluted.

"Wow."

A blush crept up her neck. "I was hoping you'd like this."

"Yes," I confirmed. "A lot."

She approached, slowly entering my space.

"Did you want to show me what you learned? I can be your pole."

She parked a hand on her hip. "I told you—it's not pole dancing. And I'm not ready to show you anything yet. I'm going to need a lot more practice."

I resumed checking my lines. "You know, if I ask you while you're tied up, you'll spill your guts."

"So don't ask." She sat next to me and put her hand on my leg. "Don't spoil the surprise, okay? I want to give you this in my own time."

Though I'd been teasing, seeing how much this meant to her had me backing down. "I promise I won't ask, darlin'."

"Thank you."

"Do you want to help look over the lines?"

"Nobody's touched those since you put them away. I think they're fine."

"Probably," I agreed. I'd cleaned them before putting them away last time, and I'd found them exactly as I'd left them. "How about you help transport them over to our bed?"

She rose and handed me a crutch. "Jesse, I want you to dominate me tonight."

My brows rose. She'd gone to great lengths to remove overt D/s from our relationship. "Are you sure about that?"

She took a breath, and I recognized her anxiety.

"Jessica, I'm not asking you to give me anything you're not comfortable giving."

"I know you're not, but I want to. I mean, I want to step out of my comfort zone. When we were first together, you did things to me—you made me feel deeper than I'd ever felt before, and that scared the hell out of me."

I set down the rope I'd picked up, and I faced her without contact. This was a decision she needed to make without my influence. "I know, darlin'. And it made you run from me." Perhaps she'd been looking for her lost artistic ability, but she'd run just the same, and then she'd dumped me.

"I'm finished with running." She wrung her hands together. "Losing you—it made me see I'd was stupid to be afraid. I'm not saying I'd be submissive in our relationship or that I want this all the time, but maybe, during scenes, I could be your sub. If you wanted."

I'd wanted that from the start, but pushing her into a role she wasn't ready to assume had proven detrimental to our relationship. What I hadn't done then and was determined to do now was listen to her. She was asking for this. I hadn't asked, offered, or expected. This was what she wanted, and I had a powerful need to give it to her.

Something had triggered this change of heart, and I needed to know what had done it. "Why? What made you suddenly ask for this?"

Her gaze remained locked to mine. "You told me being a sub was something you felt deep inside, that it was a need to give, to submit, to be dominated. I didn't understand it, and coming on top of everything else I was dealing with, I couldn't reconcile the way I responded to you with the fear that had helped me survive."

She came closer, resting her hands lightly on my chest. "Last night, you opened yourself to me. When you made love to me, you gave me something you've never given me before. You let down your guard, and you let me see you were vulnerable too. You need me. And you trust me with the deepest parts of your heart and soul. It gave me the courage to finally give you those parts of me. I know it's going to be a challenge, and I know you'll help me meet it."

She floored me. After all this time, she still had the ability to render me speechless because I was too full of wonder and adoration to think in words.

I wanted to be worthy of her trust and submission, but I didn't want her to think she was trapped in a decision she couldn't reverse. "How about we do a trial run tonight? Then we'll talk over what worked and what didn't. And you'll have your safewords. You always have safewords."

"I love you, Jesse, and I want to give you my submission."

With all the love in my Dominant heart, I kissed my submissive. She melted against me, surrendering to my mastery, and her arms wound around my neck.

When it was over, I smacked her ass. "For planning purposes, are you darlin' or Brat tonight?"

"I'll be good," she said. "I think."

"You think?" I struggled not to laugh.

"You know how sometimes my mouth runs away from me." She said it softly, as if her mouth and mind were parts beyond her control. To some extent, that was true. I could always count on her words to communicate important ideas, but they didn't always have context.

"All right, darlin'. I'm going to leave punishment out of it tonight, and we'll concentrate on torture."

She lowered her gaze. "Yes, Jesse."

Last night, she'd used my name like a title, and I found I liked it more than being called Sir or Master.

"Sit on the table and face the sofa." I'd set a thick blanket down because I planned to have her there for a while, and padding made it more comfortable.

She sat on the table with her feet on the floor, and she rested her hands, palms up, on her thighs. It was a good beginner's position.

"Spread your legs as wide as you can. Scoot closer to the edge if you need to." I stood behind her while she positioned herself because I didn't want her to be distracted by my raging hard-on. "Clasp your hands behind your neck."

146

I let her stay that way for a little while so she could settle into the position, which she did fairly quickly. She managed to be both relaxed and at attention. I touched her back, letting her know where I was, and I slid onto the table behind her. I moved her hands so she clasped them behind her back, and I kissed her neck. There was something about the curve of her neck that invited exploration with my lips. I swept her hair out of the way, raking my fingers through her curls roughly.

I pressed dozens of kisses to her shoulders, nape, and neck, and then I sank my teeth into the fleshy part of her shoulder. She cried out, and I covered her mouth. I wasn't concerned about the noise as much as I wanted her to know I was in control of her volume. I bit harder, and she whimpered, but she didn't move.

When I released her, she sighed, a small sound of acceptance and wonder.

Reaching around, I cupped her breast through the lace of the sexy bra she'd chosen to tempt me. This round globe fit perfectly into my hand. I kneaded and squeezed, working my way up to rougher treatment. I pinched and rolled her nipples. Small noises sounded in the back of her throat, but I couldn't tell if they were from pleasure or pain.

"Does that hurt, darlin'?"

"Yes, Jesse, but it feels so good."

"You want more, don't you?"

"Yes, Jesse." She breathed my name like it was a prayer. "I want everything you give me."

A year ago, if she'd said something like that, it would have been infused with sarcasm. I was finding I liked both sides of my lady. I played with her nipples while she gasped and arched into my touch. She was being very good. I wondered if clover clamps might bring out her bratty side? Perhaps I'd get to that later, after I tied her up.

"Put your hands back behind your neck."

I began with a simple design, a winding corselet around her midsection that framed her breasts. With her torso in my ropes, I sat on the sofa in front of her. She kept her gaze lowered to a point near my knees.

She was positively gorgeous. Sitting in front of me, halfway bound, she glowed with the serenity that came from giving herself completely over to someone she trusted. Her legs were spread, and I noted the string of her thong was soaking wet.

I smirked. "Are you turned on right now?"

"Yes, Jesse."

"Why? What's making your pussy so wet?"

"You. The way you touch me. The way you kiss me. The way you're looking at me."

Her gaze was still demurely lowered, so I wondered if she was aware of my expression. "How am I looking at you?"

"Like you own me."

That wasn't exactly true. I'm sure it was in my bearing, but my expression was more appreciative than possessive. Okay—she was behaving. Her guesses came from what she could see given where she was supposed to be looking.

I knelt between her legs. Her chest rose and fell on shaky breaths. "Are you afraid, darlin'? What's your color?"

"Green, Jesse. I'm not afraid. I was hoping you'd touch me more."

"I can grant that wish." I traced the tip of my finger over her clit, teasing it until the sharp point peeked out of the hood. This kind of stimulation was uncomfortable. "Like that?"

She inhaled and exhaled, breathing through the distress. "If it pleases you."

"It pleases me," I said gruffly. Then I pinched it, and she swallowed her cry. Slowly I released the tender bud. "Darlin', it pleases me that you've stayed put. I know it was hard for you to not close your legs or push my hand away."

"Not so hard." Her gaze met mine, and a happy smile lit her expression.

I kissed her, a hard press on the lips. "Lay back."

She eased herself down, spinning so she was parallel to the sofa, and I lifted her left leg. Though it was the hurt leg, it tended to feel better when it was bent, and this pose was perfect for it. I tied anchor loops around her ankle, knee, and upper thigh, and then I connected them together. To the loop on her upper thigh, I bound her wrists.

This wasn't the Shibari that had sent her into subspace before, but I watched her for any indication she might be heading in that direction. She regarded me with a pleasant smile, but her eyes weren't glazed over, which meant she was feeling good, but not flying high.

Since I hadn't expected anything other than bondage tonight, I hadn't prepared any toys. I left her there while I went and washed off my favorite vibrator.

When I returned ages later, thanks to the crutches, I found that she hadn't moved. Her gaze followed me, so she was still there.

"What's your color, darlin'?"

"Green, Jesse. A beautiful mint green."

I laughed. "All right, then. Let's help you see other colors." I drizzled lube on the vibrator, but she was so wet it might have been an exercise in redundancy. Then I inserted it into her vagina and turned it

148

to a medium pulse. "You're going to come, and I'm going to watch, so put on a good show."

Mischief flashed in her eyes. "If you untie my hands, I can put on a really good show, one that'll make you jealous of the vibrator."

She made a valid point, but I had faith she didn't need her hands, and seeing her bound and helpless was aphrodisiac enough.

"You'll be fine." I dialed up the speed. "Think of this vibrator as an extension of my cock."

"Oh, God, Jesse, what a big, blue dick you have. Oh, Jesse, you feel so good." She arched and writhed.

It looked like my Brat had made an appearance. I lifted her and turned her over so that her weight rested on her left shoulder and upper body. The way I'd bound her hands to her thigh forced her ass into the air.

The spanking I was about to deliver wasn't a punishment. It was a response to her bratty behavior, which told me she needed a firmer hand than I was using.

I rained a volley of spanks on her cheeks, spacing them out for maximum impact.

"Does that feel good, Brat?"

"Yes, Jesse. The spanking and your big, blue dick are doing it for me. I'm so close."

I turned the vibrator setting to maximum, and I fucked it into her while I smacked her ass at rhythmic intervals. "What about this?"

"Yes, oh, yes!" She cried out her climax, and I left the vibrator inside her, forcing her to seek a second peak. She wiggled her ass as I continued to spank it, but this position didn't allow for much movement.

"Your ass is so red right now, Brat. It matches your thong." I scratched my extremely short nails across her hot skin, and she moaned.

She made the noises she made when she was closing in on an orgasm. I turned off the vibrator, but I left it in her pussy.

Her body shook, from holding the position and from passion thwarted. I lifted her again, turning her onto her back. Then I removed the vibrator and replaced it with my cock. Leaning over her bound body, I fucked her with deep, hard strokes.

She watched me, her eyes wide with wonder and adoration.

"You're going to come again," I commanded.

"Yes, Jesse." Her soft whisper barely carried to my ears, but moments later, her hot pussy pulsed around my cock, and her eyes rolled back into her head.

She didn't make a single sound.

My balls drew up, and my orgasm detonated. I buried myself as deep as I could go while my seed burst into the condom.

I staggered back and collapsed onto the sofa, watching over her as I recovered. Her chest heaved, and an orgasmic blush stained her chest and neck.

Once I could move, I cleaned her up. The wet cloth I'd got when I washed off the vibrator probably felt good on her swollen pussy. She flinched, but she didn't take evasive action.

"How are you doing, darlin'?"

"Green, Jesse. I'm ready for more."

"You're insatiable."

"Where you're concerned, yes. But it's your fault."

"Is it? I always heard it wasn't wise to blame a Dom while you're tied up and can't get away."

She favored me with a soft smile. "If you weren't such a wonderful lover, I wouldn't want more."

"Smooth talker." I nodded appreciatively. "You did wonderfully tonight. I'm going to give you a reward."

Her brows lifted. "Jesse, this whole night has been one big, wonderful reward."

"Well, there's more." I untied her wrists. "Go lay on the bed." I'd planned to bind her on the table and watch while she sailed, but now I wanted to hold her in my arms while her mind was elsewhere.

She went to the bed, walking stiffly.

"Is your hip okay?"

"Yeah. It's fine."

"Your lower back?" Sometimes when she laid on hard surfaces, she had a hard time getting up.

"Actually, since I've had Bailey, my back hasn't acted up."

"Well, they say childbirth changes your body."

"Yeah," she sighed. "My feet are a half size bigger, and I found about fifty gray hairs."

I might be responsible for some of the gray, but I didn't take credit. Instead I pointed out the positives. "You like my gray."

"Gray on men is distinguished. On women, it makes us not sexy."

Snorting, I followed her across the vast room to the bed. "Jessica, you're sexy with any color hair." This was going nowhere good. "But the back thing is good. Does that mean you need less PT?"

I frowned as I thought back over the last few weeks. She hadn't mentioned PT.

"I finished PT. I'm as fixed as I'm gonna get. I have exercises to do, but that's it." She paused at the foot of the bed and faced me, hands spread wide. "I'll walk with a cane for the rest of my life, and probably, so will you. We can get a matching pair."

I didn't plan to walk with a cane for the rest of my life, but I kept my mouth shut because I wasn't stupid. "Sit down, darlin'. I'm going to make you fly."

She obeyed, scooting to the center of the mattress. I wove sleeves onto her arms, and watched her drop into subspace. It was amazing, really, the way the ropes affected her.

When I finished, I eased her back to she lay in my arms.

After ten minutes, I began the slow process of removing the rope from her torso and legs. I left it on her arms until the very end.

While she flew, I traced my fingers along the woven pattern etched into her skin.

She'd openly and freely given her submission. It humbled me, as much as I could be humble, and the itchy pain in the dark places hiding inside me was proof I was beginning to heal.

When she emerged from her stupor, I turned off the lights and made love to her.

Chapter 16

Jessica

Despite going to bed late and exhausted, I woke early. Refreshed and more relaxed than I had been in a long time, I couldn't help the feline smile that lit me from the inside. In the brightness of the morning light, I looked over at my slumbering husband.

I'd taken a real risk in asking him to Dominate me last night. Growing up the way I had, having control of my life as an adult was the single thing that had enabled me to get the help I needed to move past the trauma of my childhood and early twenties.

When Jesse had first tried to dominate me, the loss of control had been like he was ripping the scabs off fresh wounds to make them ooze and bleed again. But now I had scar tissue, and I could appreciate the closeness that came with giving that kind of control to someone I loved and trusted.

And Jesse had crafted a beautiful experience for me.

My heart swelled with love, and I wanted him to wake up with as big a smile as I had. I rolled closer and slid my hand over his thigh. He shifted, and I stroked his soft, silky shaft. It lengthened, hardening under my ministrations.

I used my foot to pull the sheet down. As I was scooting down to begin the blowjob, he pushed my hand away. Abruptly, he sat up with his feet on the floor and his back to me. He rubbed his hands over his face.

"Jesse? Are you okay?"

"Fine." Without looking at me, he grabbed a crutch and disappeared into the bathroom.

What man, in the history of the world, turned down a blowjob?

None of them.

Between last night and now, something had happened. I followed him into the bathroom to find him in the shower.

I slid back the curtain. "Jesse?"

"I'll just be a couple minutes." He'd been leaning against the wall under the spray, his hands fisted against his sides. But once I peeked in, he shifted, sticking his face under the showerhead.

Perhaps the newfound closeness we'd shared last night emboldened me. Stepping into the large, tiled shower, I rejected his attempts to brush me off. I touched his side where the scar from the bullet wound was still an angry red mass.

"Jesse, talk to me."

The tension in his body multiplied. "Are you dropping?"

"Dropping?" It dawned on me that he might be dropping. Brea had talked to me at length about Domdrop, which was like subdrop for Doms. I wrapped my arms around his waist and hugged him from behind. "Jesse, are you having Domdrop?"

"Domdrop?" He half-twisted around to express confusion, and his crystal blue gaze searched my face. "You look okay. How are you feeling? It's been a while, but last time you submitted, you dropped really hard."

It took a minute for me to remember the day I'd ended our relationship. I'd been over the subdrop, and I'd broken up with him because I wasn't ready to be anyone's sub—and he was definitely a Dom.

Like how he was trying to control the conversation right now. "I'm not having subdrop. This time was different because I gave you my submission. You didn't take it from me. But this *is* about you. What's wrong?"

Satisfied I was emotionally okay, he went back to showering.

"This isn't going to fly, Jesse. You can't open me up like this and then hold yourself out of reach."

He kissed my cheek. "I'm right here." Then he got out of the shower.

I wasn't clean yet, but I followed his ass out. The bottom half of him was already dressed, another unusual move. Jesse liked to let things air out for a while in the morning.

Wrapping a towel around my torso, I crossed my arms and nailed him with an expectant look.

Flickers of anxiety and fear crossed his features, and I watched him grapple to make those emotions leave.

I set my fingertips against his scruffy cheek. "Jesse, please talk to me."

Anxiety won the battle for facial expression. "When I was in Rio Escondido, there was a woman."

153

I tried to remind myself that, while he'd been gone, there had been a man for me, but my brain kept screaming that I thought he was dead, while he'd known full well I was alive.

But right now I needed to listen. "Go on."

"She was powerful in the village, the sister of the guy who ran it for the cartel." He closed his eyes, as if blotting out a nightmare. "Magdalena decided she wanted me, and I—I slept with her."

Something didn't add up. This didn't sound like a husband confessing an infidelity, and my heart wouldn't quite believe he would actually be unfaithful. "You slept with her?"

"I didn't want to. At first, I refused, and when I did, she would pick out a few guards and let them beat on me. Then she would restrict my food rations for a few days." His gaze fell to the floor. "I knew if I kept going on that way, they'd kill me."

He broke off, and I filled in some blanks.

"So you gave in. You had sex with her in order to survive."

He nodded. "When I was in her hut, I got more food—and sometimes alcohol, and when I kept her happy, she kept the guards from being such assholes."

Horror flowed through my veins like icicles. I could empathize with what he'd endured. I knew what it was like to not have that kind of control over my body.

"She liked to start off with a hand job because she could make me hard even though I wanted nothing to do with her. A lot of mornings, I woke up with her hand on my dick. This morning—" His voice broke, and he took a deep breath. "When David, Dean, Frankie, and Joss rescued me, I was with her. The guards tended to let her have more privacy."

I pulled him to me, and he buried his face in my neck. I held him, stroking soothing caresses down his back as he shook in my arms. It made sense now, why he'd avoided having sex with me for so long, and why he'd insisted on pinning me down and dominating me that first time. He'd been fighting more demons than I knew.

"I'm sorry," he said softly as he gripped my hair. "I didn't intend to tell you because I didn't want to hurt you like this. I don't want to lose you."

I wasn't hurt; I was outraged. "Jesse, you have nothing to apologize for. She raped you. Thank you for telling me. If I know your triggers, I can avoid setting them off."

He drew back, a severe frown marring his chin and brow, and a tempest brewed behind his eyes. "I wasn't raped. I didn't want to have sex with her, but I did it."

I cupped his face in my hands. "Do you remember when you and David found out that BS used to make Brea and me have sex with targets to soften them up?"

Briefly he nodded. This was a sore subject, guaranteed to make him entertain murderous intent toward the man who'd kidnapped me as a child. "This isn't the same thing. Nobody made me do it."

"*She* made you do it. She physically coerced you through beatings and starvation. Jesse, BS didn't rape me himself. He found other people to do it for him, people who didn't even know I wasn't there willingly. I participated in it because I wanted to survive. That's what you did. It's not different."

Thunder joined the storms in his eyes. He ripped away from me and went into the bedroom.

I wasn't going to let him go when he was like this. I'd spent a lot of time working through this issue, and I'd come to terms with it. Thanks to his bum ankle, I caught him before he'd gone too far, planting my body in front of him and moving with him when he tried to go around me.

"Jessica, move."

"No. I love you, Jesse. I'm not going anywhere."

He ran a frustrated hand across his short, wet hair, spraying us both with the droplets. "She's here with us. I hate that I woke up to my wife's hand on my dick, and the first thing I did was struggle not to vomit."

I could work with this. I'd been there too. "The first thing I learned that helped me heal was to take back control of my life and my body."

"Jessica, it's not the same. I knew what I was doing. I cheated on you."

"I knew what I was doing as well. That doesn't make it consensual, and it definitely doesn't make it cheating. Jesse, I know your heart belongs to me. And, while I might like to touch your body an awful lot, it belongs to you. Anything I do, I do with your permission. If you take that permission away, then I stop."

I stepped closer, but I didn't touch him. "When a sensation you once enjoyed takes on a negative association, the only way you can take it back and make it yours again is to give it a positive association." I dropped my towel because he needed to know he was the one with the power right now.

He exhaled hard. "I don't want to have sex right now."

"I know you don't." I spoke softly. "But please let me help you get her out of your head. Let me help you heal."

"Jessica—"

I dropped to my knees, spreading them shoulder-width apart, and I clasped my arms behind my back. I was a submissive making myself available for my Dom.

"Fuck, Jessica—why are you doing this?"

"Because I want to serve you, Jesse. I need to help you."

"What do you think is going to happen right now?" He crossed his arms, but the cadence and timbre of his voice deepened as he settled into Dom mode.

"Anything you want. I can touch you, or you can use my mouth. Or I can just stay here, kneeling for your pleasure. Or, if you're not ready, then you can go make me an omelet, and I'll go take a shower."

For a long, long time, he didn't move. My knees protested this much kneeling. In my studio, whenever I had to be on my knees to work on a piece for an extended period of time, I had pads. Even then, I got up and walked around every little while to work out the aches.

After forever had passed, he traced his thumb along my lower lip. "I had them run two STD panels. All the tests came back negative, but HIV can take up to six months to show up. Though it's a minimal risk, I'm not willing to take the chance with your health, so as much as I'd love a blowjob, we're both going to have to wait a few months."

"Or you could use a condom." Though I knew I wasn't supposed to, I lifted my gaze. "The point of this isn't to get you off, just to help you replace negative memories with positive ones. Of course, if you want, I could suck your cock, and then when you want to come, you could pull out and come on my breasts."

A shudder of desire ran through my body at the idea. I didn't know why, but it brought me close to orgasm just imagining him ejaculating on my breasts.

He chuckled drily. "You'd like that, wouldn't you?"

"Yes, Jesse."

"Kneel next to the bed."

I didn't question his order; I just followed it. Too much in a hurry to get to my feet, I crawled the short distance.

When he limped after me, I figured that his ankle was probably aching. His surgery was scheduled for the next day, so hopefully he'd be in less pain soon.

He removed his pants and sat on the edge of the mattress.

I knelt at attention with my arms clasped behind me. I would use my hands only when he told me to.

"Safewords," he said, "are for both of us."

"Yes, Jesse."

"Come play, darlin'. Use your hands, your mouth—whatever you want."

Moving slowly, I walked on my knees to close the remaining distance. Then I leaned down and kissed the tip of his cock, which was not at all hard. "Hey, little guy," I whispered. "I want to be your best friend."

"Just FYI, when you call him a little guy, that doesn't make him want to stand up and say hello."

"Shhh," I said even though it was probably a bad idea to talk back to my Dom. "You know better than to doubt my skills."

Bringing my hands around, I began by resting them on his thighs. As I kissed and licked his cock, I slid my hands higher. By the time I cupped his balls, the little guy was halfway there.

"See? We're getting along just fine." I knew Jesse liked a firmer touch, so I increased the pressure of my hold, and his cock came fully awake.

With one hand wrapped around his shaft and the other fondling his sac, I licked a line around the sensitive crown, teasing a gasp from him. Then I worked his cock into my mouth, wetting it as I went along. When I'd wet him enough, I swallowed his cock so I could take all of him.

Jesse's hands came to rest on the back of my head. The second time I deep-throated him, he took over, shoving my head down and holding it in place to force me to hold him in my throat. I struggled against my gag reflex, but I refused to tap out. This was one challenge I would meet, because failing wouldn't help Jesse begin to overcome the horror he'd endured.

He eased up, allowing me to withdraw and breathe, and then he pushed my head down and held it there again. My eyes watered, and my fingers dug into his thigh before he let go.

Then he released his hold, smoothing my hair away from my face. "God, Jessica. You're amazing. Finish me off."

I wrapped a hand around his base and got a serious rhythm going. He moaned a few times, but mostly he held my hair back and watched his dick disappear into my mouth.

Then he pulled my hair sharply, forcing me to drop his cock as he bent me back. His warm semen splattered on my breasts. My chest heaved from the exertion and the excitement of having his seed on my skin.

"Thank you, Jesse." I remembered my manners, but more than that, I was truly grateful he'd shared his horror with me and allowed me to help him.

He lifted me and laid me down on the bed. Then his face was between my legs. He licked and sucked, slurping and biting as he claimed his territory. Before long, an orgasm pulsed through my

157

tissues, and I cried out. He slowed down, licking long stripes through my wetness.

"You taste like heaven, darlin'. Pure ambrosia."

Well sated, I smiled, and then I sat up.

He knelt on the floor where I'd just been. His face glistened with my juices, and the haunted look in his eyes was gone.

"How are you feeling?" I asked.

"Like I just had an orgasm."

"Jesse."

"You transition out of being a sub really quickly." He chuckled as he got to his feet and pulled me to mine. "I feel wild and a little reckless, and right now, I'm going to clean you up."

In the bathroom, he used a diaper wipe to clean the semen from my breasts, and then he rubbed hand sanitizer over the area. I watched him work. "Wild and reckless. What does that mean?"

He shrugged. "I don't know. I think you'll have to repeat this all tomorrow, and we'll see if I'm over it or not."

My prediction leaned toward him not being over it, but I didn't want to burst his bubble. He seemed to be in a good mood.

The shower had been on the whole time we'd been otherwise occupied. He shoved me inside the cool spray.

"Jesse, I think we're out of hot water."

"Probably. Next time, you'll remember to turn off the faucet before you go chasing after me." He used the detachable showerhead to rinse my body, and then he caged me against the cold tile and kissed me breathless.

I shivered, but he only ran a fingertip between my pussy lips. Most of the cold spray fell on him, so it wasn't that bad, but it wasn't comfortable either. This must be what he'd meant by 'wild and reckless.'

His finger penetrated my vagina. He worked it around, massaging my internal tissues. "You belong to me, Jessica."

"I know." Though I wasn't in submissive mode, I wasn't quite out of it either.

"And I belong to you." His finger dropped out of my pussy, and he pressed his forehead against mine. "Heart and soul."

Hugging him to me, I gave him the comfort he so badly needed. My hand may have slipped and turned off the cold water, but mostly I hugged him.

The next morning, I did not wake him by fondling his cock because he was awake before me. This was normal because he was a morning person, and I was not. Also, he was scheduled for surgery this morning, so he'd set his alarm to a quiet setting that always failed to penetrate the thick fog of my slumber.

I opened my eyes to find him holding a plate and wearing a grin along with his usual sweats-and-T-shirt combination.

"Sylvia made you an omelet. It has veggies inside because she says you don't eat enough veggies. Well, she said you didn't eat enough—period—but vegetables specifically."

Rubbing the sleep from my eyes, I sat up.

He put a hot mug in my hands before my eyes were able to quite focus. "Coffee. Drink some of that before you decide I'm a cheerful motherfucker who needs to be taken down with a nasty glare."

Now that he'd mentioned it, I agreed that he was irritatingly joyful, but I'd missed him so much, even this was a welcome return to normalcy. I sipped the coffee. "You know, if you'd stayed in bed until after I woke up, you would be enjoying the benefits of a happy beginning right now."

He spread his hands wide. "If you eat instead of rail at me, there's time for a quickie. I'm not guaranteeing you'll get anywhere, but I will."

I ate, and I thanked him for breakfast in bed, and then I got ready to go with him to the outpatient surgery place. While I was dressing, he came into my closet—I guess it was big enough to be called a dressing room—with Bailey.

"Look who woke up in time to say hello to her Daddy and Mommy."

Bailey leaned toward me for a kiss, but rather than transfer to my arms like she usually did, she opted to stay with Jesse. She rested her head on his strong shoulder.

I petted her head. "I like snuggling with Daddy too."

Aware she was the object of our mutual adoration, Bailey grinned, fluttered her dark lashes, and patted Jesse. "Da-da."

Now, I knew she was just making noises. She was eight months old, but she'd been born almost three months early, which put her on par with most of the sixth-month developmental goals. However, the timing and circumstances were spot on. This girl was going to grow up to be one hell of a con artist.

The shock on Jesse's face transformed to pure glee. "Did she just say Daddy?"

I went with it. Normally my lies were self-serving, but after everything, Jesse needed this win. "I heard it."

We fawned over our daughter for a while, and she blossomed, playing to our sappy happy parenting. She shrieked with delight and said, "Da-da-da-da-da-da."

Nope, not a con artist. A con would withhold the prize for much longer. She was definitely a ham, though.

It ended up not mattering. Jesse heard what he wanted. His eyes were misty when he showered kisses on her face and blew on her belly to make her laugh even more.

I wanted more kids with him.

Chapter 17

Jessica

Warren drove us to the medical complex. "Call me when it's over, and I'll come pick you up."

"Thanks, Warren." Jesse reached across to shake hands with my dad. "I appreciate it."

"No problem."

"Oh," Jesse said. He reached into the glove compartment and extracted an envelope. "A little something for you and Sylvia. Words can't express how thankful I am to have you in our lives."

This had been unexpected. Even I hadn't known Jesse got them a gift. It was nice of him.

Warren opened the envelope. "Holy shit. This is too much."

Curiosity was killing me. "What is?"

"It's a fourteen-day Mediterranean cruise." His gaze moved down the page. "This has stops at so many places on Sylvia's bucket list."

"I wanted to hire a cook, but Sylvia was offended at the idea, so I figured I'd try something else," Jesse said. "It's been a tough couple of years, and you guys deserve a relaxing vacation."

Wordlessly Warren nodded. He leaned across the console and hugged Jesse. Then he came around to open the back door and help me out even though I could get out by myself. He hugged me tightly. "Call me afterward, sweetheart."

"I will, Dad."

Hearing Bailey say those syllables and seeing Jesse's reaction drove home to me exactly how much it mattered to Sylvia and Warren that I acknowledge their relationship to me. I hadn't truly understood before.

Jesse wanted to hold my hand on the way in, but between his crutches and my cane, we had seven legs to contend with. We managed something in the elevator. He pulled me against his chest and kissed me breathless.

The elderly couple in the elevator nudged each other and giggled. The taller man said, "Must be newlyweds."

The shorter man's giggle broke off suddenly. He pulled his husband to him and kissed him the same way Jesse had just kissed me.

I grinned at Jesse. "I want to always be newlyweds with you."

"I can arrange that."

The ankle surgeon shared space with a foot surgeon, a wrist surgeon, and a hand surgeon. Reading their sign left me wondering if there would be a punch line if they walked into a bar.

They took Jesse back immediately. I stayed in the waiting room while they made him do fun things like take his pants off. I totally would have helped with that part.

When he was set, the nurse brought me back to see him. It was a long row of beds divided by curtains. I sat on the lone chair and looked him over. Seeing him in a hospital setting took me back to when he'd just come home. I'd been a mess, but I'd tried to hold it together for him.

Shooing away those feelings, I smiled brightly. "Are you comfortable?"

"I'm fine. You look like you're about to vomit."

"I'm just nervous." In retrospect, perhaps I shouldn't have eaten the whole omelet. Sylvia had packed it with fixings. "When is the cruise?"

He didn't miss a beat. "In two weeks. I figured I'd be recovered enough from surgery, and you wouldn't need them so much because I'll be able-bodied."

"That was really nice of you."

He shrugged. "They've restructured their lives to be there for you and Bailey. That's really nice of them. It's the least I could do."

"I didn't know Sylvia wanted to travel."

"Most people want to travel, but I chose this because I was watching a travel show with Sylvia last week, and she just gushed over some of those places. It's mostly Greece and Rome, with a little bit of France and Spain thrown in. I had to make sure they had passports before I booked it." He flashed a grin. "I had Brea do the looking. She was up for a little friendly B-and-E while your parents were out."

We chatted, and he did a great job keeping my spirits up while we waited. When they took him away, the nurse pointed me in the direction of the waiting room.

The first thing I noticed when I entered the waiting room was Dean. He sat in the far corner reading a women's health magazine.

I took the seat next to him. "Are you thinking of transitioning?"

The corner of his mouth quirked up, and he set the magazine aside. "I'm not sure I'd make an attractive woman."

"You don't have to stop reading on my account."

"That's quite all right. I know a lot about how to flatten my abs already." He nodded toward the door from which I'd emerged. "How is he doing?"

"He's fine. I'm the one who's nervous."

Dean chuckled. "I thought that would be the case."

"Dean, don't take this the wrong way, but what are you doing here?"

He sighed. "David, Frankie, Joss, and Brea are out on a job. I'm monitoring things, but I can do that from here. It's an easy job, the kind we used to just put two people on. Brea and David are there for backup, or to prevent Frankie from killing Joss."

My eyes widened. Frankie wasn't given to violent outbursts, and the only thing I knew about Joss was he'd helped rescue Jesse. "Is he a jerk to her?"

Lifting his hands, Dean made a face that communicated uncertainty. "He keeps flirting with her, and Frankie's not one who flirts, particularly not when she's working. She's sparred with him a few times, and she definitely gets him back for stuff he says. I've asked Frankie if she wants me to hire someone else, but she said he doesn't bother her. I think she might like his brashness, but—one thing about Frankie—when she's done taking crap from someone, she's done. He won't know what hit him."

I digested this. "It sounds like you know this from experience."

"Not personal experience. I've seen it happen to others." He threw me a dry look. "Jessica, you know me better than that."

From personal experience, I knew Dean pushed when he thought he could get away with it. "So, you're here for Jesse."

"And you." He rose. "Want some coffee?"

"Sure."

A coffee station was right there in the waiting room. It was stocked with coffee, hot water for tea, and various packaged breakfast foods.

Dean returned with two coffees and a muffin. He opened the package and ate it in two bites.

"Thanks," I said as I sipped the welcomed java. "Did you skip breakfast?"

"Nope. I just like muffins. The other night when I stopped by your house to see Jesse, David and I cleaned you out of muffins."

"I wondered what happened to those." I also wondered why Jesse hadn't mentioned the visit.

"I'm not surprised Jesse didn't tell you." He brushed a crumb off his crisp, button-down shirt. "He wouldn't talk to us, and after we ate the muffins, he kicked us out."

"Oh." My heart went out to all three of them. "Dean, I'm sorry. He's dealing with a lot right now."

"I know," he said. "There was a time when my presence would have helped him process everything that's happened, but now he won't even talk to me."

Did he think I was responsible for Jesse putting distance between them? "Dean, I didn't say a word to Jesse, and I hope you won't either." I didn't want to say it had been a mistake for us to sleep together, but it couldn't continue.

"I know you haven't," Dean said. "He hasn't tried to kill me yet."

He leaned his head back against the wall behind the chair and closed his eyes. "I've been stupid enough, and I've already done too much to damage this friendship. I'm not going to do or say anything to hurt him. We didn't do anything wrong, but it's—it's a bit much for him to deal with."

Though Jesse hadn't come out and said it, I knew he blamed Dean and David for abandoning him in Central America. I wasn't sure I didn't, and so I tried to not think about it. Before this happened, I'd hoped to help repair their friendship. Now...

"Yeah," I agreed. "It's a lot."

"I miss him," Dean said. "For the past twelve years, he's been closer to me than my brothers have ever been. I'd give my life for his."

I knew how much the four of them loved and valued each other. That was why this was so hard for Jesse.

"I've never fucked up anything this bad in my life." He inhaled deeply and rocked his head back and forth. "Jessica, I just want him back. I want to do or say whatever I need to do or say, pay whatever penance I have to pay, but I want my friend back."

Twining my fingers with his, I offered support. I knew what it was like to be so close to Jesse and yet not be part of his life. Though it had been my choice, losing him had left an unrelenting ache. As I thought of a response, Dean plowed ahead. He needed a listener, not platitudes.

"Do you remember when I kissed you? And then you had a seizure that landed you in the hospital?" His gaze lifted as if he was already dumbfounded by what he was about to say. "I brought him to the hospital to see you, and then I took him home so you could rest, and that's when I did one of the dumbest, most selfish things in my life. I told him he'd jumped the gun in pursuing you, and it wasn't fair that he got to the finish line before I'd left the starting block."

164

Platitudes wouldn't help. I slowly disentangled my fingers from his. I hadn't known the real reason Jesse stopped talking to Dean. I'd thought it was due to the way Dean had treated me when I'd broken up with Jesse. I gaped, and I made a conscious effort to close my mouth.

It wouldn't have mattered if Dean had pursued me. I'd only ever had eyes for Jesse.

"I don't know why I expected him to step aside and let me have a shot. You were married and expecting your first kid." He leaned forward and put his head in his hands. "God, I'm such an asshole."

Questions whirled through my mind. How in the world could he have thought we were compatible? We had nothing in common except for the people we loved. He liked art, but he didn't love it with the same passion I did. When he'd seen my first painting, he'd told me it was nice, but Jesse was the one who understood what it meant to me to have painted it. Jesse had always been patient where my recovery was concerned, where Dean seemed to tire of my shortcomings after a few hours. If I'd broken off a relationship with Dean because he was asking for more than I could give, he would have moved on without a backward glance. And if I'd lied to him the way I'd lied to Jesse, he would have broken up with me long before I could have done the honors.

I liked Dean. I even thought he was a good lover. But I didn't love Dean, and he didn't love me. We were temperamentally too different.

I rubbed a circle on the back of his shoulder. "At least you recognize it. Admitting you have a problem is half the battle."

He sat back and regarded me through narrowed eyes. His were rimmed with fatigue and sadness, but he managed to inject enough reproof into the look to let me know he was not amused. "Okay, Brat. If you have any ideas for how to win the rest of the battle, I'm all ears."

"I don't know. You have two separate issues. The whole thing with me will fade in time. He won, so there's no sense in dwelling on an old crush you had. The Honduras thing... I don't know what to tell you. Frankly, I'm angry and heartbroken that you left him down there. I try to tell myself you honestly thought he'd died, but since he didn't, I—I don't know. He's going to need time to come to terms with what happened before he can work on restoring your friendship."

Dean's face fell. I'd never seen him bereft before. This was worse for him than Jesse dying.

My heart ached for him and for Jesse, and I thought about how Dean's alpha nature could get in his way. "Don't go away, Dean. No matter how hard and how often he pushes you away, you need to prove you're not going anywhere. Make a point to be in his life."

"Like Sylvia and Warren have done with you and Brea." He nodded. "That's solid advice."

I hadn't made the connection, but he was right. When we'd first found out we'd been kidnapped as children, Brea and I weren't sure whether we wanted to meet our birth parents. I'd come around first, probably because I had a closed-head injury that led me to make snap decisions without really thinking them through. Brea had held out for much longer. But Sylvia and Warren had installed themselves in our lives, and now I couldn't imagine not having them around.

When Doctor Sertain called me into his office to tell me about the surgery and show me some pretty disturbing pictures of the inside of Jesse's ankle he thought were really cool, Dean came with me. The two were already acquainted. Apparently Doctor Sertain had fit Jesse into his schedule as a personal favor to Dean.

"He's going to need to rest it for two weeks. Don't take the bandage off, and don't get it wet. I'll see him back for the follow-up then, and we'll get him set up for physical therapy." Doctor Sertain handed me a couple of prescriptions.

Dean tried to take them from me, but I tucked them into my purse. "I'm perfectly capable of filling a prescription."

We followed the arrows to the other side of the ward where Jesse was just waking up.

Dean took my purse. "Yeah, but if I fill them, then I have an excuse to come by and see him." He handed back my purse and touched his head. "I'm taking your advice."

Since it wasn't a comment on my skills as a wife, I let him have the prescriptions. "He won't take the pain meds."

"I know."

"I need to text my dad and let him know he can come pick us up."

Dean grunted. "I can take you home."

"Okay, then I'll text him and let him know you've got it covered."

That seemed to improve Dean's spirits. I swear—he was like a pouty child sometimes.

We found Jesse in bed with his eyes closed. A nurse stood next to him, taking his blood pressure. She smiled. "Hi, Mrs. Foraker. Who's this with you?"

"Dean Alloway."

"Alloway?" She frowned.

"It's like Calloway without the C." He dialed up the charm with a brilliant smile.

Her frown eased. "We'll say you're a relative." To me, she said, "He's waking up. Feel free to talk to him. The more he talks and moves, the better he'll come out of the anesthesia."

I leaned over and kissed his cheek. "Jesse? Come on, sleepyhead. It's time to wake up."

"Don't wanna get up, Brat."

It seemed like I had another pouty child on my hands. I touched his face and traced a line down his arm. "If you open your eyes, I'll show you my boobs."

"Don't do it," Dean said. "Hold out for more."

The nurse threw a disgusted look at both of us, and then she said she'd be back in ten minutes.

Jesse's eyes slowly opened, and he focused on Dean at the foot of his bed. "What the fuck are you doing here?"

I put my hand on Jesse's cheek and urged him to look at me. "Hey, there. The doctor showed me some really gross pictures of your bones and ligaments."

"He's unlikely to remember anything you say for the next hour or so," Dean said. "Tell him about your third nipple."

This time, I aimed a warning look at Dean.

"Dean." Jesse closed his eyes again, but he took a bigger breath, which meant he hadn't fallen back asleep. "I'm mad at Dean."

"I know," I said. "But anger fades, and true friends don't let disagreements or mistakes keep them away when it really matters."

He opened his eyes again, and he frowned at me. "Mistake? Seriously?"

"Major fuck-up," Dean supplied. "She's trying to be nice."

"That's the problem," he said. "She doesn't need to be so nice."

"Jesse, how about you tell me what you remember from the surgery?"

He tilted his head to view me from a different angle. "I was knocked out."

I shrugged. "I heard and remembered stuff when I was in a coma. Brea read whole books out loud to me, and I had to listen whether I liked them or not—and her tastes in reading are very different from mine." I preferred nonfiction, especially biographies, and she liked fantasy fiction.

"Darlin', you're pretty." He reached up to maybe touch my face, but he missed and swiped at air. He frowned at his hand.

"I don't know that looks factor into it," Dean said. "It has to do with level of sedation and your body's reaction to the medication."

Jesse grunted, but he didn't look at Dean. "Didn't hear anything."

He tried for me again, and this time, I caught his hand and held it. "Do you feel anything?"

"Irritation. Don't like this surprise."

I glanced at Dean. "Maybe you should go."

His jaw set in a stubborn line. "I'm your ride home."

"Warren," Jesse said.

"Dean's already here," I said. "Please, Jesse. Don't be difficult." I said his name like it was a title, and he responded the same way he had every other time I'd done that over the past two days.

There was more awareness in his gaze as he gave me what I wanted. "For you, darlin'."

A half hour later, Dean helped Jesse into his pants. As he'd promised, Jesse cooperated. Perhaps it was less weird to have Dean help him dress than to have my dad here.

When we got home, Dean helped Jesse up the stairs and into bed. For his part, Dean didn't say much.

I walked Dean to the door while Jesse napped. "Thank you for today. You really took my mind off waiting."

Dean smiled, but it was overtaken by melancholy. "You're welcome. I'll be back in an hour or so with his prescriptions."

Bailey was down for her nap as well, so I checked on Jesse. I was surprised to find him sitting up and waiting for me.

"I don't want Dean here."

I sat on the edge of the bed. "Jesse, he loves you and he misses you. This whole thing has been hard on him as well."

"Too fucking bad. I'll have to deal with him when I go back to work, but I don't have to put up with him in my own home." Anger drove him, keeping him up when he should have been sleeping.

"I'm sorry," I said. "He showed up and kept me company. I didn't know it would upset you so much to see him. He's been over a lot since you've been back. You haven't said anything."

"No, I haven't. One of the perks of having a house full of people is it's easy to avoid the two people you don't want to see."

Two people—Dean and David. I didn't want to fight with Jesse, not about this.

My expression must have shown my distress. He touched my cheek. "Hey, I'm not mad at you, darlin'. Like he said, you were just trying to be nice. It's one of the things I love about you—how you go out of your way to please the people you love. I'm mad at him. He left me there."

I kissed his forehead. "You're home now. Lie down and get some rest. I'm going to get some lunch. I'll check back on you in a little while, and I'll bring Bailey."

At the mention of her name, his sour mood dropped away. "She said my name."

"Yeah, well she knows who to wrap around her tiny fingers to get things done around here."

He set a hand on my thigh. "Just like her mother. You don't think I was oblivious to the way you manipulated me by saying my name in that submissive tone."

I flashed my cheekiest grin. "No, Jesse. I'm aware you can see through my manipulations."

"Brat, if I wasn't groggy from all the drugs, I would show you exactly what that manipulative smile gets you."

I pressed a kiss to his lips. "Save it up for later. Maybe even use your belt next time?"

He fell asleep with a smile on his handsome face.

Chapter 18

Dean

The aroma of oven-roasted chicken and potatoes filled the air of this elegant dining room. A scrumptious feast lay before me, but I could only pick at it.

"Penny for your thoughts?" Brea's question interrupted the glum trajectory of my internal musings. She had invited me for dinner, and she'd outdone herself. From the outset, Brea and I had established a special bond, and the fact she'd married one of my best friends only entrenched her as a vital part of my life.

I was being a poor guest. "Have you heard how Jesse is doing?"

"Oh." She waved away my concern. "He's fine. He's up and around on one crutch now. My parents left two days ago to go on a cruise."

"Yeah," David added drily. "Leave it to Jesse to show me up with the in-laws."

"He sent them on a cruise?" I wasn't surprised. Jesse was generous to those he loved, and he had every reason to love Warren and Sylvia Zinn.

"Two weeks in the Mediterranean." She heaved a sign of longing. "Jesse surprised them with it. If I don't step up, they're going to like him more than they like me."

I found that difficult to believe. Brea was a ray of sunshine, and Jesse was being an ornery jerk. "Can he move his ankle yet? Did they say how much mobility he could expect to regain?"

She peered at me curiously. "Dean, haven't you visited?"

"I tried. The last time, Jessica met me at the door and said my visits upset Jesse. She told me not to come over anymore. She said she'd let me know when he changes his mind. That was the day after he came home from surgery." This was after she'd told me to insinuate myself in his life and refuse to leave it. To her credit, she'd been very apologetic. "Does he let David in the house?"

"He does," David admitted. "Begrudgingly. Then he treats me as if I'm a stranger Brea dragged along who isn't good enough to lick her boots. He's polite when Sylvia and Warren are around, and passive-aggressive any other time."

At least David was allowed entrée. I'd been barred.

Brea looked from David to me. "You guys, he's going through some serious stuff right now. David told me what you saw when you found him, and some of the things Jessica has said... I think he has PTSD, but he won't see a doctor. I asked."

PTSD was serious. It could lead to suicidal thoughts or actions, and if that was the case, Jesse needed us more than ever.

"What did Jessica say that has you worried, Sugar?" David speared a *haricot vert* that had been cooked in butter and shallots, and he popped it into his mouth.

"She said he sleeps a lot, more than you'd expect from someone recovering from surgery, and sometimes when she catches him unaware, he's scowling and staring off into space." She pushed the remnants of her mashed potatoes around her plate. "She's subbing for him now. I'm not sure he should be dominating her if he's not in a good headspace."

I shared her concern. Jesse would rather die than hurt Jessica, but if he was in a bad headspace, there was no telling what he'd do—and it would only feed his trauma. "Your parents are away for the next couple weeks?"

"Yeah."

"I'll stop by and talk to Jessica. I wanted an excuse to go there anyway, and now I have one."

It was dark by the time I left David and Brea's place, so I parked on the street and thought about how I'd approach the house. Going to the front door was likely to get me booted, but if Jesse answered, it would be a good way to gauge his mood. On the other hand, Jessica was the one who needed to hear my warning about scening with a man who was possibly not in the right headspace.

One day, Jesse would thank me for my interference. I had no illusion that day would come soon.

I made it all the way to the front door before I lost my nerve. Perhaps I'd better do recon first so I knew what kind of situation I was getting myself into.

Jesse

A shadow darkened my field of vision, a gloomy half-thought drawing me toward an abyss. I chased it away by focusing on Jessica.

She laughed at the shock on Bailey's face when the block tower Jessica built fell down under the force of Bailey's kicking feet. "Did you kick the blocks?" Jessica tickled the bottom of Bailey's foot by dragging the tip of her finger across it.

We'd put socks on Bailey repeatedly, but after she'd pulled them off and threw them away from her for the third time, we got the message. Bailey didn't want to wear socks.

Neither did I, so I could relate.

Bailey responded to Jessica with a long, babbling diatribe. I loved hearing her talk. Like Jessica, she was very verbal. I could listen to my women forever. Bailey ended by pointing to me. "Da-da-da-da-da-da-da!"

When she'd said my name, I wasn't a hundred percent sure she knew what she was saying, but I knew for certain she understood saying those syllables to me got her my undivided attention.

I sat on the floor next to Jessica, stretching out my legs and leaning on one arm. Jessica leaned closer and dropped a kiss on my cheek. Then she gasped at Bailey. "Did Daddy come to play with us?"

For the past two hours, I'd been "laying down." That excuse was wearing thin, even for me. Now that everyone was gone and my ankle surgery was behind me, my life was settling down into a normal routine.

With that routine came some black moods that rendered me not suitable company for anyone. I did my best to contain my episodes by separating myself from my family. And when I was with them, focusing on Jessica and Bailey went a long way toward chasing away the darkness.

They were light and sunshine. Seeing them, being with them—it helped stave off the worst of my moods. When I was languishing in the depths of horribly negative feelings, I forced myself to think about them or look at the pictures I'd placed all around the room for that purpose. I knew this was the aftereffects of being a prisoner, and I was determined to work through it before it impacted my family.

Though I hadn't suffered from this before, I'd watched friends go through it. Dean went through a bad patch after one particularly brutal tour of duty in Afghanistan. He'd used alcohol to ease the darkness. I was using light therapy.

I moved into a better position, and I kissed Jessica's lips. "I love you."

Her smile turned radiant. "And I love you."

"I was poking around in your studio the other day, and I found a painting you did that I quite like." After my initial discovery, I'd spent some time studying it. Though it showed a thigh and part of an arm, it looked so real that the observer was tempted to look for the curve of her hip and waist as well. The depiction of the rope was exquisite, as was the texture in the woman's skin.

She laughed. "I'll bet you did."

"I'd like to hang it in our bedroom."

She glanced around like a teenager with her boyfriend whose parents have left the room for a few minutes. "I'm not sure I want to explain it to my parents."

I laughed and kissed her again, lingering a little longer this time. "I think it's self-explanatory."

"I was going to sell it. I may have a buyer lined up."

After what she'd gone through to get her art back, the idea she'd sell it took me by surprise. "Sell it? Why?"

She laughed. "Because that's what artists do. We make paintings, and then we sell them. If we're very good, we can pull in a decent living."

"You don't need money."

"Neither do you."

She'd asked me, again, not to return to work at SAFE Security. Though I was tempted to cut ties with two of the members there, I actually thought getting back out in the field was the best thing to banish the darkness trying to grow inside me.

Rather than respond, I kissed her deeply. On a pleased sigh, she submitted to my mastery. I loved watching her bloom under my dominance.

"You worked all morning," I said, drawing a finger along her arm. "Why don't you go soak in the tub for a half hour? Use the neck pillow to release some of that tension."

"Mmmm." She nuzzled her cheek on my shoulder. "Baby needs a bath."

"I'll take care of Bailey." I kissed her lips again because I couldn't get enough of her silky feel and the smell of her skin. "How about, after your bath, you put on one of those lingerie outfits you bought? We could scene tonight after Bailey goes to sleep."

A smile stretched her lips.

I pressed my lips to the pulse point and inhaled. "In my closet is a black wooden chest."

"Full of sex toys."

I kept forgetting she'd gone through a lot of my stuff when I'd been gone. "Yes, full of sex toys I bought to use with you. Pick out three, and I'll use those on you tonight."

A shiver ran up her spine. "Jesse, you spoil me."

That was my aim. "After your bath, put on a robe over your sexy clothes and wait for me. I'll bring Bailey to you after her bath before I put her to bed."

"Mr. Foraker, you drive a hard bargain." She giggled. "And you're so darn sexy that I can't possibly refuse."

I kissed her again, and this time, Bailey objected. She let loose with a loud, "Da-da-da-dada-da!"

We looked over to find her pointing at us, her face twisted as she scolded us.

Jessica scooped her up and covered her face with kisses, and then she handed her off to me. "You're sure?"

"I'm sure, darlin'." I set Bailey on my knee and bounced her up and down. She squealed her delight and flapped her arms. Once Jessica disappeared, her babbling took on amazing qualities. It was like she was actually talking to me. She had tone and expression and everything.

I kept her going by responding as best I could.

Eventually, she crawled up my chest, and put her head on my shoulder. I held my daughter, hugging her close to my heart, for the longest time. When I looked down, I saw that she'd fallen asleep.

No bath tonight. Jessica would understand. After all, Bailey had skimped on her nap this afternoon, so it stood to reason she'd wink out early. Moving slowly and stealthily, I carried her upstairs without using my crutch. While I wasn't supposed to be putting much weight on it, the doctor said a little wouldn't hurt. The damn thing was in a cast anyway.

I kissed my little ray of sunshine's forehead before setting her in the crib. Then I checked all the things Jessica said needed checking— like the rail on the crib, the lock on the window, and the nightlight in Bailey's bathroom.

Keeping myself in stealth mode, I snuck into my bedroom. Perhaps I'd find Jessica still in the tub or in the middle of changing, and then I could surprise her.

I found the toys she'd selected already on the bed. The vibrator, I expected. The belt, I had not. She'd talked about using it after I had surgery, but she hadn't brought it up again. The third was a pinwheel, and that surprised me as well. It was still in the package, and I wondered if she had any idea what it would feel like. I guess I was going to find out.

With a grin on my face, I meant to continue toward the bathroom, but a cold wind from the direction of the balcony stopped me. I heard the soft murmur of Jessica's voice. Was she on the phone? I hoped nothing had gone wrong with her parents.

I crept closer, my ears attuned to catch the tone of her words.

That's when I heard Dean's voice.

Dean was on the balcony of my bedroom, talking to my wife after she'd told him—reluctantly, and on my order—he wasn't welcome here.

With a frown, I melted into the shadows nearer the door to listen in, and I heard snatches of conversation through the crack in the slider she hadn't quite closed.

"Dean, I know you're upset, but you have to give it time."

"It's been long enough. When are you going to tell him?"

"He's not ready." She said more, but her volume dropped and the speed of her words picked up.

"Jessica, I'm concerned that you're sleeping with a man who—" The rest was lost in the wind as she moved away from him, and he turned to follow.

Now I could see their outlines clearly through the gossamer curtains I'd meant to be decorative, but Jessica used in case our neighbors suddenly developed the ability to see through a lot of trees and bushes.

Dean had his hands on her upper arms.

She reached up and cupped his face, an affectionate gesture she'd used with me dozens of times.

My heart stuttered, and then blood thundered in my ears so loudly I heard nothing else they said.

But I saw them. I watched as he pulled her close and hugged her. The embrace lasted for a long time, and it didn't look like she was struggling against his hold. When he finally released her, she kissed his cheek.

Then he left by climbing over the balcony railing and hopping to the grass below.

Jessica came into the bedroom, hugging her robe around her as she shivered. Lost in thought, she didn't notice me until she was right in front of me.

She stopped and put her hand over her heart. "I didn't see you come in."

"Because you were busy talking to Dean." I crossed my arms. She owed me one hell of an explanation.

Her gaze darted to the balcony door and back to me, and her sigh was equal parts nerves and guilt. "He's worried about you."

"It looked like it."

She frowned at my acerbic tone. "Jesse, I know you don't want him here."

I cut her off before she could think up a lie. "So he snuck around to climb up our balcony?" I looked outside, and I realized something. "That's not the first time he's climbed this balcony."

"Please, Jesse. I know you're upset, but he's upset, too."

Pieces were falling into place, like the fact she advocated for him even though he'd ruined my life or the way she'd touched his face just now. It was a long shot, but I had to know if I'd figured it out or if I was losing my fucking mind. "He's upset because I came back, and now he can't fuck you anymore."

Her head snapped back as if I'd slapped her. With a gasp, she backed away. It seemed more like the shock of being discovered than that of an accusation coming out of left field.

"That's it, isn't it? You weren't upset I was gone because you had Dean to keep your bed warm."

"No," she gasped. "Jesse, it wasn't like that."

The blackness closed over my soul, and it was tinged with red. "You fucked the guy who left me rotting in hell."

She shrank away as I stormed past her, and then she followed me. "Jesse, I know you're angry, but please calm down and let's talk about this, okay?"

I didn't want to fucking talk about the fact I'd spent my days struggling to not die from working under the hot sun, and my nights in a different kind of purgatory, while she was fucking the man who was supposed to have my back.

In my bed.

I studied the mattress, and a laugh escaped. "You fucking bought a new mattress. What did you think that was going to hide?" Then I realized where all my condoms had gone. He hadn't even brought his own.

"I got the mattress because the head and feet adjust, and I thought it would be better for your ankle." She clutched at my arms, but I shook her off. "Jesse, please listen."

My God—she'd made me feel like shit when she'd described the hollow hell her life had become when she'd thought I was dead. Apparently she was still a consummate liar. She'd warned me from the beginning that she was a pathological liar, but I'd foolishly thought she'd left all that behind when she'd agreed to be my wife. How stupid was I to think she'd meant it when she'd pledged to love and honor me?

Rage carried me into her closet where I tore her clothes from hangers and dumped them from the drawers. "I want you gone."

She looked at her clothes heaped on the floor, and then she faced me with her hands on her hips. "You're being really unreasonable right now."

"I'm being unreasonable?" Inches from her face, I loomed over her. "Fuck you, Jessica. Fuck both of you. You have one hour to get your things and get out of my house." Clenching my fist, I stormed past her, my cast thumping ominously against the wood flooring.

She stepped in front of me and grabbed me in a vain attempt to stop me from going. "Jesse, don't—"

I shoved her out of my way. She staggered backward and fell on her ass.

As she gaped at me, I said, "I may be injured, but I'm still lethal. Do *not* get in my way."

I left. I got in my SUV and drove. Autopilot took me to Dean's house while darkness fed my soul. I'd just lost everything important in my life, and I wanted blood.

Dean answered the door with his tie hanging loosely around his neck and a glass in one hand. "This is unexpected."

Taking one step, I leaned into the punch. Dean's lightning reflexes had him moving, but he wasn't fast enough to dodge my fury. I leaped on him, my fists flying at his face. Glass shattered, and he countered my attack. Blocking wasn't going to save him, and he knew it, so he gave me the all-out brawl I sought.

With my leg out of commission, I concentrated on using my upper body to inflict damage. Dean didn't have my limitations, but he also didn't have my determination. We rolled across the floor in a flurry of fists and elbows until he wrestled free and jumped to his feet.

Ignoring the pain radiating from my ankle and up my leg, I scrambled to my feet as well. Dean advanced, sweeping his leg out to disable me through my weak spot. To counter this move, I swept my good leg out, wrapped it around his, and took us both to the floor. Lunging, I delivered another series of punches, and I barely noticed any of the damage Dean did to me.

In the gym, when we sparred for practice, there were rules. We also had padding meant to absorb the force of the blows. For lethal hits, we used practice dummies. Tonight, I used Dean, and I didn't care if he used me. Part of me wanted him to use lethal force, to put me out of my misery. The rest of me wanted to make him hurt as badly as I did.

So when Dean got the upper hand, bringing the brawl to a close with an arm bar that cut off the flow of oxygen to my brain, I goaded him into completing the task.

"Fucking coward," I gasped. "Ch—cheating b—bastard."

Blackness dotted the edges of my vision, and his knee dug into the base of my spine.

"I'm sorry," he said. "I didn't know you were alive, and neither did she. It never would have happened otherwise."

"Liar." The word caught on the arm crushing my larynx, but I forced it out through sheer dint of will. "You—wanted—her."

"Yes," he admitted. "I wanted her, but she didn't want me, not even when we were together. It was your name she called in the heat of the moment, not mine. I was nothing more than an ineffectual bandage."

He released me suddenly, jumping back and out of my field of reach.

Having been on the verge of passing out, I rolled to my back and gasped for air. "You left me down there. You abandoned me, sentencing me to five months of hell, while you came back here and fucked my wife."

"I'm sorry. I know the words are inadequate, but there really aren't ones that work." He dragged his hands through his hair, tugging on it in a futile gesture. "I fucked up."

He paced away while I dragged myself to the wall because I needed something to prop me up. "You're right—it's not enough."

"Don't you think I know that?" He whirled, facing me with a frantic, haunted expression. "For fuck's sake, Jesse. Not a day goes by that I don't beat myself up for this. Every night, I replay every fucking step I took, looking for all the what-if's and the why-didn't-I's. The only difference between now and when I thought you were dead is now I know everything I did was wrong. Every move I made, every decision— it was wrong."

"You were a hundred yards from where I lay dying." I was miserable, and my only macabre joy was torturing him with the facts of his failure.

"I know." He roared this time. "I've never fucked up anything on so grand a scale. I fucking left you there. I fucking condemned you to months of torture and rape. Nothing I can do or say will ever make up for that."

"You wanted me to be dead because you wanted a chance with Jessica." It all came down to a woman, which was a pathetic commentary on the tattered shards of our broken friendship.

178

"No." The single syllable tore from the depths of his despair. "I was stupid, Jesse. I'll own it. Hindsight, that vicious beast, shows me I never had a chance. The playing field was always tilted in your favor. You were right that I was out of line to even bring it up. I ruined our friendship, something that was precious and dear to me, and I'd give anything to undo the damage I did."

I didn't know if losing Dean's friendship or languishing in hell for months had damaged me more.

He plopped down next to me, which showed he was either courageous or stupid, because once I got my strength back, I might still try to kill him.

Taking a handkerchief from his pocket, he handed it to me. "You're dripping blood onto my floor."

I wiped my nose and dabbed at the cut over my eye, but I didn't clean what had dripped onto his wood floor. Let it stain. Then I crumpled the cloth in my hand and squeezed out some of my frustration. "You cost me everything—my wife, my daughter, my job, and my friends."

"I should have been there," he said. "You needed more boots on the ground, but you and I both agreed on the two-person team idea, and so did Frankie and David. We were wrong, Jesse. Hubris played into it. We've always had successful missions, and I think we got sloppy. But my selfish move in asking you to step aside and let me have a chance with Jessica was a factor as well. You were pissed at me, and I was furious with you—and yes, I know you were justified and I was not. But it meant we were more committed to trying to make it work with a divided team than in making sure we had each other's backs. We're hiring more team members so we can be sure to cover all the bases in the future."

The throbbing in my neck had lessened, though it would be hours before I was breathing normally. Ignoring the pain, I turned my head and watched him warily. "Let's say one day I forgive you and David for leaving me behind. That leaves Jessica. You set out to destroy my relationship with her, and now you've succeeded. I'll never forgive you for that."

He regarded me with a steady stare. "You're not going to like what I have to say, but since you're not in any condition to walk out, you're going to listen."

I didn't want to listen. I hadn't wanted to hear Jessica justify it, and I sure as hell didn't want to hear Dean. I tried to shift my weight to get up, but agony screamed from my ankle. I looked down to see that the plaster of my cast was cracked. I'd probably fucked up my surgery.

179

"When I told Jessica you were dead, she slapped me across the face. Then she shut down. Days went by, and she wouldn't get out of bed. She stopped eating, bathing—even taking care of Bailey. Sylvia and Warren had their hands full keeping Jessica from following you into an early grave."

That was consistent with what Jessica had yelled at me in her studio. Still, I didn't see how she went from depression to fucking my former best friend.

"Frankie, David, Brea, and I helped as much as we could, but we weren't in a good place either, especially David and me. We blamed ourselves, rightly so, for how far sideways that mission went. Frankie and Brea, I think, blamed us as well, though they were kind enough not to say it."

He took the handkerchief from me and dabbed at his own bloody nose.

"If I have HIV, you're risking an infection." The warning came out automatically.

"HIV is rare in that part of Honduras. There hasn't been a new case in over a decade. You're more likely to get malaria or tuberculosis, neither of which you have." Dean dabbed some more as he absently put one of my worst fears to bed. "Almost four months after we thought we'd lost you, Jessica came to SAFE Security late one night. She was pissed, which was new for her. It was the first spark of life I'd seen in months. She'd found your financial statements. It seemed she was under the impression David and I had inherited our money, so we were the only ones who were well off."

David had inherited a trust fund from his mother, but he'd only used it to pay for Jessica's medical care. Her concern about me paying for her health care made more sense. She'd thought the tremendous cost would bankrupt me.

"You didn't inherit money."

"I know," he said. "But she thought—you know what? It doesn't matter. She was livid that you went on a dangerous mission when you didn't need the money. She felt betrayed, and right or wrong, it jolted her out of her malaise. She vented to me, railing against all of us for our selfish need for danger and adventure."

And she'd repeatedly asked me not to go back to work at SAFE Security. Even before that fateful mission, she'd dropped hints about how I could just work on technology and stay home. I closed my eyes because I sensed the worst was yet to come.

"Then she kissed me. It was anger and loneliness more than passion, but one thing led to another. And she ended up crying at home for two days before she'd even talk to me again. It seemed that she felt like she had been unfaithful." He closed his eyes. "I hated seeing her like that, Jesse. It was almost worse than watching her try to die while we watched. She'd turned all that pain inward, unleashing it on herself. And so I talked her out of self-hatred and into my arms by telling her it would be therapeutic for both of us."

Tension ran through my whole body. I hated the whole situation, and it didn't make me blame her less. Even *she'd* known she was cheating on me, and yet she'd chosen to continue doing it.

"Slowly, she began to emerge from the worst of it. I ordered her to eat five small meals a day, and she began to gain back some of the weight she'd lost. When you saw her, she'd gained about fifteen pounds."

And she'd still been frighteningly thin.

"She spent a lot more time with Bailey, and that was good for both of them. Before, she'd taken care of her on autopilot—really Sylvia and Warren stepped in and cared for her—but now she was mentally present. She went back to her therapist, which was enormously beneficial, and she started working in her studio again, making furniture. I don't understand the furniture thing, but whatever. I guess it kept her busy and helped her be less depressed. She still cried a lot, but now it was a few times a day instead of a constant flow."

He tapered off, and I glared at him. "So, you're saying it's okay that you fucked my wife and ruined my marriage, because if you hadn't, she'd be dead?"

"No, you asshole. I'm saying she was out of her mind with grief and any decisions she made during that time were a function of her survival instinct and not a rational application of her thoughts and feelings. I'm saying she loves you, and the only thing that's going to ruin your marriage is you."

I'd done that already. "I threw her out."

"Get her back."

It wasn't that easy. I had darkness inside me, and even now I was in its grip. "She's better off without me."

Dean lumbered to his feet, his hulking mass moving far too gracefully for such a big guy, and he went to a table we'd knocked over during our brawl. He righted it, and then he took something from the drawer.

"When I saw the difference in Jessica from a few sessions of psychotherapy, I began going myself." He handed me a card. "I know you're hurting, Jesse. I know you're battling demons we can't see. And I'd fight with you like this every day if I thought it would help, but it won't. Call the number. Go see someone. She's not better off without you. None of us are."

181

Chapter 19

Jesse

My leg was definitely fucked up again, but I didn't care. A vision of Jessica beat a steady rhythm in my mind, and it wasn't an old image. Sprawled on the floor, her thick robe gaping open to reveal the lacy green top of a sexy teddy—and a hint of fear in her eyes—she stared up at me.

Never once, in the whole time I'd known her, had she been afraid of me. I was her rock, her refuge. No matter what else was going on, she'd always known I'd be there for her. In the past few weeks, she'd willingly stripped away her defenses to bare her soul to me, and I'd literally tossed her away.

Dean drove me home, but I didn't invite him to come inside. The wounds were still too fresh, the cuts ripped open and renewed by being forced to hear Dean's side of the story.

I could tell the moment I opened the front door that the house was empty. No furniture was missing, but the sense it was a home where a family lived was utterly absent.

Upstairs, the pile of her clothes was not significantly smaller. She'd taken a single bag, the staple of her vagabond existence before she'd come into my life.

I checked Bailey's room, not expecting to find her because I knew Jessica wouldn't leave her behind. This room had more things missing. She'd loaded up most of Bailey's things, but she'd left hers behind.

She was well and truly gone.

I went back into my bedroom, but pictures of Jessica were everywhere. Her smiling face mocked me for my failure to keep the darkness from chasing away everything I loved. The ache in my chest broke, shattering into tiny shards that ripped up whatever hadn't been destroyed in Rio Escondido.

Limping down the stairs, I went to the liquor cabinet and filled the wreckage of my insides with a liquid numbing agent.

Jessica

Glancing down at the baby seat where Bailey was peacefully slumbering despite the maelstrom going on inside me, I pounded on Brea's door once again.

David answered. From his robe and his tousled hair, I deduced I'd interrupted some sexy time. I didn't care. He looked at me, probably seeing the mascara streaked down my cheeks, the bags in my hands, and the baby carrier, and his eyes grew wide. "Jessica, are you okay?"

"Can I come in? Jesse threw me out, and I need a place to stay." I got it all out without breaking down in tears.

After Jesse had stormed out, I'd gathered some clothes and packed up Bailey's things. The numbness wore off as I got into the car and drove to Brea's place, and by the time I'd parked in the garage adjacent to the building, I'd been a wreck. It had taken me almost a half hour to get myself under control enough to get Bailey and a couple bags out of the car.

He stepped back. "Of course. Your room is right where you left it. Give me a minute to untie Brea, and I'll send her to you."

Brea and David had turned a corner of the room into a nursery. They'd purchased the same crib and bumpers for Bailey that she had at home, citing a desire to make her feel as comfortable here as she did at home.

She didn't stir as I changed her diaper and kissed her cheek before putting her down for the night.

When I got pregnant with her—on purpose—I had intended to raise her by myself. I'd wanted her more than I'd wanted anything in my life, even a relationship with Jesse. But then we'd worked through our differences, and I'd fallen head over heels for him with a love I'd never imagined possible.

In my heart of hearts, I knew it wasn't over. Nobody who loved me the way he did would let this tear us apart. In the morning, Brea and I would put our heads together, and we'd come up with a strategy to pull off this most important con.

But right now, I felt like someone had punched me in the gut.

I washed my face before going out to the living room, where I found Brea waiting for me. Holding her arms open, she rose and met me halfway. In the familiarity of my sister's embrace, I reaffirmed the strength that had made me a survivor.

She led me to the sofa, and she sat down so close to me that our thighs touched. "Tell me everything."

David appeared with a tray that he placed on the coffee table. "Tea and leftover cake. Cake always helps."

He was sweet and thoughtful, and I was fortunate to have him in my family.

That thought generated moisture in my eyes, and I blinked away the tears. I was not going to cry. Jesse wasn't dead. He'd lost his way, but as long as he was here, I had hope.

"I had just finished taking a bath when I saw someone on my balcony. Since Dean is the only person I know who uses that door as an entry, I went outside to see what he wanted."

David arched his brows. "You didn't let him in?"

I shook my head. "Jesse... Jesse flipped out the last time Dean came over. At first, he was just mad, but then he made me tell Dean he wasn't welcome anymore. He's been moody lately, spending a lot of time sleeping or locked in his office. The few times I've intruded, I've found him staring off into space, lost in thought. Bad thoughts—the expression on his face is always hard and hateful."

Brea put her arm around me. I'd already confided in her about this, and from what Dean had said, she'd voiced our concerns to David and Dean.

"Anyway, I went out there, and Dean wanted to know how we were doing. He asked if Jesse had been to see a therapist yet, and I said he hadn't, that I hadn't brought it up because he wasn't ready. So far, I've been able to help him get to a good headspace. He likes spending time with me and Bailey. It's when he's the happiest."

"Jessica, he needs more help than you can give him," David said. "From what you've told Brea, it sounds like PTSD, which makes sense, given what he went through."

"I know," I said. I'd planned to talk to him about seeing someone soon. With my parents gone, being alone with him and Bailey had been really nice. I finally had the family I'd always craved. "When Dean went away, Jesse was in our room. Somehow he put together that Dean and I had slept together when I thought he was dead, and he was livid. He threw all my clothes in a pile on the floor, and he told me to get out. I tried to stop him, but he knocked me out of the way and stormed out."

A few seconds of silence pressed on me as they absorbed what I'd said.

David rubbed his hand on the back of his neck, a sign that he was puzzling something out. Then his gaze searched my face. "He knocked you out of the way? Did he hit you?"

"No, he shoved me, and I fell. Then he said that he might be injured, but he was still lethal, and not to get in his way. He gave me an hour to get out, and he left. I don't know where he went."

A sharp intake of breath told me that Brea was pissed. "He threatened to kill you."

"No." I was horrified. "I think he just wanted me to stop getting in his way. I was trying to prevent him from leaving so we could discuss the problem."

"No, Jessica, that's not what happened." David's lips pressed together, and he used breathing techniques to bring his blood pressure down. "You were afraid enough to leave your home. It doesn't matter what you think he might have meant—it was a threat, a warning that he could use lethal force to get you out of his way."

"Jesse would never—"

David rose, cutting off my protest. "He's not himself right now—that's what you said, and it's what you've been saying to Brea since the surgery. The truth is you don't know what he would and wouldn't do."

I stubbornly refused to vilify him, and my phone rang before I could think of anything to counter David's assertion. I looked at the caller display. "It's Dean."

David took the phone. "Hi, Dean. It's David. Jesse was there? He... Are you okay? Is he okay? Jessica is here. He threatened her and threw her out." He listened for a while, nodding his head even though Dean couldn't see. "Yeah. Agreed."

He ended the call and handed my phone back. "Jesse went over and fought with Dean. After they kicked each other's asses, they talked. Jesse isn't in a good place mentally. Dean is sitting in his car outside your house because he's afraid Jesse might do something stupid like come over here and drag you back."

If Jesse asked me to go back, I would—no dragging required. Since Jesse hadn't shown up or called, I feared something infinitely worse. "If he's in a really dark place, he shouldn't be alone."

"That's what Dean said. I'm going over there. You guys lock up and go to bed. I won't be back anytime soon."

He left.

Brea handed me a cup of tea and a plate of cake. "Okay, first thing, we need to get Jesse to agree to therapy. Talk therapy, not the sexual therapy you've been trying to use. It's not working."

I begged to differ. It worked in the short term, but it wasn't a long-term solution. Even my liaison with Dean had been a short term therapy. Healing came from the inside, but hope came from knowing that no matter what, the people who loved you weren't going to give up and go away.

Okay, fine. She was right—it wasn't working.

Jesse

"Dude, you're beyond pathetic."

Even in my dreams, Dean's fucking voice wouldn't go away.

"If you're wondering what that smell is, you're lying in a pool of vomit."

Now David's annoying voice invaded the peaceful oblivion of my slumber, and it made my head hurt.

Not only did my head hurt with a vicious, pounding headache, but my ankle was killing me. Awareness returned, and I took stock of my injuries. Nose, eye, head, shoulder, both hands, ribs, ankle—my whole body felt battered and bruised.

The wetness on my cheek and the sickly sour smell confirmed David's assertion. I rolled away from my sick and opened my eyes.

"There he is." Dean stood over me. Wearing the same blood-spattered clothes as last night and sporting two black eyes, he peered down at me. "You look worse than I feel."

David handed me a wet hand towel, and he knelt to clean up the floor with another one.

I wiped my face and looked around. I'd spent the night sleeping on the tiled bathroom floor. It took a minute, but detailed memories from last night slammed back into my brain.

"Jessica? Bailey?"

"They're at my place," David said. "Where they will stay until you get your head out of your ass."

"My head's out." Actually it felt like it had spent time in a blender on the slice-and-dice setting. "I want my wife and daughter." I glared at Dean while I said it, emphasizing that Jessica was *my* wife and Bailey was *my* daughter.

Ignoring me, Dean turned on the shower and adjusted the temperature.

David regarded me impassively. I noted the white lines around his mouth and the disapproval in his eyes anyway.

"They're not coming back," he said. "Not until you get some therapy."

I knew I needed to talk to someone, but I resented David for leaving me to die. "I want you both out of my house."

Dean hauled me to my feet and tried to lift my shirt over my head.

186

I jerked away and glared.

He crossed his arms. Despite the black eyes, the broken nose, the bruise swelling on his face from a well-placed right hook, and blood on his shirt, Dean managed to still come off as suave and sophisticated. I fucking hated him. And I loved him. It hurt to think about either feeling.

"Jesse, we're not leaving. We know you're in a bad state right now, and this is the point in a friendship when our actions speak louder than words."

I blinked. "You're not leaving? Wow. Where was that mentality when you left me rotting in Rio Escondido?"

His gaze didn't waver. "We're not here to litigate that. You have a legitimate complaint, and we have no defense that will make up for what happened. Right now, you're a mess, and unless we can help you put your life back together, you're going to lose your family."

I jerked a thumb at David. "He just said they weren't coming back. Seems like you should have come up with a more coherent strategy. Get out."

"No," David said, his quiet resolve grating on my last nerve.

"I don't fucking want you here!" I shouted at the top of my lungs, which caused a sharp pain to stab through my eye and into my brain. This time, when I vomited, I made it into the toilet.

A cold cloth pressed to the back of my neck. I tried to throw it off, but David immobilized my arms and Dean held the cloth in place.

When I stopped fighting, David released his hold. "You threatened to kill Jessica last night."

I'd never do that. No matter what, I'd never harm her. "Fuck off, David. She didn't say that."

"No. She tried to rationalize how you telling her to get out of your way because you are 'lethal,' only meant that you wanted her to stop getting in your way." David hauled me to my feet and propped me against the wall next to the shower. His light brown eyes glittered hard with a warning. "Of course, we've seen you kill people before, so Dean and I know that's not an idle threat."

I closed my eyes as I tried to recall exactly what I'd said. I'd been angry, and her getting in my way had triggered a culmination of all the times my ankle injury had thwarted me from gaining freedom. I'd lashed out at her for so many reasons, most of which had nothing to do with her.

"Fuck." I muttered the curse. "She's never coming back. She's better off without me." I, on the other hand, didn't want to face an existence where she wasn't by my side.

"Not true, dumbass." Dean got my shirt off this time because I didn't resist. Then he went after my pants.

David put the plastic bag over the cast they'd put on my leg after the incisions had healed. It was cracked, and so I needed a new one anyway. The bag was the least of my concerns.

"Do you think you can shower on your own, or do you want me to wash you?" Dean grinned as he made the offer.

David pursed his lips. "Dean, you know—we'll be supportive if you want to come out of the closet."

Dean only grinned louder. Now I knew what Jessica meant when she said I was too fucking cheerful in the morning.

I got in the shower and closed the curtain. Jessica's shampoo mocked me from the shelf where she kept it. I put it out of my head and focused on cleaning my various wounds.

All told, Dean had gone easy on me last night. I had bruises and scrapes, but I frequently came away with many more when I sparred with him.

"You'll eat a light breakfast, and then we're taking you to see Doctor Wilkins." Dean's voice intruded once again.

"Who?"

"Wilkins. He's an Army vet who specializes in treating people like us."

I snagged a towel, dried off, and wrapped it around my waist before opening the curtain.

Dean lounged on a chair Jessica said didn't belong in a bathroom even though she used it to sit on when she put lotion on her skin. He smiled when I emerged. "Gargle, and that'll take care of the rest of the smell."

"Is Wilkins your therapist?"

"No. That would be a conflict of interest." He handed me a folded stack of clothes.

"You can leave," I said. "I know how to get dressed."

He shook his head. "We're not leaving you alone for a second."

I knew, from past experience, that Dean was comfortable being present for all bodily functions, so I didn't threaten to take a dump while he watched. Instead I glanced around. "David left?"

"He's making breakfast. I love a man who cooks."

"Doesn't work on me," I informed him as I put on my pants. "You fucked my wife. I know which side your bread is buttered on."

He shrugged. "Bread is a rectangle with six sides."

After breakfast, they took me to the same office where I took Jessica to see Nikki. Great. We could book our shrink appointments for the same time and carpool.

Adam Wilkins was an Army vet who'd lost a leg and three fingers in Iraq. Since he was in a wheelchair, I had to estimate his height, and I put it right around mine. He had a muscular build, the kind that came from regular weightlifting and vigorous aerobic exercise. He greeted me with a firm handshake before wheeling ahead of me to his office.

The office had minimal décor. Furniture consisted of a sofa and two upholstered chairs with a table between them. Off to one side was a desk with nothing on it. On the walls, Wilkins had framed his diplomas and license.

I sat in the center of the sofa, which was too soft to allow me to sit up straight, so I perched on the edge.

Wilkins transferred to a chair. He sat back and smiled. I noted that his eyes were kind of light brown mixed with yellow and green.

"So, you deal with PTSD?"

"Yes," he said. "Though generally we wait until there's a diagnosis before slapping a label on things."

"Did Dean tell you why I'm here?" I didn't know where to start.

"He mentioned why your friends and family are concerned. Why don't you tell me, from your perspective, why you're here?" Again he smiled. It was a strong expression, but there was absolutely no judgment in it.

"I lost my shit and threw my wife out of our house."

"The short version is no fun," he said. "You can either start at the beginning, or we can work backward. Do you want to start with what happened to make you throw your wife out, or did you want to start with what happened on the battlefield?"

The battlefield was inside my head. None of it was easy to talk about, so I started with pushing Frankie out of the plane over a Central American jungle.

Two hours later, I felt lighter. There was something about unburdening myself to an impartial but sympathetic third party that made a difference. I had a lot of work ahead of me, but for the first time, I felt hopeful I could navigate my way back to my life.

I found David and Dean waiting in the cookie-and-cry room, as Jessica called it. While I didn't feel much like crying, I did help myself to two chocolate chip cookies.

They trailed after me.

"We could grab some lunch, and then go get Jesse a new cast," David said. "I'm hungry."

"Jessica." I hobbled to the parking lot on my single crutch. "The cast can wait. I need to see Jessica."

David unlocked his SUV. I got into the back, and Dean got in next to me.

189

He grinned, but it lacked his usual arrogance. "Want to talk about it?"

"No."

Wilkins had agreed with me that it would take time before I would be at a place where I could forgive David and Dean. He counseled me to not banish them from my life because then I'd never deal with it.

"Jesse..." Dean trailed off, pressing his lips together as he gathered his thoughts. "We're not taking you to see Jessica until we know she'll be safe with you."

Even yesterday, I would have punched him for saying that, but right now I was glad my wife's life was filled with people who were looking out for her.

"I understand your concern," I said. "But she's the one I owe an apology to."

He scrutinized my face. "We never meant to hurt you."

I lifted a hand. "Dean, never, ever again talk about your affair with my wife. I think I made my feelings about that perfectly clear when I rearranged your face."

He arched a brow. "So, you're over it?"

"Yeah." I jutted my chin at him. "But from now on, you aren't to comment on her appearance, beauty, or any other physical attribute. You are to refrain from hugging or kissing her, and you are to never call her by any nickname."

"I accept those terms." A slow smile spread across his face, and shitheadedness lit his eyes. "May I say that you're looking ravishing today?" Then he undid his seatbelt and flew across the seat. He had his arms around me before I knew what hit me, and the fucker kissed my cheek.

From the front seat, David busted a gut from laughing.

Jessica

David had been texting me updates all day, so I knew they were en route.

Brea snorted in disgust. "They're going to want lunch, and I didn't make enough for three hungry men."

I picked up the leftover chicken and potatoes we'd dug out of the fridge. "Then we'd better eat all this in the next ten minutes."

When the front door opened, Brea stuffed the last bite of cake in her mouth. She hadn't been as concerned about sharing the chicken as she had been about not wanting to divide the last slices of cake. I shared her sentiments.

She leaned toward me conspiratorially. "Do you think he'll get on his knees and beg?"

I couldn't see Jesse ever doing that, but until last night, I'd never imagined he could be so cold and unreasonable. "That's not necessary."

Bailey hadn't taken our challenge to heart, and so she was still happily munching on shredded chicken, cold pasta, and cereal, all of which were spread out over the tray of her high chair.

Jesse appeared in the wide opening separating the kitchen from the dining room with David and Dean hot on his heels. He paused, his gaze locked on me.

I wasn't going to make the first move.

"Can we talk?"

Ball was in my court. I'd begged him to talk last night, and he'd shot me down. But playing tit-for-tat games wasn't going to help, so I rose. "Brea, will you watch Bailey?"

Bailey seemed to notice our company for the first time. She flung a piece of chicken as her arms waved. "Da-da-da-d-d-da!"

He went to her and got down on one knee because his cast made squatting impossible. "Good afternoon to you, my sweet girl." He leaned in for a kiss, and she had a similar idea, but she hadn't developed the habit of closing her mouth for a kiss. She ended up crashing into his chin with her mouth open. He kissed her forehead. "Be good for Aunt Brea while Mommy and I go into the other room."

He got up and motioned for me to precede him into the next room.

In the dining room, I turned around. "We could go to my room."

"If you're comfortable with that," he said. "I thought you might want people in hearing distance."

I took his hand and led him to my room. In all the time I'd known Jesse, I'd never seen him this nervous and uncertain. Even when he felt that way, he was practiced in the art of hiding his emotions.

The sitting area was missing from the room. They'd taken out the sofa and chairs to make room for the crib and changing table. I sat on the bed and patted the space next to me. "I won't bite."

Careful to keep his distance, he perched as far from me as he could get. He rubbed his hands on his thighs. "I feel like I'm about to propose and I'm not sure of your answer."

"Huh. I guess it's good I went and married you without asking what you wanted."

My joke had the intended effect. He laughed nervously, and it broke some of the tension. His gaze met mine. "Jessica, I'm messed up."

"I know."

"Do you?" He looked away, and a shadow passed behind his eyes. "I mean, I'm really fucked up, and I didn't used to be."

"Jesse, only a sociopath wouldn't be affected by what you went through. David told me you went to therapy today. I'm glad. I've been meaning to encourage you to go, but I wasn't sure if it would make you mad or sad or what."

He bowed his head and rubbed his palms on his thighs again. "I've been a bastard to live with. I'm sorry."

I laughed. "Jesse, you haven't been that bad. There were moments, sure, but I saw how hard you were trying to be the man you were before." Since he had chosen a spot so far away, I scooted closer until our knees touched. "When you go through bad stuff, it changes you. You're never going to be exactly the same, and that's okay. I don't expect you to be."

"I'm not sure who I am anymore."

I touched his knee. "Do you love me?"

His head whipped up, and he nailed me with all the urgency in his heart. "Yes, Jessica. I love you so very much."

"Do you want to stay married to me?"

"Yes. Forever."

"And you agree to pretend that thing with Dean and me never happened?"

"Hell, yes."

"And do you want to be a father to your daughter?"

"Yes."

"And do you want to have a couple more kids?"

"Yes. Wait."

I'd thrown him off with that one. I giggled. "No taking it back."

"I'm not willing to risk your life. That hasn't changed."

I shrugged. "We'll discuss semantics later."

He closed his eyes and breathed. The fingers on his thigh tapped, counting out a staccato rhythm. When he opened his eyes again, the air of panic disappeared. "I'm not going to let you derail this discussion."

"I know. I said we'd talk about it later."

"Jessica, I want to ask you to come home, and I'll understand if you need me to leave."

"Leave?" I wanted us to be together, not apart in a different configuration.

192

"Yes. I threatened you. At the time, I didn't even notice what I was doing, but it doesn't matter. There's no excuse or defense for what I said or did. I can only say I'm sorry."

"I forgive you."

His mouth gaped. "Just like that?"

"No, not just like that. I've put a lot of time into thinking about it, and I don't want to hold a grudge. I want you, Jesse. I want our family. It means a lot to me that you're seeing a therapist and that you apologized. If there's one thing I've learned in my eventful life, it's that nobody is perfect. People mess up, some worse than others, and when that happens, you have a choice to make. You can either move past it—together—or you let it splinter what you've built. I'd rather move forward with you than without you."

A sheen of tears wet his eyes, and a single drop squeezed out onto his eyelashes. I wiped it away, and he hugged me to him, crushing me in his arms.

"I'll never fuck up like that again. I promise."

I stroked his head because his face was buried in my breasts. "I know. It's just like when you kept those submissives when you should have released them—you never fuck up the same way twice."

He lifted me, moving me to the center of the bed where he laid me down and covered my body with his. He claimed my lips in a hungry kiss. When I was breathless, his attention moved to my neck.

"I've never missed you as much as I did last night."

"Wow. That's impressive."

He rolled to put me on top, and he slapped my ass. "Bratty comments will be dealt with in this manner."

I spread my legs to straddle his thigh, and I ground my pussy against that large muscle. "If you spank me, I'll deal with it in this manner."

He twisted his fingers in my hair, tugging lightly. "I see how this is a vicious cycle that promotes your bratty behavior."

"You love it," I teased, and then I sucked hard on his neck.

"Ah, vixen. That's gonna leave a mark."

"It'll blend in with all the other marks. Dean did a number on your face, but wow—he looks so much worse."

"Brat, do me a favor?"

I lifted my lips away from the second hickey I was in the process of creating. "What's that?" I knew better than to give blanket permission when he was still angling for anal.

"Never mention Dean when we're in bed."

Grinding my pussy harder, I reached into his pants and wrapped my hand around his huge erection. "Is this like how you don't want me to be bratty, or is this like, if I do, you'll teach me a lesson by ramming your dick down my throat?"

He hissed as I traced my fingertip along the crown of his cock. "Neither. It's a favor, something you do for me because you know it'll make me happy."

I planted a kiss on his lips. "Yes, Jesse. I'll do you that favor."

He hadn't seemed to notice that, in all my gyrating, my pants were around my ankles. That might be because his cast was in the way. In the blink of an eye, I kicked off my pants, bared his cock, and sank down on it.

We both gasped. He felt so good inside me, filling me with more than just his cock. I felt the power of his love blunting the edge of every painful shard that had threatened to destroy our love. I felt the strength of his determination and the potency of his courage.

I pushed his shirt up as I undulated.

With a groan, he stilled my hips. "Darlin', there's a condom in my pocket."

In my quest to trick him into the kind of sex that led to conception, I'd forgotten his concern about HIV. "You know, there's next to no risk. You tested negative."

He set his jaw firmly and used his Dom voice. "This isn't up for discussion."

I melted. "Yes, Jesse."

Reluctantly, I eased off his cock. He dug into his pocket and rolled the condom over his slick penis.

"You brought a condom to therapy?"

He pursed his lips. "I found it in David's backseat, and I hoped it was a sign." With that, he flipped me over and sank into my pussy in one practiced move.

As he thrust into me, I caressed his face and arms. "I love you, Jesse."

He paused long enough to kiss me. "Back at you, darlin'." Then he did that thing where he swiveled his hips to drive me insane.

"Harder," I begged. "Faster. Please, Jesse."

I urged him with whispered pleas. Delicious heat spread in my core, enveloping me in a sweaty, love-filled haze, until I cried out my climax.

He thrust twice more, and then he followed me over that cliff.

We held each other for a long time.

Epilogue

Jesse

"You have the ring?"

Frankie snorted in disgust. "For the fiftieth time, I have the ring. Who do you think is stupid enough to try to take it from me?"

"I just don't want you to lose it."

"Name one time I've ever lost anything important," she challenged.

I couldn't. "Sorry. I'm nervous."

"Why? You've technically married her twice already."

"Yeah, but the first time I didn't even know about, and the second time was a small, hasty exchange of vows. This is the big event."

Outside of this house, over a hundred people waited to witness me marrying Jessica.

Frankie fixed my tie even though it was probably fine. Dean had already been by to make sure my appearance was up to his standards.

"It's going to be fine," Frankie said. "Everybody is in place. The catering service has taken over the kitchen. The cake is beautiful. The wine is breathing. The summer weather is perfect—a little on the hot side, but not humid. What else? Nothing. All that's left is for you to promise to love and cherish a woman you already love and cherish." She muttered an oath under her breath in Farsi.

Frankie was my best man. When I'd first told Jessica about my selection, she'd been mad because she'd wanted Frankie to be her bridesmaid. She'd tried to persuade me by putting to use the belly dancing lessons she'd been secretly taking with Brea and Frankie. I had to admit she stated her case very well with the way she shook her hips and moved her arms. However, I'd insisted on solving the dispute the fair way—I'd tied her up and made her climax until she gave Frankie to me.

Frankie walked me to the dais on one end of my back yard, and she left me there to go do her part.

From his position in the center of things, Dean smiled. Yes—we'd selected him to perform the ceremony. It was a peace offering, but I wasn't sure whose it was.

Dean whispered, "Nervous? Don't worry—if you faint, I'll watch you fall."

Nothing was going to ruin today. I grinned, and then I faced the long aisle where my bride would appear.

First came Brea and Frankie, arm in arm, since Brea was the maid of honor. They were followed by Julianne Terry, a friend of Jessica's from Michigan, and David.

Then came Jessica. Warren walked her down the aisle. I'd like to say I noticed her dress, but I only noted it was white and bell-shaped. My gaze remained glued to her face. Radiant with happiness, she glowed.

Dealing with my issues these past six months hadn't been easy, but having her by my side to help me through the worst of it had forged an unbreakable bond of love and friendship between us. I knew that no matter what life threw our way, we would weather that storm together.

We said our vows, and after a long, nearly indecent kiss, she whispered in my ear. "I'm pregnant."

I held her tighter.

Michele Zurlo

Michele Zurlo is the author of the Awakenings, Doms of the FBI, and the SAFE Security series and many other stories. She writes contemporary and paranormal, BDSM and mainstream—whatever it takes to give her characters the happy endings they deserve.

Her childhood dream was to be a librarian so she could read all day. Some words of wisdom from an inspiring lady had her tapping out stories on her first laptop, and writing blossomed from a hobby to a career. Find out more at www.michelezurloauthor.com or @MZurloAuthor.

Lost Goddess Publishing

The Doms of the FBI Series

Re/Bound (Doms of the FBI 1)
Re/Paired (Doms of the FBI 2)
Re/Claimed (Doms of the FBI 3)
Re/Defined (Doms of the FBI 4)
Re/Leased (Doms of the FBI 5)
Re/Viewed (Doms of the FBI 6)
Re/Captured (Doms of the FBI 7)

The SAFE Security Series

Treasure Me (SAFE Security 1)
Switching It Up (SAFE Security 2)
Unlocking Temptation (A SAFE Security Short)

The SAFE Security Trilogy: Mercenary Hearts

Forging Love (A SAFE Security Novella: Mercenary Hearts prequel)
Coming Fall 2019:
Drawing On Love (Mercenary Hearts 1)
Broken Love (Mercenary Hearts 2)
Shards of Love (Mercenary Hearts 3)

Awakenings

Letting Go
Owning Up
Serving Sophia

Safeword: Oasis Series by Michele Zurlo

Wanting Wilder
Mina's Heart

Paranormal by Michele Zurlo
Dragon Kisses 1-3
Blade's Ghost

MM Romance by Nicoline Tiernan
Nexus #1: Tristan's Lover by Nicoline Tiernan
Nexus #2: The Man of His Dreams by Nicoline Tiernan

Anthologies
BDSM Anthology/Club Alegria #1-3 by Michele Zurlo and Nicoline Tiernan
New Adult Anthology/Lovin' U #1-4 by Nicoline Tiernan
Menage Anthology/Club Alegria #4-7 by Michele Zurlo and Nicoline Tiernan
Discovering Desires Anthology by Michele Zurlo

Bear's Cove Series (MM/MPreg) by A. J. Stone
Dak's Omega
Tanzil's Second Chance
Perfect Blend: Kofi's Omega

Draco International (MM/MPreg) by A. J. Stone
Amaricio's Omega
Koren's Omega Neighbor
Zeke's Reluctant Omega

www.ingramcontent.com/pod-product-compliance
Lightning Source LLC
Chambersburg PA
CBHW032000170626
46807CB00006B/2570